PATRIOT ACTS

ALSO BY GREG RUCKA

KEEPER

FINDER

SMOKER

SHOOTING AT MIDNIGHT

CRITICAL SPACE

A FISTFUL OF RAIN

A GENTLEMAN'S GAME

PRIVATE WARS

PATRIOT ACTS

GREG RUCKA

BANTAM BOOKS

PATRIOT ACTS
A Bantam Book / September 2007

Published by Bantam Dell
A Division of Random House, Inc.
New York, New York

Book design by Carol Malcolm Russo

Library of Congress Cataloging-in-Publication Data
Rucka, Greg.
Patriot acts / Greg Rucka.
p. cm.
ISBN 978-0-553-80473-7 (hardcover)
1. Assassins—Fiction. 2. Mistaken identity—Fiction. I. Title.

PS3568.U2968P38 2007
813′.54—dc22
2007006927

Printed in the United States of America
Published simultaneously in Canada

www.bantamdell.com

10 9 8 7 6 5 4 3 2 1
BVG

THIS IS FOR JERRY,

WHO HAS BEEN MY FRIEND FROM THE START

AND WILL BE MY FRIEND AT THE END

TRUE PATRIOTISM HATES INJUSTICE IN ITS OWN LAND MORE THAN ANYWHERE ELSE.

—CLARENCE DARROW

PATRIOT ACTS

PROLOGUE

I have never wanted to kill anyone as much as I wanted to kill the son of a bitch in front of me right now.

He's standing thirty, maybe thirty-five feet from where I'm lying hidden in the reeds and mud of this marsh. Not the easiest shot in the world but not the hardest, either, and I've got a submachine gun set to three-round burst to help my chances, and I've got his head in my sights, and all that remains now is for me to get on with it, to get down to business. I've been lying here for almost four hours, feeling the autumn cold seep up from the wet earth and into my body, waiting for this moment, waiting to close the trap. Waiting for this.

Right now, in this moment, his life is mine.

I can't pull the trigger.

I list all of the reasons he must die. I conjure the faces of his victims, the small handful of them that I know about. The neighbor who was in the wrong place at the wrong time and suffered for it; the reporter who died as preamble to more death; the friend, stabbed in the heart while I watched, too far away to save him. He died in my arms, a good man who left this world too early in fear and pain.

Three people, all of whom had the misfortune to know me. Three murders added to the sea of the dead that this man now in my sights has caused. That's what he does, you see, he murders. He does it for money, and he does it so well and so carefully that he's considered one of the ten best professional assassins working in the world today. One of The Ten, they call him, the same way they call him Oxford because they don't know his real name.

My finger refuses to budge.

I give myself more reasons to kill him. The least of them is the gun that Oxford is holding in his hands. That gun—or at least its bullets—is meant for me, and for the woman I have given my word I will protect. The woman who has both destroyed my life and recreated it. The woman who, like Oxford, can bring death like birdsong on a breeze, who they call Drama because they don't know her real name.

Her name is Alena, and right now she and Natalie Trent are speeding far away from this place, to a house where she will be safe.

Leaving me, here, now, trying to decide who it is I will become.

Something gives me away. Oxford turns and the weapon in his hands finds me, and now I can add self-defense to my many reasons to cut him down. It isn't as if I've never killed before. People have decided to point guns at me in the past, and once or twice they've ended up dead as a result of my response. If there was ever a time to fire my weapon and kill this man, it is now. It is him or it is me, and still I can't manage it, and I think that perhaps it will be me.

Then his left knee evaporates in a cloud of blood and bone.

He staggers, losing his aim on me, searching for the muzzle flash, and I watch as his hip bursts, and the sound of the second shot barks through the darkness. He twists, falling to his last knee, and then the back of his head opens. The sound of the third shot chases him as he topples into the marsh water.

I'm up and running already, racing along the trail, knowing who it is I'm going to find, but not understanding why I'll find them. When I reach them, Natalie Trent is helping Alena down from her sniper's perch. Then Alena is hobbling towards me on her one good leg. I catch her before she can fall. She puts her arms around me, pressing harder, and I think it is because she wants to, rather than because she needs to.

"He would have killed you or you would have killed him, and I couldn't let it happen." Alena's voice is thick with her tears. "I couldn't let you die for me, you understand? I couldn't let you become me."

I think about all of the dead.

"It's too late," I say.

PART ONE

CHAPTER ONE

Natalie Trent drove, speeding us away from Allendale and the body of the man I had been unable to kill.

She drove fast at first, trying to put quick distance between ourselves and the place where Oxford's body now lay, but once we left the Franklin Turnpike for US 202, she slowed to the speed limit. From inside her coat, she pulled her cell phone, pressed the same button on it twice without ever looking away from the road, and then moved it to her ear.

"About thirty minutes," Natalie told the phone, softly. "I've got both of them with me—yes, *both* of them. He's going to need a car."

She listened for a moment to the reply, murmured a confirmation, then ended the call and dropped the phone back into her pocket. She checked her mirrors, left then right then rear view, and when she did that, she met the reflection of my gaze. She tried a thin smile, and it looked as tired as I felt.

"Dan says he'll have a car waiting for you," Natalie said, paused, then added: "You're still going through with it?"

"I'm wanted for murder," I said. I didn't say that the murder I was wanted for was probably the wrong one, the death of an FBI agent named Scott Fowler. I didn't say it because I didn't need to. Scott Fowler had been a friend to both Natalie and me, a dear friend of many years, in fact. Had been, right until the moment he'd shuddered out his final breath while I tried to save him from the knife that Oxford had buried to its handle in Scott's chest.

That was Oxford's revenge, the way he had worked. He'd killed Scott because he could, and because he knew it would hurt me, and he had been right. He'd killed Scott Fowler because Scott Fowler had been unlucky enough to call himself my friend.

That he hadn't, for instance, killed Natalie Trent, or any of those other people who had the audacity to call me their friend, to care for me, wasn't for lack of trying. It was because we'd barely managed to deny him the opportunity.

Natalie frowned, putting lines to her beautiful face, then shifted her attention back to the road and said nothing more. Beside me in the backseat, Alena shifted, turning her head to watch as a New Jersey State Police car raced by, lights and sirens running, heading in the opposite direction. At Alena's feet, and mine, lying flat and forlorn, Miata pricked up his ears, raised his muzzle, then lowered it again, more concerned with the tension inside the car than anything that might be happening outside of it. He was a big dog, a Doberman, strong and loyal and silent as the grave. The first two were in return for the love Alena had given him; the last was because the man Alena had taken Miata from had cut the dog's larynx, to keep him silent.

Alena watched the police car disappear into the darkness behind us, then turned back and glanced at me, then quickly away again when she saw I was watching her. With the back of her left hand, she wiped at her eyes, deliberately erasing the last of her tears. If they embarrassed her, I couldn't tell. I imagined they did. The last time Alena Cizkova had cried, she'd been locked inside a Soviet prison cell with men three and four times her age. She had been eight at the time.

One shot would have been enough to kill Oxford, and God knew she could have put the shot where she wanted it to go. But Alena had used three instead, and the first two had been revenge, pure and simple. Until very recently, I'd been living with her and Miata at their home on the island of Bequia. Alena had brought me there to protect her life, and I'd succeeded, but with qualifications. Another woman, entirely innocent, had died at Oxford's hands. Then he'd taken the use of Alena's left leg with a blast from a Neostad shotgun that discharged while he and I had grappled. The shot had found Alena, turned the muscle and bone beneath her left knee to ground chuck. Since then, there'd been no opportunity and no time to seek truly appropriate medical attention, and now Alena Cizkova—sometimes called Drama—who had once commanded millions of dollars for her ability to visit death upon anyone for a price, needed a brace and a cane to walk.

So Alena had returned Oxford's favor. I wondered if Oxford had realized what was happening before the last round found home. If he'd understood who it was who was shooting him. Time dilates in moments like that, and he was smart, and more, he was quick. He'd probably understood. It was probably the last conscious thought he'd had.

Alena had exacted an assassin's revenge. Just fast enough to limit Oxford's ability to strike back, just slow enough to let him realize what she was doing to him, and why.

The three shots though, regardless of their significance, had been a mistake. One shot, maybe that would have been ignored by a slumbering resident jerked suddenly awake. One shot, he or she could have believed it was just their imagination. But three, in quick succession? No doubt someone had called the cops.

It was the first mistake I'd known Alena to make, and it was significant as much for its singularity as for the reasons I suspected that lay behind it. It wasn't an error of planning, nor an oversight. Nor was it an error in judgment. She had made it deliberately, because she wanted to. She had wanted to punish Oxford, and not just because of what he'd stolen from her body.

She had wanted to punish him for what he'd done to me.

She and Natalie should have been halfway to the safe house in Cold Spring by the time I put Oxford in my sights. Somehow, Alena had convinced Natalie to turn around, to double back, and that must have been quite the trick, because I knew Natalie. She and I had been friends for nearly a decade, colleagues for just as long, and even business partners for a couple of years. We'd fought each other, loved each other, and carried each other through very dark days. We'd seen each other in glory and despair, with warts and without. I knew just how damn stubborn she could be, and how seriously she took her job. There was only one thing that would have convinced Natalie to risk the safety of her principle.

The safety of a friend.

They had done it for me.

That was why Alena couldn't look at me right now.

And that was why, as soon as we reached the safe house in Cold Spring, as soon as I made certain that Alena would be protected, I was going to leave.

■ ■ ■

We crossed the Hudson on the Bear Mountain Bridge and the water was black beneath us, and the sky still heavy with stars. It took another seventeen minutes to reach Cold Spring, and another ten after that to locate the safe house off Deer Hollow Road, where the street tapered out into the surrounding woods. We were maybe half a mile south of the Cold Spring reservoir, perhaps a mile east of Lake Surprise, and there were no other houses on the street. The safe house itself was a small two-story structure, old, pushed back from the road and surrounded by trees. All of its lights appeared to be off. The only things noteworthy about it at all were the three vehicles parked nearby, a Mercedes-Benz SLK 230 Kompressor on the driveway beside a Ford minivan, both of which I recognized as belonging to the security detail, and then a twenty-year-old Honda Civic. Even in the relative darkness of the night, I could see the Civic showing its age.

Natalie swept the Audi into a slow turn, then reversed into the driveway, killing the engine. I got out first, Miata following on my heels. Natalie emerged next, immediately moving around to Alena's side to give her a hand out. It was late October, predawn in the Lower Hudson River Valley, and the air had a bite to it, cold and a little moist, rich with the smell of autumn.

The front door to the house opened, and Danilov Korckeva stepped out, a serious-looking pistol in his right hand, held against his thigh. He made for us briskly, looking past me, up the street, checking the approach. Then he glanced over to where Natalie was helping Alena out of the vehicle, and the anxiety on his face flickered for a moment as he gave her a smile, then faded altogether for an instant when Natalie returned it. Then Dan put his attention on me, and however sweet he was on Natalie Trent, I didn't rate, because the anxiety was back, and now he was scowling. Past him, in the darkened doorway, I could just make out one of the security detail, another of the Russians standing post, night-vision goggles waiting on his forehead and a Remington shotgun close at hand.

"What happened?" Dan demanded when he reached me, hissing the question. "You were going to cap the fucker and do the vanishing act. What happened?"

I moved around to the back of the car as Natalie used her free hand to pop it open with her remote. She had Alena out of the car now, supporting her with one arm as Alena got her cane beneath her. I lifted the trunk, took hold of the submachine gun I'd failed to kill Oxford with, and the HK PDW.

"What the fuck happened?" Dan asked a third time, more insistently, his voice lower.

Alena said something in Russian, softly, and it didn't sound hostile, but whatever it was, Dan reacted as if she'd put a knife to his throat. He stood six four, which put him almost five inches taller than both Alena and myself, and he had at least fifty pounds on me, probably as much as double that on her, and most all of it from bone and muscle, not from fat. I didn't know his age, but it had to be somewhere in the early forties, which gave him ten years on each of us. With his shaved head and his black goatee, he vibed Satan-as-bully, and looking at him you got the impression that he'd just as soon break your neck as get drunk on vodka with you. He'd been Russian *spesnaz*, essentially their equivalent of the Special Forces, and he these days was hooked in tight with the organized crime running out of Brighton Beach. He called Alena "Natasha" or "Tasha," for short, presumably because it was the name she'd used when they had first encountered each other. How he knew Alena I didn't know and I'd never asked, but however he knew her, one thing was clear.

She scared the living shit out of him.

When I met his eyes as I handed him the PDW and said, "Get rid of this," the look he gave me said that now I did, too.

"Can it wait until morning?" he asked. "I'll have to pull a guard off the house otherwise."

"Morning's fine."

"It'll go in the Hudson."

I went back into the trunk, hooked the strap on the go-bag, and pulled it onto my shoulder. It was a small nylon duffel, nothing fancy. Inside were two pairs of underpants, one clean shirt, a toothbrush, a set of fresh socks, and what was left of the half million dollars I'd held back from Oxford's money. By my guess, there was about three hundred thousand left, but I wasn't sure, because I hadn't counted.

I pointed to the Civic, asked Dan, "That's for me?"

He looked vaguely embarrassed. "The best I could do so quick, Atticus."

"As long as it gets me to Newark, I'm happy," I told him.

He looked relieved, but not by much, then turned to follow Natalie and Alena as they made their way into the house. I went to the Civic, found the driver's door unlocked; when I opened it, the dome light stayed off. I appreciated that, and I appreciated that Dan had taken the time to disable it. Then again, from the shape of the car, it was just as possible that the bulb had died.

I tossed the go-bag onto the passenger seat, pulled the keys from where they were waiting in the ignition, and dropped them in my pocket. I closed the door again, took a moment for another look around, another listen to the surroundings. The sky was still dark as pitch, and the only sounds I heard were from the woods, rustling dead leaves and shifting branches, and then, from somewhere above me, the sound of something solid knocking on wood. A tree house was just visible in the branches, perhaps twenty-five feet from where I was standing, maybe fifteen feet or so from the ground. There was a figure moving inside, and he raised a hand to me, and I raised one back. Another of Dan's Russians, this one on overwatch. Whoever was up there was probably very cold and very bored, but again I appreciated the precaution.

Miata nudged my left hand with his muzzle. He'd hung back to wait for me, and I reached down and gave him a scratch behind the ears. He looked up, fixing me with those soulful dog eyes, and I swear it was as if he knew what was going to happen next. Dogs' eyes are like that. Sometimes you can see exactly what they're feeling; sometimes, you see exactly what you're feeling yourself.

"Yeah," I told him. "Stop wasting time, right?"

By way of answer, Miata turned and headed up the path to the house.

I followed the dog.

Natalie and Dan were in the kitchen, which seemed to be the only room with its lights on, and that was fine with me because there was no way to see into the kitchen from the outside. Looking from the exterior, the house would appear dark, and that was how both I and Natalie wanted it.

"Who's in the tree house?" I asked, taking off my jacket.

Dan's expression was one of both disappointment and surprise. "You saw him?"

"Not soon enough."

That mollified him, and he grinned. "That's Vadim up there. He's my boy."

Natalie arched an eyebrow. "You've got a son?"

"Nineteen," Dan said, then added, "He has promise."

I hung my jacket on the back of the nearest chair, fighting

off a wave of sudden exhaustion while listening as Natalie and Dan continued discussing the security arrangements for the safe house. Oxford's death diminished the threat against Alena, but none of us was willing to say it was gone, not yet. Three hours before Oxford had planted his dagger in Scott Fowler's heart, Scott and I had met with two men at a Holiday Inn off Times Square. Two men who, we'd assumed, had been holding the end of Oxford's leash. One had been a big stack of jovial threat who had done most of the talking, but the other had been a quieter and more thoughtful piece of menace named Matthew Bowles.

Bowles and his partner hadn't been the instigators, though; they were middlemen, the ones responsible for tasking Oxford, for directing him at some other's request to clean up the mess that Alena and I had become. But Oxford had become a liability to them. In the end, Scott and I had persuaded Bowles and his partner to cut their losses. We'd watched Bowles make a four-second telephone call that terminated Oxford's contract, firing the assassin with all the ceremony and care of ordering take-out.

Oxford hadn't liked that. He'd liked that I'd stolen most of the money he'd made from two decades of killing people even less.

That was when he'd begun murdering anyone who'd ever had the misfortune of calling themselves my friend.

He'd killed Scott in Madison Square Park while I was close enough to see it and too far away to stop it. Scott had died in my arms while Oxford had fled, unnoticed and unmolested. The irony of that—if there was an irony to be found—was that I was now wanted for Scott's murder, for the murder of a federal agent.

There were ways out from beneath the charge, of course. Most obviously, I could just turn myself in to the authorities and confess the whole story of everything that had transpired. It could probably work. Until I'd disappeared to Bequia with Alena, I'd had a good reputation in the New York security community; I'd had some respect and even a modicum of brief fame. With a strong lawyer and a little good faith, the truth behind Scott's death would be revealed. At the least, I could be exonerated for the murder of my friend.

But that would require Alena's corroboration, and as Alena was known in certain law enforcement and intelligence circles as Drama, and as Drama was wanted in connection with something in the neighborhood of two dozen murders-for-hire, the odds of her corroboration being seen as credible were pretty damn low. If she walked into the Federal Building in lower Manhattan, the only way she'd walk out again would be in full restraints, with a phalanx of guards, on her way to arraignment.

If she walked out at all.

Someone had hired Oxford to kill her, after all, and that someone was most likely connected with the government. Just because Oxford was currently bloating with swamp water in the Allendale Nature Preserve didn't mean another attempt on Alena's life wouldn't be made.

Even now, we didn't know who had bought the hit. We didn't have the first idea.

I had given Alena my word that I would protect her. I had sacrificed friends and future because I believed her when she told me that she was a killer no more. I had promised her that she would be safe. The best way I could keep that promise was to button her up someplace safe and secure, and that someplace was this house in Cold Spring. Natalie would run the security, and Dan would provide the muscle and the firepower. Nothing fancy, just a safe place that could be secured and controlled for a week, maybe two at the outside. Long enough to be sure that the threat to Alena was gone, that Oxford was the end of it. Long enough for me to disappear someplace far, far away. It didn't matter where.

Just someplace where the people I loved didn't die because of the things I'd done, or the man I'd become.

Miata padded off into the darkness, in search of Alena, and I listened with half an ear to Natalie and Dan, standing around the kitchen table, discussing the security he'd put in place. Vadim up in the tree house had been a last-minute addition, it seemed, placed up there while Illya—the guard on the front door—had been dispatched to find me a car. While they talked I found myself a nearly clean glass and filled it with water, drinking it down. I was still wearing my Kevlar, and while it was a light vest, about as thin and comfortable as these kind of things ever managed to be, I was warm in it.

I thought about taking it off, leaving it behind, but I could just imagine what Alena would say if she saw me remove it. She'd call me a fool, and ask me if I wanted to die, and if I answered that things, for the moment, seemed to be safe, she would have snorted that near-contemptuous snort of hers and left it at that.

Natalie had given me a pistol before my meeting with Oxford, and that I did remove, setting it on the table. If I was going to be catching a plane anytime soon, it'd be best to go light. The vest could be ditched easily enough at the airport, if needed; the gun would be harder to dispose of, and since I didn't know where she'd acquired it, I didn't want to risk it being traced back to her. Better to leave the problem for Dan and Natalie to solve.

"There are three," Dan was telling her, indicating a rough drawing he'd made on a piece of paper that rested on the table. The drawing was a map of the house and the immediate area, and it looked quickly done, but more than serviceable. "Not counting Vadim on overwatch. He's got a rifle up there, and night-vision."

"And hopefully a blanket," I said.

"You've got coms?" Natalie asked Dan.

Dan reached into the outside pocket of his jacket, held up a Nextel mobile phone. Natalie nodded slightly, and he dropped the phone back where he'd found it.

"What about the other three?"

"Illya's on the door, you saw him as you came in. We loaded his shotgun with the Brenneke rounds, better for dealing with vehicles if a vehicle should come. Yasha is covering the back door, and Tamryn is sleeping upstairs, in the room next to Tasha's."

"So six altogether, counting you and me."

"You think more?"

"No, six should be plenty, at least for tonight."

They both looked at me.

"Dandy," I told them.

Dan considered my lack of enthusiasm, then said, "I'll go check on Tasha, make sure she's comfortable."

He left the room, shutting the door behind him.

Natalie and I stared at each other. After a couple of seconds of silence, I said, "I'm not sure it's safe to leave the two of you alone. I'm thinking I'll come back to find a gaggle of little red-haired Russian thugs-to-be shaking down the nearest kindergarten."

"He's Georgian, not Russian."

"He's also got a nineteen-year-old son behind a rifle in a tree house outside. Talk about a motivated family."

Natalie grinned, but then it froze. She shook her head slightly. She didn't want to banter, she didn't want the jokes. I didn't blame her. There was a lot of history between us, history that stretched back to a time and a place where we had been very different people. Her father, Elliot Trent, and his company, Sentinel Guards, was *the* be-all and end-all of security firms in Manhattan.

She'd left his company to form a new one with me. She'd turned her back on her father and his Secret Service connections and his five hundred employees and the corporate accounts, and instead thrown her lot in with me when we hadn't stood a chance in hell of surviving.

It was the way she was, always looking to pursue a challenge, maybe because it would have been so very easy for her to live a life with no challenges in it at all. She was beautiful, she was smart, and Elliot Trent was a wealthy man. He hadn't even wanted her to join Sentinel, and when she'd gone into business with me, he'd all but disowned her. As far as Elliot Trent was concerned, I was a danger not just to myself and others, but to the profession as well. If anyone had told him that my profession seemed to have changed recently, he would have taken it as proof confirming all of his worst suspicions.

"You don't have to go," Natalie said, finally. "You can stay."

"I'm not going to take the risk."

"You think maybe, just maybe, you're being paranoid?"

I nodded. "But that doesn't mean I'm wrong."

"Oxford's dead."

"But not whoever the hell it was who hired him in the first place. That threat is still out there, and I want it bearing down on me, not on her and not on you."

Her brow furrowed as she considered her possible counter-arguments, and then she sighed sadly. "Any messages?"

I thought about it, then shook my head. My association with Alena had already cost me all of my friends but Natalie; what relationships remained wouldn't survive what would happen next. I'd disappeared once without a trace. Doing it again was going to be one time too many.

"You're sure?" Natalie asked.

"There's nothing I can say."

"Not even to her?" She indicated the floor above us with her head.

"There's nothing I can say."

"Maybe you should think of something. It was her idea to go back for you, Atticus, not mine."

I shook my head again, hoping Natalie would take that as my request to let the matter drop. I wasn't surprised when she didn't.

"She's in love with you, you know that, right? That's why she made me turn around, why we came back."

"It doesn't matter."

"Of course it matters, Atticus." She looked at me with honest incredulity. "It's the only thing that matters."

"Don't be a fucking idiot."

"What?"

"Give me a goddamn break, Nat," I said. "You don't really believe that. It's all that matters? It doesn't matter at all. Not at all, not one bit. Not to Oxford or Bowles or any of that lot, and sure as hell not to Scott. What matters is survival. That's all that fucking matters."

"Don't tell me what I do or don't believe." Her look reflected my sudden anger, turned it back on me, and it crept into her voice even though I knew she was fighting to keep it out. "Survival isn't just drawing another breath. It has to be more than that."

"Then I'm right," I said. "You are a fucking idiot."

She shook her head, hard, as if trying to knock the words I'd said free with the motion, and I know she would've said something more in response, but the door from the hallway opened again, and Dan returned.

"She's fine," Dan said. "Cranky, that's how I know."

"She's not the only one," Natalie said, looking at me. The

anger she'd been reflecting was gone, replaced by confusion, and it made me feel guilty, but I wasn't about to explain.

Dan reached around his back, beneath the same thin black leather jacket he seemed to always wear no matter what the weather, and came out with a pistol. He held it out, offering me the butt end.

"Just in case," he said. "It's clean. You can dump it with the car."

It was a Glock 34, simple and straightforward and infinitely anonymous. The magazine was fully loaded, seventeen rounds. I tucked the pistol into my pants at the small of my back.

"We'll take good care of her for you," he told me.

"I know you will."

"She wants to see you before you go."

"Then I should see her," I said, and turned to head upstairs.

"Atticus," Natalie called after me. "Idiot or not, I'm right. It's the only thing that matters."

They'd put her in a small room on the second floor, beside the bedroom where Tamryn was sleeping. The lights were off, and she was sitting on the edge of the bed, Miata with his head in her lap, petting him.

When she saw me, she said, "Why do they keep putting me on the second floor when I can barely climb the stairs alone?"

"Because it's easier to fall down than to climb up?" I suggested.

She snorted, then pushed Miata gently away and got to her feet, using the headboard as a support. Her cane was leaning against the wall nearby, but she didn't go for it, instead making her way slowly to where I was standing just inside the door. The progress looked painful, and when she reached me she put out her hands, resting them, palms flat, against my chest, and I thought she would give me her weight, but she didn't. There was enough light to see her face, just barely, but not enough to read what was painted there when she looked at me. I couldn't feel her hands through the vest, but I imagined that they were warm.

"I have to go, Alena," I said.

"I don't know how to do this, Atticus," she said, and the frustration in her voice sounded more pained than angry. "I have never had to do this. I have never had to say good-bye to someone I did not want to see go."

I didn't say anything.

She moved her left hand, raised it as if to rest it against my cheek, but then dropped it back to my chest, as if afraid that the touch would burn her. Even in the darkness, I could see her scowling.

"I want to kiss you," Alena said, suddenly. "May I do that?"

"You can do that," I told her.

She moved her hands up my chest once again, this time lighter, splaying her fingers, as if reading me in Braille. When they reached my shoulders, she began to lean in, then balked, pulling back. She tilted her head to her right, tried a second approach, pulled back once again. Her head tilted to the left, and that seemed to make her feel more confident, and she held my shoulders more firmly, and this time I knew she would go through with it.

I met her mouth with my own, felt her lips tentative against mine, and there was only a light brushing of skin, dry and softer than I had thought her capable of being. Then she did it again, this time with certainty. Her fingers moved to my neck, then into my hair, and she pulled herself into me. I put my arms around her, tasting her and holding her, and she made a sound into my mouth, almost mournful.

Then she let me go, reaching out for the dresser with one hand, using it to support herself as she made her way back to the bed. She sat slowly, in exactly the same place she had before.

"Good-bye, Atticus," Alena said.

I left her sitting there.

CHAPTER TWO

It turned out I was right; they were coming after me.

I'd just thought they'd give me more time before they did it.

Three minutes out from the safe house, following Foreman Road, the reserve light for the gas tank lit up on the Civic's console. There was no tone, no warning buzzer, but there didn't need to be. It was a hard light to miss.

My first thought was that, in his haste to acquire a car, Illya had forgotten to check how much gas was in the tank. Then I thought that there was no way in hell that Dan would have permitted that kind of mistake, no way in hell he would have supplied me with an escape vehicle that wouldn't be able to manage my escape.

So maybe it was a fault in the console someplace, a short in the warning light or a skewed sensor in the tank.

I was willing to believe that, until I saw the headlights in the rearview mirror.

They were distant, maybe a hundred feet back, but riding high enough to throw reflected glare into the Civic. As I watched, the lights came closer, then held steady. Maybe fifty feet off. A good covering distance. Not so far away as to lose the target; not so close as to risk unnecessary exposure if the target did something unexpected, hit the brakes, for instance, or threw a U-turn.

I told myself that it didn't mean anything, that it was a public damn road, and that other vehicles would thus be using it. I told myself that, yes, while it was half past four in the morning and only assassins and their students and the people who protected them would be awake and up and about in the sleepy little Putnam County town of Cold Spring, that was no reason to become alarmed.

The Glock was on the seat beside me, wedged beneath the go-bag, and I reached over for it, moved it into my lap. The Civic was an automatic, and I took both hands off the wheel long enough to rack the slide, to make the pistol ready. Then I slid the barrel beneath my right thigh, on the outside, so my weight would keep it from bouncing around should I do anything to anger the Laws of Physics, but so I could grab it in a hurry if the need arose.

I had a very strong feeling that the need would arise very shortly.

The lights behind me were steady, still keeping their distance. The sky was playing in shades of black and blue, and I couldn't tell the make of the vehicle. From the height of the headlights, I guessed it was a pickup of some sort, or maybe an SUV.

That damn reserve light was still on, still warning me that I was low on fuel.

I felt my pulse begin to race.

If the tank had been tapped, punctured, or drained just enough to get me going but not enough to get me where I wanted to go, there was no telling what else had been done to the vehicle. No telling if a bug had been planted, if an explosive had been placed. That the car hadn't blown up when I'd started it was small consolation; it's easy enough to rig a charge in two phases, to prime when the engine starts, to detonate when it stops.

I didn't much like thinking that, because it meant that when the car died, I would, too.

There was a turn coming up, onto County Route 10, and I made the right, and when I did the lights behind me seemed to move closer, just a bit, as if whoever was handling the vehicle behind me wanted to keep me in sight.

We'd passed a Citgo station on the way to the safe house, in the direction I was currently heading. It couldn't be more than half a mile from where I was now. I'd noted it because there'd been nothing else around, just the pumps and a garage and a lot and the encroaching woods.

That was what threw the switch for me, and I saw it all so clearly then, saw it as if I had planned it myself. I was about to be ambushed; I was already being herded into the kill zone.

Whoever had planned this hadn't wanted to hit me at the safe house, and that made sense; there had been a lot of guns at the safe house, and it would have made taking me out difficult. So they'd let me get mobile, to isolate me, but they'd done so with an eye to controlling how far I could go, and where. With the reserve light on, of course I would stop at the first gas station I could find.

There would be two teams, then: one in the follow vehicle, to monitor my progress, to act as the stopper if I tried to reverse and double back to the safe house. The second team would be in position already, waiting at the gas station, but in contact with the first, in the follow vehicle. Maybe on radio, maybe on cell phones, it didn't matter. The point was, they would know I was coming, and they would be ready for it when I arrived.

Then I would turn into the station and roll up to the pumps, and before I could even get out of the Civic, the follow car would pull alongside and the team that had been waiting would emerge from their cover. They'd shoot into the vehicle from each of their directions, forming two cones of fire, and trapped in the Civic, I'd find myself unable to do anything but die.

I could see it as clearly as if I had planned it myself.

I could see, too, that there was no way to avoid it. I was already in the mouth. Passing the station by wouldn't free me from the teeth. The follow vehicle would simply keep me in sight, and the second team would catch up, and they'd either wait for the Civic to choke to a halt, or they'd force me off the road, then take me there. There were plenty of places they could do it, plenty of stretches with nothing but trees and darkness and nothing else. Worse, continuing on would only take me further from the safe house. I had to get back there, had to make certain that I was the only target.

The gas station came into view maybe a quarter of a mile ahead of me, to the left of the road. Sodium lamps shining orange through the trees, bathing the pumps beneath, turning the edges of the asphalt lot blue. I could see the darkened office, and beside it the darkened garage. The illuminated Citgo sign rose above the branches atop its pole, a shining marker for my designated grave.

In the rearview, the lights from the follow vehicle had grown brighter. The driver was closing the gap.

I slowed, signaled, and turned into the ambush.

CHAPTER THREE

The second team had come in a Ford sedan. The sedan waited at the opposite end of the lot from where I entered, positioned almost directly between the two rows of pumps. My headlights splashed across it as I turned into the gas station, and I could see the car parked facing towards me. Its front doors were already open, and two men were standing behind them, wearing bulky winter coats and facing each other, as if conversing over the roof of the car. In the moment of illumination as my lights found them, I marked them both as Caucasian, each standing with his hands out of sight, hidden behind their respective doors. The one at the driver's side door wore a watch cap, the other was bald.

There were two rows of pumps, three pumps apiece, and spaced to allow for four lines of cars to refuel simultaneously. I oriented the Civic towards the right-hand row on the inside, continuing to tap my brakes, as if bleeding off speed in preparation for a stop. With my left, I reached out to unlock my door, then rolled down the window. A gust of cold autumn air, smelling faintly of gasoline and motor oil, filled the car.

The follow vehicle turned into the station behind me, and I saw that it was a Jeep Cherokee, either green or black; it was hard to tell with the sodium lights. If it was coming to ram or pin the Civic, I was done, and for a half-second of pure terror, I thought that was exactly what it intended to do. But it pulled the turn tighter than I had, and I realized why; he didn't want to risk getting hit by the cone of fire that would come from the Ford. Instead, the Jeep's driver was going to come parallel, past the pumps on my right. I glanced over, saw only one occupant, the driver behind the wheel, also Caucasian, his hair dark. He didn't look my way.

I put more pressure on the brakes, brought the Civic to a stop, turning the wheel slightly to the left, leaving the engine running. There couldn't be much gas left in the tank, but the Civic wouldn't need much to do what I wanted it to do. I had the Glock in my right, ready. At the Ford, the two men were still pretending to speak to one another, not looking my way. It was a big tell. At almost five in the morning in a deserted gas station, when a new car pulls in, shining its lights at you, you look at it. If you don't, you're hiding something.

To my left, the lights in the garage and the office were dark. If they'd been that way when Natalie had driven us past, on the way to the safe house, I couldn't recall. I hoped they had been. If not, it meant someone had been working but wasn't anymore.

The Cherokee passed the row of pumps, now turning slightly to the left about fifteen feet past the last one, coming to a stop, its driver's door angled roughly in my direction. Ford, Cherokee, and Civic now described a chevronlike shape, with me in the Civic at the apex. It was a strong firing solution; if I tried moving forward, the shooters would tighten their cones of fire. If I tried to run, they could cut me to ribbons from two angles.

The Cherokee came to a stop, and that was the go-signal. The driver reached for something on the seat beside him, his weapon, and then I had to ignore him, because the two at the Ford were more trouble, at least at the moment. Each of them had already turned in my direction, their hands coming up from where they'd been hidden behind their doors, and each held a submachine gun, an MP5, but the barrels were extended, suppressors fixed in place.

I tapped the accelerator lightly at the same time I opened my door, swung my legs around and slid out of the Civic, into a crouch, and I didn't hear the shots as they opened fire, but I heard the impacts, the sound like rocks being driven into the body of the car, the sound of the windshield cracking. The Civic was still in drive, and it kept rolling forward, doing no more than four, maybe five miles an hour, and I stayed with it, stayed low, using the open driver's door as a shield. Another battery of silent shots slammed into the car, but nothing penetrated, and that was as I'd hoped. Between the two panels and the window glass, it would take a meaner round than the suppressed nine-millimeter the MP5s could fire to cut its way through.

I kept moving with the Civic as it rolled steadily forward, staying low. If I'd done it right, the car would be on course to meet the Ford, though it would take the better part of a minute to get there. It was going to be a very long minute, especially with three people shooting at me.

I reached out for the door, pushed it fully open to give me the most cover I could manage, then released it and went to a two-handed grip on the Glock, and it was only then that I realized that I wasn't afraid. I was vaguely surprised to discover that I wasn't truly worried at all. It's not that I didn't recognize the danger I was in, and it wasn't that I didn't acknowledge how perilously close to my own death I was standing. But as I moved, as I shifted my weight and stutter-stepped to keep pace with the car, as I brought the Glock up to kill the one wearing the watch cap, I felt precise, sure, even certain. I had done everything I could to even the odds, I had a plan, and either it would work or it wouldn't, but there was only one way to find out.

I came out quick, sending five shots from the Glock at the shooter in the watch cap as fast as I could pull the trigger. He was the priority target; he was at the driver's door of the Ford, and that made him the driver, and I didn't want him getting behind the wheel and turning the tables on me.

My shots rang out, one atop the other, and the gunman wearing the watch cap jerked, then toppled back. The clatter of his MP5 hitting the ground rang across the lot, and I heard his partner, the bald one, call me a motherfucker, but I'd already hunkered back behind the cover of the Civic by then. Another battery of silent gunshots rattled the car.

"Fuck!" the bald one was shouting. "Fuck! Sean's down, fuck!"

The outburst surprised me, not for the profanity, but because I'd taken them for professionals, and I'd expected them to remain professionally silent. Then again, perhaps I'd surprised them. After all, they'd quite possibly thought they'd caught me dead-to-rights and I'd just put them on notice that, no, I wasn't planning on going quietly.

As if in answer to the outburst, the predawn filled with the bark of an automatic rifle. No suppression on this weapon, and the reports were angry and loud, and it had to be the shooter from the Cherokee getting into the act now. This time, glass shattered rather than cracking, and in my periphery I saw the instrument gauge explode inside the Civic. Past my left shoulder, a gasoline pump sparked, the LEDs on its face shorting out.

"Where is he? Where the fuck is he?" the bald one shouted. "Mark! Do you have a shot? Do you have a shot?"

"Shut the fuck up!"

"I can't see him! I can't—"

"Grant! Shut up, he's—"

I pivoted in my crouch to face the Civic, letting it roll past me. As the rear panel came even, I leaned right and snapped off two shots in the direction of the Cherokee. Its driver, Mark, was at the rear of the Jeep, using it both as a brace for his rifle and as cover for himself. He'd probably exited from the passenger's side, coming around as far from me as possible, and I had been right, the rifle was an automatic, an AR-15.

Both of my shots missed, smacked into the SUV, and I barely managed to tumble back behind my moving cover before Mark returned the favor, sending another battery of rounds my way. The trunk on the Civic snapped open, the latch destroyed by a penetrating round, and brake lights exploded, and behind me I heard glass shattering in the office, or maybe it was in the garage.

"You get him?" The bald one sounded shrill, his voice pinched and overloud with adrenaline. "Son of a bitch! Mark! Mark, you get the cocksucker?"

"Dammit, Grant!" Mark shouted in response. "Shut the fuck up!"

"Fuck! Fuck fuck fuck!"

Grant's voice descended into muttering, then silence, and there was a pause, a moment of almost silence that might have lasted three seconds or maybe lasted ten, as each of us with a gun tried to figure out what to do next. The Civic was still tenaciously rolling forward, but slowing, losing momentum, and the engine was beginning to cough and splutter. A radio crackled from the direction of the Ford, but I couldn't make out the transmission, or if anything was actually being said at all.

The Civic and I were coming parallel to the Cherokee, and I was going to have to do something about that. Maybe the MP5 in Grant's hand couldn't penetrate the Civic, but the AR-15 my new friend Mark was packing fired .223s, and it fired them quick, and at tremendous velocity. Cold-rolled steel or not, Mark's shots would have no trouble punching through my car.

"Wait for him!" Mark shouted, suddenly. "He's gonna break—"

I sidestepped along with the Civic, then broke cover again and pounded six rounds at Mark and his AR-15 as fast as I could, one after the other, pure suppression fire. It was a lot of bullets and a lot of noise, and it came at him fast, and it had the desired effect. He wrenched himself back, around the rear of the Cherokee, swearing furiously. Another rattle of rounds clattered against the Civic from the suppressed MP5.

The Glock had seventeen rounds, and I'd blown through thirteen of them. Or maybe fourteen. I wasn't sure. Optimistically I had four left. I swung back to face the inside of my open door, realized that the Civic had almost reached the end of its journey. I shoulder-rolled out from the cover of the door, this time going left, and as I came up I fired two shots at Grant and his bald head, less concerned with hitting him than with keeping him preoccupied. Both rounds smashed the Ford's windshield, beside where he stood, and he started to duck back behind his open door.

Then the Civic hit the Ford, and the Ford hit Grant, in the form of the door he was trying to use for cover. It wasn't a fast impact, and it wasn't—relatively—a hard impact, but it was still the impact of one car hitting another, and that was enough; that had been what I was after all along.

Grant grunted and went down and out of sight as if someone had dropped a bag of bricks on his head, and I went after him immediately, trying to capitalize on the moment and the brief advantage it gave me. Mark was screaming a warning to him, and there was another rapid string of barks from his AR-15, but I was vaulting the Ford's hood then, the Glock in my right, and I didn't dare look back and I wasn't about to stop. I cleared the gap between the Ford and the passenger door, saw Grant on the ground, and somehow he'd managed to keep hold of his MP5, and somehow he managed to raise the muzzle in time, and somehow he managed to pull the trigger.

He'd set his MP5 to three-round burst, so that was what he fired, and that was what hit me. Rounds slammed into my chest, the sensation like being struck with a club very hard and very fast. I landed on my feet, but for some reason ended up on my right side, practically parallel to where Grant lay on his back, the MP5 still in his hands. Each of us moved to kill the other.

I was faster, and put two rounds from the Glock into his head.

Then I dropped my pistol, took his MP5, popped the magazine, and gave it a read. Eighteen rounds remaining. I slapped it back into place, ran the bolt, and then rolled onto my back, and when I did that, it felt like something tore open in my middle, low in the belly, ripping me apart with a line of acid and fire. I threw a hand out towards the Ford, reaching into the open compartment. Using the seat, I pulled myself upright with one hand, clutching the MP5 with the other, and the pain flipped, exploded, and everything from my right hip on down told me that I should, under no account, ever try moving like that ever again.

There was a tremendous amount of blood all over the ground beneath me, or so it seemed to me. Already, it had soaked my jeans. Some of it was certainly Grant's.

Just not much of it.

There were two marks in my vest, where rounds had hit and died against the Kevlar. The highest was in the upper right quadrant of my abdomen, the other roughly middle, about where my navel was. The blood I was spilling was coming from further below. With my free hand, I reached around to the small of my back, beneath the vest, and discovered a hole in my body that couldn't have been much larger than an apple. Maybe a Fuji. Maybe a Braeburn. When I brought my hand back around, it shone black in the night, covered with more of my blood.

I wasn't hearing Mark or his AR-15. There was a good chance he didn't know I'd been hit, that all he knew was that there'd been a quick exchange of shots, and now there was silence. But he wasn't calling out, either, wasn't asking Grant for his status, which meant that he figured either I'd killed Grant and was still alive and kicking, or that Grant and I had killed each other. Certainly, if Grant had killed me, Grant would have announced the fact the same way he'd announced everything else that he'd witnessed.

I was getting cold, and it wasn't just the night.

When Alena had begun teaching me, she'd done so, first and foremost, by showing me her training regimen. "Showing," in this instance, had meant making me do it with her, and the first month of the process had been a living hell, had very well nearly killed me. It wasn't just the diet and the exercise, it had been the *choice* of exercises. Between the swimming and the running and the combat practice, she'd thrown in ballet and yoga. Everything she did, everything she'd taught me, had been about one thing: control of the body, how to make it do what you wanted it to do, the way you wanted it done, when you wanted to do it.

Breathing had been one of the very first lessons. How to breathe properly.

I took a breath, forced myself to do it right, to bring it in deep to the lungs, to let it out slowly. I took a second one, then a third, and then, when I felt I wouldn't have to scream when I moved, I shifted myself away from the side of the Ford, turning as best as I could to face the front of the vehicle. When I moved, it felt like I was literally ripping myself in two directions, as if everything below my pelvis was grinding itself to paste, and an ocean roar grew suddenly in my ears, and the night all around me turned white.

Then the night came flooding back, and I knew I had blacked out, that I'd lost seconds, hopefully only a handful. I'd pitched forward, almost doubling over, and I'd dropped the MP5 in my lap. That had been lucky, and it had probably saved my life, because if Mark had heard it hitting the pavement, he'd have forgotten about coming slow and careful. I got my breathing under control, took hold of the MP5, and forced myself to sit upright again.

Grant's body lay to my side, his eyes open and unmoving. Through the open front doors of the Ford, I could see his partner, the one he'd called Sean, flat on his back. His eyes were closed. He had a boyish face, clean-shaven. The watch cap had come off when he'd fallen, and the hair on his head was cropped close, either brown or black. I couldn't see where I'd hit him, but the blood that had spilled from beneath his body made me think wherever it had been, it had been high in the torso, maybe even the neck. I couldn't tell if he was breathing or not.

The blood slicking my hands made controlling the MP5 hard, and I fumbled with the burst selector, trying to get it off three-round and onto full-auto. Then I listened for Mark and his AR-15 to approach. I hoped it wouldn't take long. The way I was bleeding, long was something I didn't think I could experience for much longer.

Something scraped the pavement, a faint sound, and it could have been nothing more than a leaf blowing across the lot. I raised the MP5 to roughly even with my head, supporting the barrel with my left, keeping my right on the trigger, pointing the muzzle downwards, towards the ground at an angle. It was counterintuitive, and it was risky, but it was the only way to turn a direct-fire weapon like the MP5 into an indirect-fire one, and indirect fire was the only way I could see out of this.

Firing like this—skip-firing—relied on the inherent strangeness of ballistics. Bullets don't behave like billiard balls. Despite what movies and television portray, they don't ricochet at perfect angles. This is why soldiers and cops don't press themselves against walls for cover; if the angle is right and the surface hard enough, the bullet won't bounce away, but rather will ride along the plane, sometimes as high as an inch or an inch and a half above its point of impact. If you're leaning against the wall the round is riding when that happens, you can end up with a very nasty, very lethal surprise.

I didn't like doing it, and I didn't have terrific faith that it would work, but I didn't see any other choice. I was bleeding badly, I knew it, maybe even bleeding out. I had an MP5 with eighteen rounds versus an AR-15 with quite possibly a reloaded magazine. Even if I had been able to stand for a straight-on fight, I was pretty certain I'd lose.

C'mon, I thought. *C'mon, come and get me, you bastard.*

It was what he had to do. His night, like mine, had become a total clusterfuck, and now he had to end it, one way or another. From the setup for the ambush, it was clear they hadn't expected that I would make them. But I had, and now Mark was down two buddies and all alone, and the last he'd heard had been Grant's shots and mine, and now he didn't know what was what. Like me, he was running out of moves and out of time. He could either climb back into his Cherokee and bolt, or he could approach the Ford and finish the job. And since I hadn't heard the Cherokee starting up again, it was going to be the latter.

Distantly, somewhere ahead and in front, I heard the clack of a magazine being fitted into place, a bolt being slid back. He'd made his decision; he was coming to finish me, reloaded and ready. Probably swinging around behind the rear end of the Civic, using it for cover.

The ocean was rising once more in my ears, and the edges of my vision were beginning to lose color again. Sitting the way I was hurt, and I was sure it made the bleeding worse. If I waited any longer, the chance that I'd pass out seemed more and more likely.

My finger was slippery on the MP5's trigger, but I got it down, laid a spray at the pavement, sweeping the barrel in a slight arc in front of me. I tried to count the shots, let up when I hit ten, but I was probably off by one or two.

There was an immediate scream of pain, and I heard first the AR-15, then Mark, hit the ground. He continued to scream, and he was loud, and I didn't blame him for that. One of the rounds must have found a foot, maybe destroying a toe, maybe coming at him a little higher. There are a lot of bones in the foot, most of them small, and all of them delicate. There was a reason he was screaming.

I readjusted my grip on the MP5, pulled the trigger again, sprayed at the ground again, but this time I kept the trigger down until the weapon went dry.

Mark stopped screaming.

I tried very hard not to start as I began lurching towards the Cherokee.

CHAPTER FOUR

To this day, I'm still unsure as to how I got into the Cherokee, how I got it turned around and headed the right way on County Route 10. I have a vague, distorted memory of reminding myself to breathe, and that getting to the vehicle itself was agonizing, not just because I was hurt, but because I had to do it quickly. My right leg had become beyond useless, and my left had been desperately trying to follow suit. How I managed to drive the vehicle at all remains a mystery; I must have used my left foot to work the pedals.

But there were things that I knew, and the most important among them was that I had to get back to the safe house, and I had to do it fast. The whole gunfight couldn't have lasted more than a minute, maybe two minutes, tops, but with the noise and the coming dawn, I was certain that what passed for law enforcement in Putnam County generally, and Cold Spring specifically, would be arriving soon. While the cop who found me might very well get me to a hospital, he or she wouldn't get me to the safe house, and the safe house was where I needed to go.

The first truly clear thing I remember is almost overshooting the entrance to Foreman Road, wrenching the wheel too hard and almost too late, and nearly sending the Cherokee and myself into the trees. I remember seeing that the sky was starting to burn with red, that daylight was beginning to illuminate the car, and that I seemed to have gotten my blood everywhere.

And I remember turning down Deer Hollow Road, seeing two big black Chevy Suburbans parked in the street almost directly in front of the house, each facing it. Dan and Alena and one of the Russians were all at the minivan, and the Russian I didn't know was holding a rifle in one hand, and somehow I knew that he had to be Vadim, Dan's son. Miata was jumping into the minivan's back as I lurched to a stop, and all of them had turned to watch me arriving, and all three of them were pointing guns at me. I was just lucid enough to realize why they were doing that, that they didn't know it was me behind the wheel, that they'd never seen the vehicle before.

Dan had a shotgun at his shoulder, and I could see blood spatter on his left cheek, and Alena had a pistol, a .45, and there were two bodies lying in front of the house, the legs of a third just visible through the door. Smoke was drifting lazily from somewhere inside, catching on the slight breeze outdoors. The two bodies that I could see wore tactical vests over their body armor, black pants and black boots. Each of them was missing most of his head. Two more MP5s rested on the ground, close to where each of them had fallen, and they were suppressed models, identical in all ways to the ones I'd encountered at the gas station.

Whoever had tried to do me had sent a team to the house, as well, probably within minutes of my departure.

I stopped the Cherokee maybe twenty feet away from where they were all pointing their guns at me, and I actually turned the engine off before moving to open the door. The Cherokee was an automatic, too, and I didn't want it to roll into anyone.

Alena shouted my name when I tumbled out of the car, but it was Dan who ran to help me up.

"I can't stand," I told him from the ground.

He swore in Russian, trying to get me back to my feet. There were powder burns on his face, along with the blood spatter, and that meant he'd been firing at close range, indoors. Whoever it was who'd come after them, they'd managed to breach the house.

"All right," Dan said, hooking an arm under me and carrying more than supporting me in the direction of the minivan. "We're going. You're losing blood, we have to do something about your bleeding."

"Where's Natalie?" I asked him.

"She's not coming."

"Where's Natalie?" I asked him.

"She's not coming, Atticus. We discuss this later, okay?"

I looked at him, and it was difficult to focus.

"Where's Natalie?" I asked him.

Dan shook his head, said something to Alena in Russian. They were trying to get me into the van; Miata was worriedly snuffling around the interior. The other Russian, Vadim, was already moving around to the driver's side, ready to climb behind the wheel.

"I'm going to sanitize," Dan told Alena, then turned and sprinted back into the house.

"Where's Natalie?" I asked Alena.

"They hit us maybe a minute, two minutes after you left," Alena said, and she had a knife in her hand, a switchblade, I didn't know where it had come from. The blade snapped out, shining in the thready dawn light. She began cutting my jacket off me.

"Two teams, front and back. Illya rabbited; it looks like he set us up."

"Where's Natalie?" I asked again.

Alena finished cutting the jacket off me, closed the switchblade, then started on the straps to my vest. I watched her working, her mouth closed tight, lips pressed together as if to seal in any potentially dangerous words. When she pulled the vest free from my body, something fell onto the running board, and I looked down, saw that it was a bullet, and guessed it was the one that had been inside me, that it had caught between my back and the vest. Looking down made me dizzier, so I looked up again, back to Alena.

"We have to stop this bleeding." She took a piece of my torn jacket, wadding it quickly in her hand and then pressing it against my belly. With her other hand, she moved mine on top of it. "Hold this here, don't let it go."

"Alena," I said. "Where's Natalie?"

She looked up from where I was spilling blood and met my eyes, hers deep and brown and full of the sadness they seemed to always hold. After a moment, she turned her head slightly to Vadim, spoke to him in Russian. Vadim responded, and from his inflection I knew he was asking a question, possibly about her sanity. She repeated what she'd said before, and he answered quietly, and I heard him opening the door, climbing out of the van once more.

"Where's Nata—" I started to ask.

"Vadim will take you to her," Alena said.

Natalie was in the yard behind the house.

She lay on her side, about eight feet from the rear door. The Sig Sauer she had given me and that I had returned to her earlier that night lay on the ground, maybe six inches from her thigh, near her outstretched fingers. The backyard had once had a lawn, but the lawn had long since overgrown, and with autumn, that overgrowth had gained a layer of fallen leaves. The rising sunlight brought out their color, made their oranges and reds and browns bright and beautiful. The reds almost matched the red of her hair.

They didn't go with the blood around her body at all.

Vadim held me steady while I looked down at my friend's body, and Alena stood on my other side, close enough to touch me but not doing so.

"Who?" I asked her. I could hear the ocean noise beginning to rise in my ears once more, feel the edges of my vision starting to contract.

She pointed with the hand that wasn't holding her cane, and I saw the body of a man, perhaps forty, maybe fifty feet away, lying facedown, beside one of the trees that framed the narrow yard. He was white, his hair shorn close to the scalp. He wore the same gear that the others in the front wore, but instead of an MP5, he'd been carrying a rifle.

"Vadim killed him," Alena told me.

There were another two bodies, these closer, off to the right. One of them was missing most of his throat. The other had been shot multiple times in the head and neck.

I shook my head, and the world didn't stop spinning when I was finished doing it.

"No," I said, and it was getting harder to make the words. "Who did this? Who made this happen?"

"I don't know."

"I'm going to kill whoever did this." I think I told it to Natalie. I might have been saying it to Alena.

"I know."

I could hardly hear her over the sound of waves filling my ears. I forced myself to look away from the body of my friend.

"I'm going to kill whoever did this," I repeated.

Alena nodded, blurring in my sight. Her mouth moved, and I saw Dan step into my dwindling periphery, then start forward, one hand shooting out to catch me before I fell. Vadim tightened his grip on my arm, but it wasn't enough, and the last thing I saw before I couldn't see more was the face of Natalie Trent, of my last friend, beautiful as she had ever been, as she slept forever on a blanket of leaves in the New England fall.

CHAPTER FIVE

I woke up twice before the flight.

The first time, I was lying on my back on something cold and hard, and I could smell garlic and onions and frying meat. When I opened my eyes, I saw two large colanders and a stockpot and what looked like a twelve-inch skillet hanging above me from various hooks. Between a tarnished copper saucier and a pasta steamer hung a bag of Ringer's solution, and the line from the bag seemed to be running down and into my arm. Dan and Vadim were on one side of me, and there was a woman I'd never seen before on the other, and her nose looked like someone had trapped it in a vise and forgotten to ever release it. Dan still had powder burns on his face, but the blood spatter was gone.

There were voices all around me, some very soft, all of them speaking Russian, and the woman with the fascinating nose was wearing surgical gloves, and the gloves were stained with blood. It took me a moment to recognize that it was likely my blood that stained them, that she was probably working on me as I watched, and that explained the extraordinary amount of pain I was feeling.

"Please tell me I'm not getting surgery in a kitchen," I said.

Dan and Vadim and the woman all looked down at me in surprise.

Then the woman looked at Dan and began shrieking at him, clearly berating him, and Dan shouted back at her, and Vadim reached for something out of my sight. I felt a needle breaking through my skin, felt something warm and heavy filling my veins, and I fell gratefully back into darkness.

The second time I awoke, I was in a bed, in a room, in the dark. Light filtered in from the street through windows somewhere behind me, but it was weak, street lighting, and I thought it must be late in the night. The sound of music thumped up through the floor and then through the bed from someplace beneath me, a bass line more felt than heard, and behind that, barely audible, I could make out the susurration of traffic running along streets that sounded slicked and puddled with rain.

The bed was a big one, maybe a king, and I was beneath the covers, and my clothes were gone. Alena lay beside me, sleeping above the sheets, and she had her clothes on, but had removed her boots. A pistol rested on the nightstand nearest her, along with a cell phone, and I tried reading the time on its display, but couldn't focus my eyes, couldn't manage to make things stop looking so blurry. It took me another few seconds to realize that was because someone had removed my contact lenses.

I wondered where I was going to get a new set of glasses.

Paws came scratching across the hardwood floor, Miata making his way to me, and I felt his breath against the back of my hand. I raised my arm and stroked his neck for a few seconds, and then he pulled away, and I listened to the sound of him settling once more on the floor nearby. I shifted experimentally in the bed, trying to reposition myself, and the pain that erupted from my right side, from my gut down through my knee, made me gasp, and filled my eyes with water.

Beside me, Alena made a noise in her sleep, perhaps responding to me, but more likely experiencing, once again, the nightmares that were her youth.

The pain lasted for several seconds before it drifted away reluctantly, and it must have been a minute or more before I was willing to try moving again. This time, I limited myself to moving only my right leg, and the pain returned as intense and hateful as before. Maybe because I'd known it was coming, I managed to remain silent.

The hurt retreated, taking its time to do it. When I finally closed my eyes again, I saw Natalie's body, lying in the leaves.

I stared at her until sleep took me back where I belonged.

The plane was a Gulfstream V, and it was waiting on a piece-of-shit runway in Montauk, on the ass-end of Long Island, and I didn't get a good look at it from the outside, because Dan and Vadim had to carry me on a stretcher into the plane. Once inside, I had a great view of the ceiling, which was painted a robin's egg blue. It seemed an oddly cheerful choice, and I supposed whoever designed these kinds of things had gone with the color to conjure a greater sense of flying free in the wild blue yonder.

The pilot stood at the door of the cockpit as I was loaded inside, a long stick of a man with a two-day growth of gray and black beard on his face, wearing a suit with a wide array of wrinkles. Our eyes met as I was carried past him, and the boredom he showed me was so absolute I wondered if he wasn't loaded up with painkillers the same way I was.

They carried me almost the whole length of the plane, then settled me on a leather-covered bench near the galley. As soon as I was down and safe, Vadim slipped past his father, heading back the way he came. Dan looked down at me with a frown for a moment, then sighed and sat down on the bench opposite me.

"I want to sit up," I told him.

"Atticus," Dan said. "You really don't."

I rolled my head to the side to look at him. He looked tired, and I imagined he hadn't grabbed much sleep since everything had gone to hell at the safe house, however long ago that had been. I didn't know. My sense of where I stood in the passage of time had been almost entirely destroyed. It wasn't the first time I'd experienced the sensation, and each time it happened to me, I liked it less and less.

"Help me sit up," I told him.

Dan sighed heavily, but moved to assist me. If he did it because he was still afraid of me, I couldn't imagine why. The condition I was in, I couldn't have convincingly threatened a wet paper towel.

It took effort, and more help than I had hoped I would need, but together we got me propped into a nearly upright position, with my back to the galley wall, and a view of the length of the plane. I swore a couple of times while we did it.

"Don't swear," Alena said, limping down the aisle, Miata following at her heels. She had a duffel bag, gray canvas, over her shoulder, and it must have made moving with the cane difficult, but she gave no sign of it. "You can't breathe properly if you're swearing, and why the hell is he sitting up?"

The last was directed at Dan, and for a moment, I thought he would actually throw up his hands in exasperation. "He tells me he wants to sit!"

Alena dropped the duffel onto one of the leather-covered seats, then dropped herself into the one across from it, facing me. She scowled. Miata continued past us, snuffling his way into the galley.

"The bullet creased the iliac crest on your right side as it exited. The bone needs time and rest to heal. If you insist on moving, you will prolong recovery, and potentially do greater damage. Bad enough that I'm half lame; now you're trying to cripple yourself, as well?"

"Imitation is the sincerest form of flattery," I said.

Vadim returned, carrying a bag of his own, this one smaller than Alena's duffel, black, with a silver Nike swoosh on its side. He gave me a grin, then bent to stow his luggage in one of the lacquered wood cabinets acting as a divider between portions of the cabin. The plane wasn't terribly large, but a lot of effort had gone into the main cabin design, and there was plenty of space. Slight tears marred the leather upholstery around me, and I could see faint scratches on the lacquer in places, and it struck me that the Gulfstream probably got a lot of use.

Finished, Vadim closed the cabinet once more, then dropped into a seat of his own, pulling an iPod from one of his jacket pockets. From where he stood at the cockpit door, the pilot called out to us, asking if we were ready to go. That surprised me, not because he seemed to actually care, but because he sounded American, and not Russian.

"They're ready," Dan said, and he got to his feet. He switched into Russian, asking Alena something, and while I was starting to pick up words here and there, I couldn't really understand it. But I heard the name "Illya," and that was enough.

"You know where he is?" I asked.

They both looked at me, Dan with vague hostility, Alena with curiosity.

"Not yet," Dan admitted. "But we'll find him. We'll find him, and we'll take care of him. *I'll* take care of him."

"But you don't know where he is."

"I said that I will find him."

"And you think he doesn't know that? There's no way Illya's still in New York, Dan. He got out, and he got help to do it, most likely. You're going to have to cast a very wide net before you find him again."

Dan clenched his teeth, showing me one of his thick fingers. The anger was an anger I understood, the anger of betrayal, and I didn't take it personally that he was consequently directing it at me.

"But I *will* find him, Atticus." It was a growl, half threat, half oath. "I will find him, and when I do, I will pay him back for what he did. He sold us out, he got two of my boys killed and your Natalie, he goes down for that. For that, he pays."

"He pays for that," I agreed. "But not until after I've had a chance to talk to him."

"The fuck—"

Alena interrupted. "It will take you a while to find him, I think, Dan. Atticus is correct."

"This kind of thing, it has to be answered quickly!"

"Not until after I talk to him," I said, and I said it deliberately, and I said it softly, and I said it as clearly as I could. In his seat, about to put his ear buds into place, Vadim stopped what he was doing, turning around to look at first me, then his father.

"Tasha, tell this guy—"

"Find him," I told Dan. "Watch him. Track him. Mark him. But don't touch him, Dan. And don't let him make you. Once you have him, you let us know."

"I have to take care of this!"

"You will. But I'm going to need him first."

I moved my eyes from Dan to Alena, and I saw she was with me, that she understood what I wanted, and why, and more, why it was important.

She spoke quietly, in Russian, and Dan made a face like he was having trouble controlling his temper, and then he actually did throw his hands in the air. When they came down again, he pointed his finger at me a second time.

"I don't do this for you," he said. "And I don't do this for Tasha, you understand? I do this for Natalie, because I liked her, and she liked you. But because I do this for Natalie, Illya is *mine*, you understand? His life is now mine, no one else's. No one kills that walking fuckhole but me, understand?"

"I understand."

Dan grunted, turned away, slapping Vadim on the shoulder. The younger man got to his feet, and the two of them exchanged a rough hug. Vadim had drawn the short straw on the height gene, because he only reached Dan's shoulder, which put him at, perhaps, chin height on me and Alena. But he had his father's body type, the same strength of chin and jaw. When the two of them embraced, it was clear that the blood running between them was thick.

Dan released the young man, this time slapping him lightly on the cheek, then made his way to the front of the aircraft. He stopped at the door, looked back at us.

"I will see you when I see you."

"You didn't even see us here," Alena responded.

Dan turned to the pilot, still waiting at the cockpit door. "How many passengers you carrying?"

"One," the pilot said. "Some kid I'm taking back to the home country."

"That's right. One."

Dan looked back at us, then at his son, a final time. Then he went out the door, disappearing down the stairs.

"Buckle up," the pilot told us.

Seven minutes after takeoff, the pilot came over the intercom.

"International waters," he said.

I shifted carefully on my bench, looked over to where Alena had taken a position opposite me, her legs stretched out in front of her, as if she was imitating my posture. Her head was turned to the window, resting her forehead against the glass. Miata lay curled in the aisle between us.

Without looking at me, Alena asked, "Are you ready to talk about what happened?"

"If you're asking do I feel up to it, yes, I think so."

"Then tell me what happened."

I told her what happened, as best as I could remember. Everything from the moment I'd left the safe house in the Civic to my broken memories upon returning. I ended with her and Vadim taking me to see Natalie where she lay in the yard.

She never stopped looking out the window as I relayed it to her, and her questions were few. She was curious about the AR-15, because she said that had been an anomaly in the weapons load-out. The MP5s were, strictly speaking, MP5SDs, and apparently, all but two of the people who'd been trying to kill us had carried them.

"Tasked from the same source," Alena murmured, more to herself than to me. "Each group, tasked from the same source for their op."

"Your turn," I said. "What happened at the house?"

She drew a deep breath through her nose, exhaling it strong

enough that it formed a mist on her window. Then she swung her legs off the bench, turning so she could sit facing me.

"Natalie was trying to protect me," Alena said. "Remember that, Atticus."

Then she told me what happened at the safe house.

CHAPTER SIX

The window in Alena's room at the house in Cold Spring looked out over the backyard, not the front, and so she had not watched me go. But she had heard the sound of the Civic starting, had heard its wheels turning on the leaf-strewn road, and because she had never had to say good-bye before to anyone she did not wish to see go, she remained motionless, and listened for as long as she could. She listened until the sound of my departure faded into the night.

When she said this to me, she told me that she would have been embarrassed to admit it, except that doing so is what had given the first warning, because by doing so, she heard two things she hadn't expected.

The first was the sound of an engine, of a vehicle coming down the road (she admitted that, for a moment, she had hoped it was the same vehicle, that I was returning for some reason, but almost as quickly as she'd thought that, she had dismissed the idea: I was not returning). Then she heard another one behind it, and she understood that two vehicles were now approaching the house.

The second was the sound of the front door closing.

It was these things that provided the warning, or, more precisely, provided Alena with the warning at the same time that Vadim, in his tree house and with his rifle and his night-vision goggles and his phone, saw the two Suburbans coming quickly down the road towards the house, their headlights off. Being a good boy, and being trained by his father, he did what he was supposed to do. He got on his radio and told Dan that the house was about to be hit.

It was then that Vadim heard the front door closing, and turned just in time to watch Illya run for the trees.

(Vadim, who had disconnected himself from his iPod long enough to listen to what Alena was telling me, was eager to offer his version of events at this point, interrupting to say, "I asked Dan if I should shoot the little shit-eating motherfucker." His English was flawless, his accent pure Brooklyn. "Dan said not to, he said Illya wasn't the problem, and he told me to stay down and out of sight until the fuckers who'd arrived started into the house.")

Many things began happening at once, then, Alena told me. She heard movement downstairs, and Dan shouting for the guard at the back, Yasha, to get ready, that they were about to be hit. She heard Natalie running, already starting to climb the stairs. Miata, too, had realized that something was wrong, and had gotten to his feet, following Alena as she had half hopped, half limped out of her room and into the one of the guard next door, Tamryn.

Alena shouted to Tamryn to get the fuck up, then grabbed his shotgun and spun back around to take a position at the top of the stairs. The shotgun was another Remington 870, the same make and model that Yasha and Illya had been issued by Dan ("He got a deal on them," Vadim explained), but unlike Illya's, both Yasha's and Tamryn's had been loaded with three-inch double-ought buckshot, which would be more effective at close range, inside the house.

Tamryn had scrambled out of bed, drawing his secondary weapon, a Smith & Wesson 910 semiauto ("How do you know that?" Vadim asked her, and Alena looked at him as if the question was beyond idiotic, and answered, "Because I saw it, Vadim." She was always very precise in matters of equipment and gear, not because she was particularly obsessive about the tools of the trade, but because she felt it was her professional obligation to know and understand what each tool was, and what it could do), and rushed to follow her out. By the time they'd each left the room, Natalie had reached them, and Dan was close at her heels. On her way to the stairs, Natalie had grabbed Illya's discarded shotgun, which she now tossed to Dan.

None of them had managed to take any reasonable, or even effective, defensive position at this point, which was unfortunate, because it was at this point that the people who'd arrived to kill them entered the house.

("They poured out of those Chevys like their dicks were on fire," Vadim told me. "All gung ho, 'Let's go, Marines!' attitude and shit, but professional about it; they were trying to keep it down, at least until the shooting started. I really don't think they thought anyone was going to be shooting back at them, you know?")

They came through the door in good entry formation, Alena said, covering their angles. The lights were still off in the house, and they tried to be quiet about it. From where she, Natalie, Tamryn, and Dan had been trying to take position, they could see the shapes of their attackers in the ambient light. But they had all still been in motion at the breach, and that made them easy to spot, and it was the attacking force that opened fire first.

There was an initial barrage of fire from the MP5s, eerily quiet since the weapons were suppressed, and maybe as a result, their voices had seemed so much louder.

"Target, top of the stairs!" one had shouted. "With the shotgun, take her, *take her*!"

From the volume of fire that poured in Alena's direction, she had no doubt they were referring to her, and not to Natalie.

Tamryn went down almost immediately, before he could get a single shot off. He'd been on Alena's left at the top of the stairs, and one of the first bursts meant for her had gone wide, and taken him instead. Alena, Natalie, and Dan had all returned fire, but none of them had scored hits. This didn't bother Alena, since it wasn't the object of the exercise, as far as she was concerned.

The object of the exercise, so to speak, was to get herself, Natalie, Dan, and Miata out of the house alive. If they could force the assault team back out the front door, then they would have secured an effective crossfire, and Vadim could pick their attackers off at his relative leisure.

Outside, in the tree house, Vadim had been lining up his first shot as the assault team had been taking up their formation. Three of the team had broken right, away from him, looking to go around the back of the house, but the rest of the group—there were eight in all—had taken up positions for the entry.

Now Vadim heard the barrage of fire from inside the house, and he felt that qualified as permission to do some shooting of his own. He fired, and put a .308 round through the head of the man furthest back in the assault team. His rifle wasn't suppressed, and everyone heard the report, and this threw the entry team into chaos. One of them tried to immediately reverse direction and make for the cover provided by the Suburbans. The remaining three continued trying to gain the house.

"They went total bugfuck when I took their first guy down," Vadim said. "They were all shouting to each other, trying to keep some sort of control of the situation. I only wish I'd been quicker, you know?"

Back on the stairs, Dan, Natalie, and Alena were continuing to lay down fire. The initial furious exchange of bullets had abated, and Dan had dropped his shotgun and dived past Nat and Alena, to where Tamryn had gone down. One of the assault team tried to capitalize on the move, coming around the door frame again, and Alena and Natalie both opened up on him simultaneously.

The man fell, and Alena said she was certain it was Natalie who had made the kill.

(I found that hard to believe, but did not say so. If Alena thought that crediting Natalie with the kill would somehow make me feel better about what happened to her, she was wrong. It didn't mean I couldn't appreciate the effort, or see it for what it was, but she was wrong.)

Then Dan threw the smoke grenade that Tamryn had been carrying, and it landed in the front hallway just as Yasha entered from the kitchen, firing wildly with his own Remington. The second shooter at the door put a burst straight into his chest, and Yasha fell at almost the same moment the grenade detonated and began filling first the hallway, then the house, with white smoke. Again, Natalie and Alena returned fire, and the man who'd killed Yasha pitched forward and didn't move again.

At which point Natalie dropped the shotgun, switched to the

Sig Sauer I'd returned to her, grabbed hold of Alena's left arm, and said, "We are getting you out of here *now*!"

Dan took hold of Alena's right arm, handing her the little Seecamp .380 he kept in his pocket, and together with Natalie, they hoisted her to her feet, and began working their way down the stairs, planning to exit at the rear of the house. They still didn't know how many people they were dealing with out front, and they didn't know if more would be arriving.

What they did know was that Alena had been verbally identified as the shooters' primary target. To deny the enemy that target meant they had to get out of the house, and that meant going out the back.

In the tree house, Vadim was having trouble getting a good shot on the two shooters he still had to deal with. He'd fired off two more rounds, each to no effect, now leaving him with only four in the rifle before he'd have to switch to the revolver his father had given him. He didn't have a reload for the rifle in the tree house with him, because none of them had considered that they might need to repel an attack of this magnitude.

To make matters worse, Vadim was getting very worried about the three he'd seen breaking for the side of the house. From his vantage point, with the beginnings of dawn's light starting to flow out of the forest, he could see the treeline surrounding the backyard, but not much of the yard itself. With the remaining shooters outside, throwing occasional bursts of fire at him, he couldn't risk switching targets, nor picking up the cell phone resting by his knee.

Then smoke had started pouring from the front of the house, and the two shooters that Vadim couldn't get a bead on saw it, and one of them wheeled back to the door, bringing his MP5 to his shoulder.

(Vadim wasn't sure why he did this, and Alena explained the reasoning before I could. Until the smoke began pouring out of the house, the shooter could believe that his back was covered. But once the visibility behind him went, there was no way to determine what might be happening inside. More importantly, it meant that there was no way for the shooter to visualize anything that might come at *him*. Therefore, not wanting to leave his back exposed, he'd turned around, hoping that the Suburbans would provide an adequate defense against Vadim's sniping.)

Regardless, in turning he showed Vadim the back of his head through the side windows of one of the Suburbans. Vadim fired once, and the man fell forward, the top of his skull turned to mist. The remaining shooter returned fire, trying to suppress Vadim, then broke for the side of the house. Vadim dropped him before he made the corner.

In the house, they'd reached the hallway on the ground floor, and Natalie was leading Alena along, towards the back door. She'd let go of her, holding the Sig with both hands, in a high-ready position, being careful to clear each room before they passed through it. Miata had trotted close beside Alena as she'd struggled along. Her damaged leg made the going much slower than she'd have liked, but the brace running from her ankle to her knee kept it from becoming impossible. Dan stayed at the rear, covering their backs, having switched to his main pistol, a Springfield Armories TRP, which he, too, was holding in the high-ready position. Smoke from the grenade was everywhere, and while it didn't actually make it harder to breathe, the visibility in the house was next to zero, and it made for a tense trip through the ground floor.

They reached the door into the yard, and Natalie had thrown it open, then stepped back into cover. Nothing happened, and she looked back to Alena and Dan, and they both nodded, and all of them, including Miata, started out into the creeping dawn.

When they were all five, maybe six feet outside, Dan's Nextel squawked inside his jacket, Vadim trying to raise him over the radio. Almost instantly, probably cued by the sound of the transmission, two of the three who had gone to flank came around the side of the house, on the right, bringing their MP5s to bear. Natalie turned, putting herself in front of Alena, half blocking her with her own body, as Dan stepped forward, each of them preparing to fire. It's likely, in that instant, all three of them thought they were going to die.

It was Miata who saved their lives, because before any of them had even realized the two shooters were coming around the corner, Miata had known. Either he'd caught their scent or he'd heard their movement, but for whatever reason, when the two with MP5s made the corner, Miata was already halfway to them, running hard.

The result was that the two shooters each had to switch targets, because neither of them knew which of them Miata was aiming for, and waiting to find out would have been too late. When you have eighty-seven pounds of furious Doberman bearing down on you, teeth bared and making not a sound as he charges, panic isn't just a reasonable response; it might well be the only response.

One of the two fired off a burst, but it was panicked, and his shots went low, passing beneath Miata as he leapt at him. The shooter screamed, dropped his gun, and fell, pretty much all at once. The second shooter, who had been pivoting out of Miata's way, now realized what he'd done and tried to self-correct. Before he had a chance, Alena and Dan opened up on him, each of them firing double-taps that scored hits in the face and neck.

In the cascade of their shots, then, came the other one, and the part of Alena's consciousness that tracks these things in the middle of gunfights thought it was Vadim's rifle, but thought also that the shot had come from the wrong direction. She turned, trying to locate the source, and that was when she saw that Natalie had gone down, and that was when she saw the last shooter, with his rifle, just inside the treeline, and she knew that the rifle was pointed at her.

(What must have happened, Alena said, was that the shooter on the rifle had lined up a head shot on her, and most likely had been about to take it, when she, Natalie, and Dan had reacted to the other two coming around the corner. Natalie's attempt to shield Alena from the two shooters and their MP5s had moved her into the sniper's path of fire, as well. Alena was adamant about this, and I was inclined to agree with her; if Natalie hadn't moved when she had, the way she had, the bullet that struck her would certainly have hit Alena, instead.)

Dan checked Alena with his shoulder, sending her onto the ground, practically falling on top of her, firing the TRP as he fell. With the range and the motion, if he had managed to hit anything, it would have been a miracle, and since people like us didn't rate miracles, he didn't hit anything at all. The shooter with the rifle fired again, missing, then readjusted and reacquired, readying to make his third shot. This time, he'd score a hit, whether on Alena or on Dan they didn't know, but they were on the ground, and the next bullet was going to kill one of them, certainly.

Then, from the tree house came the sound of shots, Vadim firing his last two rounds at the man who had killed Natalie Trent, doing to him what he had done to her.

CHAPTER SEVEN

Vadim found a bottle of champagne and three micro pizzas, pepperoni, in the galley when he went to look for lunch. He seemed genuinely surprised that Alena and I would decline to share such a feast with him, returning to his seat and his iPod with a rolling of the eyes that did more to convince me of his nineteen years than anything else had thus far.

After a moment, Alena pulled herself to her feet and put on water for tea. I looked out the plane window and saw land beneath us, painted in white. Ice or snow. We were headed for Europe, I knew that, Eastern Europe almost certainly. I wasn't sure of the range of the Gulfstream V, but supposed we'd have to land to refuel at least once before reaching our final destination.

Alena made two trips back from the galley, traveling slowly and carefully so as to keep from spilling the hot drinks. She brought mine first, then returned with hers, and took her same seat once again.

"Black tea," she said, making a face. "No herbal, nothing without caffeine. I'm sorry."

"We'll survive," I told her, thinking about how, once upon a time, I'd thought caffeine was a major food group all its own. Now it was no longer a part of the diet, neither mine nor hers, at the top of the list of verboten stimulants, in fact. Aside from being addictive as, say, nicotine, caffeine drains the adrenal gland. Considering how much Alena and I relied on adrenaline to do its job, that was something neither of us wanted.

"How many days have I lost?" I asked.

"Three and a half. Dan wanted to move you sooner, but I wouldn't let him. You lost a lot of blood. You almost died."

"We could have made the trip sooner."

"It was not in my mind to risk it. You nearly died, Atticus."

I considered that, then said, "And you wanted to see how what happened in Cold Spring would play out. See what got reported in the media, maybe."

Alena brushed hair back from her cheek, and as she did, the Gulfstream banked slightly, and sunlight came flooding through the windows. Where it touched her head, the copper of her hair seemed to burn.

"So how bad is it?" I asked.

"No, that's not what they did."

"What do you mean?"

"It didn't make the media, Atticus. None of it. From the time we fled the safe house until just this morning, when we left Brighton Beach, there was never as much as a whisper that anyone had died in a gun battle in Cold Spring. There was never as much as a whisper that anything happened there at all."

"There must have been something. Some report."

"No. Nothing."

I removed my newly acquired glasses, rubbed my eyes with my other hand. The glasses had been waiting for me this morning, and while the prescription had been correct—or at least, close enough that my eyes had been able to compensate—their fit was bad, and they dug into the skin behind my ears. I folded them closed, set them on the shelf beside me.

"Natalie," I said. "There should have been at least something about Natalie."

"And I am saying to you that there wasn't, Atticus. There was nothing at all."

She stared at me, a little blurred in my sight, but her expression seemed almost entirely neutral, her sad brown eyes meeting my own. She was waiting for me to say it, to put the words to what she had already concluded, but I wasn't willing to, not quite yet. Not until I had at least made an effort at providing an alternate explanation.

My problem was, no alternate was offering itself for use.

"Dan did not need to sanitize the house," Alena said. "They would have done that for us."

"Whoever 'they' are."

"You know who 'they' are, Atticus, at least in the abstract, at least as much as I know it. There is only one possible explanation to satisfy every question, from who hired Oxford, to who tried to kill you, to who tried to kill me, to who did kill Natalie as a result."

"There could be others."

"With the ability to enforce media silence regarding what happened, to cover up the deaths of almost a dozen men? With the ability and the capital to assemble, finance, and deploy two coordinated strikes against both you and me with perhaps less than three, maybe even two hours of notice? There was no expectation that you would be arriving at the safe house, Atticus, remember that. The initial plan had been that you would deal with Oxford while I was taken to Cold Spring. You were never to join us there."

"Natalie called Dan from the road, told him that I was coming in with you two, that I'd need a car."

"The car that Illya acquired, yes. Which is probably when he informed his masters that you would be coming to the safe house. Masters who, in all likelihood, are responsible for Illya's disappearance. The team that ambushed you could have been an element of the larger team that assaulted the house; they could have been split off when it became apparent they needed a new contingency to deal with you, when they realized they needed to stage an ambush."

The tea bag in my cup was floating on the surface, on its side. I poked it back down with a finger.

"That's something that's been bothering me," I said. "Why didn't they just hit all of us at the house? Why did they think it was necessary to hit me separately?"

"They identified you as the greatest threat."

"Greater than you? I find that hard to believe."

"They knew I was wounded. They wanted to isolate you. That's why they forced you into an ambush, away from the safe house."

"Stupid on their part."

"Perhaps. They were having to adapt very quickly, remember. And their assessment of you was correct; you broke their ambush, and you killed all three of them without dying yourself. There are not many who could have survived that."

"If they'd kept the whole team together, hit us as soon as we'd arrived at the safe house—"

Alena moved her left hand, a slight gesture, side to side, impatiently. "Don't make assumptions, Atticus. We do not know if they were in position when we arrived. It is just as likely that they had to call for more men to set the ambush as it is that the three who attacked you were part of the larger unit."

I snagged on the word "unit." "You think they were military?"

"Not active duty, no."

"Civilian contractors."

"That would be my suspicion, yes. And we both know who civilian contractors contract *with,* Atticus." She ran a hand through her hair. "As I said, we both know who 'they' are."

I put my tea down, on the shelf, beside my glasses. I was tired and I was sore, and I hurt in body and heart. I let my head fall back against the cushion behind me, closed my eyes.

Natalie Trent was still resting on her bed of leaves.

"I love my country," I said softly. "But I fear my government."

Beside me, Alena said, "With good reason."

Then she reached across the aisle, and took hold of my hand, and held it until the government I feared was far, far behind us.

PART TWO

CHAPTER ONE

It took three years, two months, and twelve days for us to find where Illya Tyagachev was hiding.

Within three weeks of arriving in the Georgian capital of Tbilisi, I was out of the woods and beginning to heal, and to heal fast. Maybe it was because I'd been in the best shape of my life when I'd been shot, better even than when I'd been twenty and full of juice and pounding the ground in the Army; maybe it was simply my bullheaded resolve that, between Alena and myself, at least *one* of us needed to be able to rely on their legs to do what they were told.

Whatever the reason, I bounced back quickly, and was able to move around, unassisted and with only minor discomfort, before the end of November. I wasn't doing handstands during yoga, and the ballet training was off the table, but if I had to, I could serve in a pinch. Vadim was still traveling with us, and he helped pick up my slack, further acting as our legman, gopher, and extra gun.

We spent New Year's Day that year at the Sonnenhof Clinic in Saanen-Gstaad, looking out at the snow-covered mountains of the Bernese Oberland. Alena had undergone her first surgery only two days prior, a combination exploration and cleanup where a team of orthopedic surgeons had gone into her leg to visualize the damage Oxford had done there. They'd removed the remaining bone debris and the last of the shot that had been missed by the first doctor who'd worked on her, back in Kingstown, St. Vincent.

The operation took just under three hours, and the doctor leading Alena's care, Frau Doktor Marika Akrman, told us afterwards that it had been "very productive."

"But there is, I am afraid, not so good news, as well," she said. Her English was precise, the accent very German. "What we feared due to the delay in your treatment has come to happen, and the anterior cruciate ligament will have to be replaced. In addition, the tendons that were severed have retracted. If you had come to us sooner, we might have been able to reextend and reattach them. Unfortunately, that is no longer possible."

Frau Doktor Akrman was in her fifties, with a girlish face and blond-white hair. When she frowned or smiled it made her look a lot younger. She was frowning when she added, "I am sorry to tell you that I do not think you will ever be able to dance as you once did."

Alena and I took the news stoically. That had been our story, that Alena had been teaching ballet in Moscow, a bystander making her way down the street caught in a cross fire between two rival gang factions. It wasn't the most creative lie, but it worked, because it wasn't much of a lie at all. I'd found the report of the actual gunfight through a Google search, and it was easy enough to put Alena on the scene as a woman named Sinovia Gariblinski, an innocent victim who had recently wed an American software designer more than willing to pay for his new bride's expensive surgeries.

In fact, the money behind the surgeries—the money behind *everything* we did, how we traveled, how we lived, all of it—was Alena's and Alena's alone. Her "blood money," she called it, the wages she had been paid for the nine men and two women she had murdered as one of The Ten. There was a lot of it, hidden in trusts and accounts and investments around the globe, carefully folded into the safety of private banks. One of the first things Alena had done when we'd reached Eastern Europe was reach out for her attorney, arranging a meeting between him and the two of us in Warsaw. She'd liquidated some funds and redistributed others to new hiding places. After all, I'd been able to leverage Oxford through his money; she didn't want the same thing happening to us.

"How much more of this will she have to go through?" I asked Dr. Akrman.

The Frau Doktor inclined her head, accepting my concern for my spouse. "Another two procedures, I think. We will have to reattach the bones in the tibia and fibula, as discussed, and bolt them back into place. Then a final operation, to replace the anterior cruciate. Of course, you will need to look into appropriate physical therapy once you get her back home."

"How long until I regain the use of the leg?" Alena asked.

"If you dedicate yourself to the physical therapy, not long." Frau Doktor Akrman smiled a practiced smile, attempting to remove the sting from what she had to say next. "But without the tendons, the strength in your left leg will be severely diminished. Running and jumping will be difficult, and I would strongly advise against even attempting to try."

Alena smiled, too, saying she understood, and Frau Doktor

Akrman left, and as soon as she was out of the room and the door was closed, Alena pulled the pillow from behind her head and threw it across the room. The pillow hit the television in its open cabinet on the opposite wall, then fell to the floor. Alena cursed in Russian.

"Don't swear," I told her. "You can't breathe properly if you swear."

She turned the cursing at me, glaring, and I gave her a big grin in return. She tried to keep glaring at me for another second or two, but my grin won, and finally she had to look away, out the windows and at the glorious winter view, to keep her bad mood intact.

"It's better than I hoped," I said.

"No running?" Alena demanded. "No jumping? How is that better?"

"You'll be able to walk without assistance, without the cane. You'll be able to swim."

She grunted a sullen acceptance, and I left it at that.

The last operation was performed that March, five months after we'd fled the States, and it was a shorter procedure than the second, and at the end of it Frau Doktor Akrman declared it a success. Alena was discharged from the clinic eight days later, and we made our way back to Georgia by roundabout route over the next three days. She was on crutches, and despite the Frau Doktor's optimism, we both knew it would be a while before she could move about reliably on her own.

Vadim had located a new house for us outside the city of Batumi—the fifth we'd stayed in since fleeing the U.S.—down in the south along the Black Sea coast. It was easy to find places on the coast to rent or buy, and the Georgian economy being what it was, a little of Alena's money went a very long way. Most of the dachas the Party bigwigs once used were uninhabited or had been converted to summer rentals, and if we were willing to pay in cash—and we always were—almost anything we needed could be obtained in relatively short order, from vehicles to accommodations to weapons.

The house was larger and more ostentatious than I would have chosen if I'd made the pick myself, with too much space for only three people and a dog. The last of the Georgian winter was still with us, and keeping the house warm was a nightmare. Vadim acknowledged all of these faults, but then justified the choice by telling us that there was an indoor pool, and that it was heated.

I was growing very fond of Vadim.

Alena and I made the first, stuttering attempts at resuming our respective training regimens. We swam a lot, slowly resumed our routine of morning yoga. Alena still couldn't incorporate ballet into her workout, but she took great glee in watching me attempt it, and never failed to find something wrong with the way I was moving, with a *jeté* here, an *entrechat quatre* there. I didn't mind; I enjoyed my feeble attempts at dance, the way it focused my mind inward, honed my awareness of my own body.

We brought up a physical therapist from Batumi three times a week to work with Alena. He worked with her in the pool, mostly, and with weights, sometimes, and after watching them together during the first half-dozen or so of their sessions, I left them alone. Vadim tailed him the first four times the therapist left the house, and his assessment was, and I agreed with him, that if this guy was going to try and kill any of us, it wouldn't be because he was working for someone who wanted him to do it.

■ ■ ■

Twice since the year turned Dan had contacted us via e-mail sent from anonymous accounts. There had been no sign of Illya, and in February, Dan offered the theory that whoever he'd been working for had tied up that particular loose end with a hollow-point to the base of the skull. Alena was inclined to agree. I wasn't so certain.

In early April, we received a third e-mail, and in it Dan asked if we could perhaps do without Vadim, that he had work for him back in Brooklyn.

"He's missing him," Alena confided to me while watching my attempts at dance the following morning. "So he says he has work, because Dan doesn't want us to think he is weak."

"He misses his son. How is that weak?"

"He believes admitting such things makes one vulnerable. It can be exploited."

I thought about what Natalie had said to me six months earlier in the kitchen of the house in Cold Spring, and what I'd said to her in return. Her words had seemed so saccharine and manipulative at the time, an attempt by her to convince me to stay, and I'd resented her like hell for making something that was already difficult all the harder.

At night, when I closed my eyes, I still saw her on her autumnal bed. It didn't help things that the last words I'd exchanged with her had been bitter and spiteful ones.

"It can," I said, and left it at that.

At the end of April we moved to a smaller house outside the resort town of Ureki, and the next morning we sent Vadim back to his father. The boy was glad to go, though he tried to hide it. He missed New York, and he had friends there he wanted to see. I could almost remember what that was like.

The following day the weather turned unseasonably ugly, as if reminding us it was still winter, but Alena, Miata, and I went down to the shore for a walk anyway. We did some shopping for the house, bought some fresh-caught sea bass for dinner. In the grocery store, I saw Alena hovering over the selection of wines, and she caught me looking and then moved on to gather fruits and vegetables. Georgians, as a rule, loved to drink, and loved their wine, but Alena was not Georgian, she was Russian, born—she thought—in Magadan, and further, she never touched alcohol. Since I'd begun training with her, I didn't, either.

We took our walk, getting cold and wet, trying to enjoy the empty beach and the quiet, but it wouldn't take. When we'd been in Bequia, both of us had known Oxford was coming, that it was only a matter of when, not if. That knowledge had followed us, cast its pall on the mood and the environment. Even at the best of times in Bequia, it had been impossible to truly relax.

So it was here, some six and a half months since the attempts on our respective lives. It didn't matter that there'd been nothing, no threat, no signs of danger since that murderous night in Cold Spring. Our enemy remained, unnamed and unknown and potentially very powerful, and just because they hadn't found us yet didn't mean they had abandoned their search. As it had been with Oxford, we lived with the knowledge that we were hunted, and that the hunter might find us at any time.

Yet we lived with something else now, too, something that we hadn't truly had in Bequia, even with Alena teaching me. We had been tested, after all, first by Oxford, then more cruelly by Cold Spring, and we had remained true to each other, had defended each other, had supported each other. For Alena, it must have been an extraordinary sensation, bewildering and perhaps even frightening. There had always been someone who had wanted to hurt her, or use her, or kill her, or there had been the promise of the same. That promise remained, but this time it was different.

This time, she had someone with her that she could trust absolutely.

With Vadim in the house, it had been easy to push any thoughts of intimacy aside as inappropriate, even if, as an excuse, it was a feeble one. Vadim didn't care what we did, and, being nineteen, probably imagined that we were doing far more together than we could've possibly done, anyway. With the addition of fabulous lingerie.

But Vadim was gone, the house was ours, and when Alena looked at me, I could see everything she felt for me, and everything she wanted. It was all there, and it was so raw and so sincere that I had to look away, because it scared me. It scared me a lot.

Because Natalie had been right. Every single thing she'd said to me had been right.

The house, like the one in Batumi, was murder to keep warm. A woodstove served as the major source of heat, positioned in the main room. Miata went straight for it as soon as we were inside, dropping to the floor to bathe in its glow, and we knew that meant the house was safe. Each of us trusted his ears and his nose far more than our own, and if he wasn't reacting to anything, that was because there was nothing to react to.

We did a sweep anyway, confirming what we already knew, then unpacked the groceries in the kitchen. Alena went off to change out of her soaked clothes, and I went to the stove and fed it a couple more logs, annoying Miata as I did so, because it forced him to move out of my way. The fire came back strong, and I used a stick to close the door on it, then cleaned the rain from my glasses. A few droplets fell from my hair, spat and sizzled when they hit the cast iron. From the back of the house, I heard the little stereo in Alena's bedroom switch on, the strings and harmonies of "Eleanor Rigby" coasting softly down the hall. Her music tastes were eclectic, almost exclusively confined to the Beatles and their catalogue, with the occasional opera or string concerto thrown in for variety. After another moment, I could make out the sound of running water, the shower in the bathroom starting.

I removed my coat and boots, put them nearby, so they could dry out, then moved the pistol I'd been carrying at the front of my pants and set it within reach on the wobbly wooden coffee table that had come with the house. I pulled a chair of my own closer to the stove, and proceeded to let it do the same thing for me that it was doing for Miata. It was warm and it was comfortable, and the stiffness that had been rising in my right hip was abating. I felt drowsy, realized that it would be very easy to nod off right here, and realized also that there was really no reason that I shouldn't.

When I heard Alena's voice, I had no idea that she was back in the room.

"Atticus?"

I sat up and turned, and she was standing on the edge of the rug, her bath towel wrapped around her body, and that was all she was wearing. With her hair wet, it looked closer to black than to red. She shivered.

"I told you," Alena said. "I don't know how to do this."

"You've got to be freezing," I said.

Her brow creased with her frown. "It's not my first time. I don't want you to think that."

The only response I could think to that was to get up and go to where she was standing. I knew what she was trying to say, but she had also told me enough about her youth that I knew what she wasn't telling me, as well. When the girl is eight and in a prison cell, the "first time" is the last thing you can call it.

She had crossed her arms around her middle, and as I approached she wouldn't meet my eyes, instead focusing on my chest. Her expression had shifted, turned to something between determined and sullen.

I kissed her, the way I had wanted to kiss her back in the house in Cold Spring.

"It's all right," I told her. "It's mine."

We moved to Kobuleti the following winter. It was another resort town, roughly midway between Batumi and Poti, and the town wasn't meant for great things, but great things had been thrust upon it. When Abkhazia, in the north, had seceded, it had taken Georgia's best beaches with it, the ones of soft sand and alluring landscapes. Kobuleti's beach was rocky, flat, and utterly uninspiring. But it was Kobuleti's beach, and it was safe, and wealthy Muscovites and young Georgians came every summer to soak up the heat and wade the water. Kobuleti had responded, and now there was a resort that took advantage of the nearby mineral springs, two new hotels with all the amenities, and several flourishing boutiques and restaurants. During the high season, from the beginning of July until mid-September, the town was packed. Walking down the main street on a summer's night, music poured from every other café and bar as each venue pulled double duty as a nightclub.

During the off-season, though, Kobuleti shut down, turning into one of those quiet seaside communities that made me remember my Northern Californian youth. The tourists left, as did most of the attendant service workers, and everything grew quiet, and the world around the town contracted. Walking the rocky beach on a cold November morning, the sky and the Black Sea sharing the same battleship shade of gray, the only noise that of the water and the gulls, it could seem like the whole planet was nothing but a small town surrounded by pines and water.

We'd bought a house two and a half miles from the sea, on the north side of town, the right size for the three of us. Secluded, far enough back in the woods that you couldn't trip over it by accident, but not so far away that we couldn't see someone coming if a visitor wanted to drop by unannounced. The house had been a summer cottage for some minor Party official once upon a time, then sold as a rental property, and subsequently had seen more than its share of abuse.

The first thing we did when we moved in was to make it secure. We installed an alarm system with motion detectors and two cameras, covering the immediate approaches from the front and the back. We hooked up external lights to complement the cameras, and to give us visibility if anyone wanted to pay us a visit during the night. We replaced all of the locks, and a couple of the doors.

Then we discovered that the roof leaked, and instead of paying for someone to come up from Batumi to fix it, we decided we would do it ourselves. Then we found mold in the walls and carpet, and set about tearing out the old and installing the new. When we pulled up the carpet, we found there were hardwood floors in almost every room, and we decided we liked those better, so we had to finish them. Everything needed a fresh coat of paint. Cracked windowpanes had to be replaced. The pipes were lead in many places, and had to go.

The house became our project, how we spent our hours when we weren't training in the woods or the makeshift gym we'd built in the garage. We read books on home repair and carpentry and renovation. We bought tools. We drove all over the country in search of building supplies and fixtures. Partly, we did it as a way to keep busy, but partly we did it because, without our ever saying so to the other, we'd both decided that this house outside of Kobuleti was going to be our home.

It wasn't that we'd forgotten. I could still conjure the memory of Natalie effortlessly, the picture of her as she lay in death as clear as today in my mind. But after two years of lurking apprehension and no sign of Illya Tyagachev, with word from Dan coming less and less often, it had become impossible to simply mark time. Since it was impossible for me to do what I truly wanted to do—what I had come to feel I *needed* to do—it became necessary to do something else.

A little over seven months after we'd bought the house, Rezo Raminisshvilli, who ran one of the two cafés in town where we went for Internet access, mentioned to Alena that another of the summer cottages about a mile and a half from ours was going to be demolished. Whoever now owned the property wanted to put up a more modern abode, and felt that starting from square one was the best way to do it. We headed out the same afternoon to see if there was anything we could salvage, and were delighted to find that not only were most of the windows intact, but they were the original fixtures, and in reasonably good condition.

We salvaged five of them, brought them back home, and set to work repairing and installing them. They'd been painted multiple times, and the paints used had been lead-based, so I had them out on sawhorses in the back, and was working on stripping the third of the five. It was hot—it could get quite hot in the summer, even along the coast—and I stopped to drink some water and catch my breath. Miata was lying on the threshold of the open back door, in the shade, half asleep, and Alena was fitting one of the finished boxes into place, alternately shimming and hammering. She was wearing a white tank and blue bootleg Levi's she'd bought the last time we'd been in Batumi. I could see the scar, thin and white, that curled along the inside of her left bicep, from a man in Afghanistan who hadn't liked her politics, or lack thereof. She hadn't cut her hair since we'd left the States, and it was down to her shoulders now when she wore it loose, but at the moment she'd tied it up and back in a hasty ponytail.

I drank my water and I looked at Miata, and I looked at her, and I looked at myself, and then I burst out laughing.

"What?" Alena asked. She spoke in Georgian. Mostly, we spoke in Georgian or Russian, as a habit. "What is it?"

I kept laughing. Miata had raised his head, sleepy and perhaps annoyed at my interrupting his nap. That made me laugh harder. I wasn't hysterical, and Alena could tell that, and that probably helped to keep her from thinking that I'd lost my mind. She scowled at me just the same, folding her arms across her chest, waiting for me to share the joke. She had to wait a while, because when she did that, I laughed even harder.

Then, finally, I was able to get it under control.

"What's so fucking funny?" she asked.

I managed to stop laughing long enough to gesture vaguely at the house, her, and the dog with my hammer, and to say, "Bonnie and Clyde play house."

It took her a few seconds, staring first at me as if trying to determine if I truly had lost my mind or not, then finally looking at those things I'd indicated. She frowned at Miata. She frowned at the house, with its missing windows and half-finished floors. Then she looked down at herself, at the handful of nails in one hand and the hammer in the other, and the penny dropped, and she, too, started laughing.

Laughing at our domestic fucking bliss, and the irony of it all.

■ ■ ■

Twice a week we'd check for a message from Dan.

We would go to one of the Internet cafés in town, get a cup of tea and surf the Web and check up on the news of the world. While we were at it, we'd check the LiveJournal of a man named Billy Kork. Billy Kork was sixteen, lived in Newark, and posted every few days or so about all the kinds of things you'd expect a sixteen-year-old from Newark to post about. He posted about music, and school, and movies, and television, and girls. He posted a lot about girls. Sometimes, he shared his poetry. His poetry was very, very bad.

When we saw that another of the very, very bad poems had been posted, we'd log in with the user name and password Alena had chosen, and access the private-message portion of the blog. Once there, we'd find a message from Dan, forwarded to us by Billy Kork. If a response was required, we would post one, and thus carry on an albeit truncated and stilted conversation.

It was a good system, simple, and difficult to crack. To have intercepted the communication would have required the intercepting party to know, first, that Billy Kork was Vadim; second, that "mountainclimber998" was Alena and myself; and third, at least one of the account passwords. The odds of discovering the first were very, very low, but within the realm of possibility. The odds of discovering the second were even lower, because the only way to learn that we were mountainclimber998 would've been from either Dan or Vadim. Learning the third, especially the password for mountainclimber998, was impossible.

Which is not to say that it was a foolproof system, because it wasn't. On our end, if someone knew what they were doing and hit the computer after we'd finished with it, they could have recovered enough information to know what was going on, despite the fact that I made a point of clearing the browser's cache after each session. On their end, it was possible that someone could bring a federal warrant to bear on LiveJournal and its servers, forcing them to open the accounts, and thus gain access to our communication that way. But if the federal government knew enough to know that it was Dan and Vadim communicating with us, then surely they would know a lot more, and the Men in the Black Balaclavas would have come calling.

As that had not yet happened, we could reasonably assume we were safe.

In the beginning, the messages had been status reports. They mostly apprised us of Dan's search for Illya, and the frustration he was having in locating the man who had betrayed us. Sometimes he'd give us an update on what was happening in New York, what was going on with the few people I'd asked him to keep tabs on. But these days, the very, very bad poems, and thus Dan's messages, were fewer and further between. Even the blog itself was beginning to suffer from a lack of attention, with Billy offering his opinion less and less often as Vadim himself lost interest in the façade. I couldn't blame him; he'd kept Billy Kork alive for over two years. That's a long time to tell the same joke.

Still, twice a week, we found ourselves an Internet café, and we checked Billy Kork's blog.

Two months after our third New Year together, on a rainy and cold Monday morning, the message came.

I'd settled at the computer in the little café, a place called *Khval Dghes,* which translated to "Tomorrow Today," Miata flopping at my feet. He was getting old, and both Alena and I suspected arthritis was beginning to affect his joints; on the days when it rained, days like today, he was slower, though as attentive as ever. Alena was at the counter, ordering our tea and chatting with Rezo's wife, Irema.

We'd been around long enough that we were known in Kobuleti, that we were locals, and we were reasonably sociable as a result. Better that the community know us and like us, better that we be good neighbors than bad; that way, should anyone come calling asking questions, we stood a chance of hearing about it. Being antisocial would have only drawn unwanted attention, and the wrong kind of speculation. As it was, we were the nice-but-strange couple renovating that house outside of town. It was assumed that we were married, that we had American money, and if they wondered why we'd chosen to live in Kobuleti, their imaginations were happy to supply plenty of theories. With Alena's limp and the silent Doberman, they would have talked about us anyway.

I surfed for a few minutes, checking the news, then running the same searches I always did, plugging in the names that still mattered to me to see if the people they belonged to showed up on the Web. I found a few articles and stories, skimmed them. A girl I had known and cared for apparently had sold her first novel for a six-figure advance. I was mildly surprised to find a story about an ex-girlfriend dating a reasonably famous computer guru. When I typed in "Natalie Trent" I got multiple hits, but none of them for the one I cared about. As far as I knew, there'd never been so much as an obituary for her.

On an impulse, I did a search for "Elliot Trent" and got much the same result. Alena joined me as I tried it again, this time adding "Sentinel Guards," and that came back with a surprise. She moved her chair closer beside me, leaning in and resting her chin on my shoulder, reading as I did.

"He sold it," she said. "He sold his company, Sentinel Guards."

"Yeah."

"'Citing declining health.'"

"It's a better excuse than a broken heart," I said. "His health's fine. It's his will that's broken."

"You're so sure?"

"He was a widower, Natalie's mother died from breast cancer when she was young. I can't remember Natalie ever mentioning Elliot so much as dating another woman. It was just the two of them. And now he's outlived his daughter, as well."

Alena stayed silent for several seconds, leaving me to my thoughts, which weren't particularly pretty at that moment. Then she said, "You should check."

I shook it off, nodded, and typed in the address for Billy Kork's LiveJournal.

" 'February's wind, it blows so cold,' " I read, aloud. " 'Is this my bones, as they grow old?' "

"In the name of God," Alena groaned, burying her face against my shoulder, "please stop."

I pointed at the screen. "You sure? The third stanza is all about his acne trouble."

"Check, damn you," she said.

I logged in as mountainclimber998, tapped in our password, then followed the appropriate link to reach the private messages.

2330 NORTH WILLAMETTE BLVD.
#202
PORTLAND, OREGON

Alena and I stared at the monitor, neither of us speaking. At my feet, Miata stirred, repositioned his head to rest on my shoes.

"Tbilisi to Berlin—" I started to say.

"No," Alena disagreed. "We take the ferry from Poti to Sochi, to Russia. Sochi to Krasnodar, by plane. Krasnodar to Istanbul, by plane. From Istanbul to London, from London to target."

I pulled my eyes from the words on the monitor to look at her. Her expression had hardened, her mouth drawn to a tight line. She turned her head, met my gaze.

"To target," I echoed.

"To target," she confirmed.

CHAPTER TWO

The condominium was built on the edge of a cliff, over-looking a place called Swan Island, presumably because once upon a time, swans had held a great fondness for the place, or maybe because the land below, spilling into the wide swath of the Willamette River, had been owned by a man named Swan. I didn't know, and I didn't bother to find out, because I didn't care to. That wasn't why I'd come to Portland.

There were two buildings in the complex as you faced it, each block about four stories tall, and from the looks of things, I figured the condos were two stories each within. It gave the place height enough that anyone taking a leap from one of the upper balconies would be lucky to get away with a broken leg and nothing more. If someone were to take a header, the cement poisoning would be fatal.

It was seven in the morning, and it was raining cold and

steady, and when I looked opposite, across the river, I could just make out the tree-covered mountains to the west through the veil of falling drops. I was sitting in a Nissan Pathfinder, with Danilov Korckeva behind the wheel and Alena seated directly behind me. According to my watch, we'd been on the ground in Portland for precisely twenty-seven minutes. Thirty hours earlier, we'd left Miata in the care of the Raminisshvillis and made our way to Frankfurt, instead of London, catching a direct flight on Lufthansa to, what I was informed by the signs at the airport, was the City of Roses. I hadn't seen any roses yet. Like learning about the origins of Swan Island, I didn't think I'd have the time.

Dan had arrived two days prior, on the Gulfstream. Vadim had made the trip with him. Together, the two had put Illya Tyagachev under immediate surveillance, each of them taking turns.

"You're positive it's him?" I asked. The words sounded strange to me, the English still alien on my tongue.

Dan nodded. "I made the ID myself, Atticus. Here, we go around the back, you can see the approaches. His place is on the second floor, second apartment from the south."

"Lives alone?"

"Far as we can tell, yes. Haven't taken a look at the apartment. Didn't want to do anything that might warn him. I don't want to lose him again."

"Probably wise," I told him.

Dan spun the wheel, and we turned up North Holman, now heading roughly east, but then he swung an almost immediate right, and we were heading south again, this time coming along the block at the rear of the condominiums. Houses were spaced evenly on both sides of the street as we approached, with shallow lawns running down to the sidewalk. The houses showed their age, beaten with weather and use. The nicest place in the immediate vicinity seemed to be the condos themselves.

We'd seen a black iron security fence at the front of the complex, with a call box and a gate. The fence enclosed a parking lot at the rear, with berths for each automobile built under the walkway for the second-floor condominiums, providing meager shelter from the rain for driver and vehicle. The fence was eight and a half, maybe nine feet high, with vertical bars, no crosspieces, to deter attempts to climb it. A motorized gate ran on a track, closed for the moment, where the cars could enter and exit, and perhaps six feet north from that was a smaller gate, for pedestrian traffic. There was no one in the lot as we went past, but most of the berths were full. I counted the spaces from the south side, saw that the fourth one was empty. Assuming each condo had a companion berth, and assuming the odd-numbered ones went with the apartments on the second floor, Illya Tyagachev was missing his car.

"Where is he now?" Alena asked from the backseat.

"Working, he drives a cab," Dan said. "Graveyard shift. I didn't want Vadim following him all night long, he might've made that. I told him to get rest, instead, so he's back at the hotel."

Alena hissed softly with displeasure.

"When does he get off work?" I asked.

"Another hour—he drives midnight to eight," Dan said, quickly, as if trying to assure us that his lack of surveillance didn't translate to a lack of information. "Heads home, crashes, gets up again around four in the afternoon, heads out again."

"To his other job," I said.

Dan had turned us away from the condos, had us on a main thoroughfare heading south, back towards the heart of the city. He shot me a glance, vaguely suspicious.

"You know about the other job?"

"He didn't pay for that place on a hack's salary," I said. "And if he did what he did to us for money, I'm sure it was spent long ago. There's another job, got to be. That's probably how you found him."

"There is another job," Dan confirmed. "He sells meth."

"Russians," Dan told us. "Add in the others: Ukrainians, Armenians, Kazakhs, Uzbeks, Tajiks, all the rest. Over sixty thousand of them are here. That's why Illya came here. He didn't want to leave the U.S. of A., but he couldn't leave his people, either. He probably went to Seattle first, maybe San Francisco, we haven't been able to track all his movements yet. But he ended up here, maybe six, seven months ago."

Dan leaned his chair, threatening to topple backwards on the people eating their McDonald's burgers at the table behind him. We were in the food court of an indoor shopping mall. The court was on the third level, open in the middle with a view down to the ice rink below, where maybe two dozen boys and girls were wobbling about on skates. Music drifted up at us, distorted, the Vangelis theme from *Chariots of Fire.* Between that, the cavernous acoustics, and the ambient noise of shoppers and diners, there was little chance of being overheard.

"Anyway, he finds where the Russians are, you know how it is. Meets the people he needs to meet, gets himself a gig running meth from the labs outside of town to the sellers here in the town. Lot of meth here. They have a lot of the wide open spaces here in Oregon; you need that if you cook meth. Stuff stinks like shit in sunshine."

I nodded. When he said "Oregon," he said it "ore-ee-gone."

"You know the people he's working with?" I asked. "That how you found him?"

"One of them I know from the old days. He heard from a friend who heard from a friend who heard from a friend that I was looking for this guy, that it was personal for me. Illya, he changed his name, he calls himself Maks Dugachev now."

"And you're *certain* it's him?" I asked again.

Dan sat forward, bringing his chair down with a slam, getting angry. "I told you, I checked for myself, I made visual confirmation. This is personal for me."

"And the people, your friend's friend's friend, you trust this guy?"

"I told you, I trust him."

"How do you know him?"

"It doesn't matter! I know him, he won't fuck with me, he understands the personal, okay?"

"It matters to me," I insisted. "It matters if he tips 'Maks' that we're on to him."

Dan shot me a look, then spoke to Alena in Russian, asking why the hell he should put up with my bullshit. She'd been sitting with her chair turned away from us, chin on the railing, gazing down at the skaters. Without looking back, she told him that he had to put up with my bullshit because my bullshit was her bullshit, and if he didn't like hearing it from me, he could hear it from her instead, and that the questions would be the same, but her patience for the answers would be much shorter.

She sounded only vaguely annoyed when she said it, and she never raised her voice, and Dan looked from her back to me, sighing.

"His name's Semyon, okay? Semyon Pagaev. We were outside the White House together when the hard-liners tried to take Yeltsin in 1993. This man, I trust him with my life."

It took me a moment before I remembered that the White House he was referring to was the White House of Russia, where the Supreme Soviet had been housed. Now it held the Russian cabinet, if my memory was serving me right.

"This satisfy you? Are you happy now?" Dan demanded.

"Almost. How'd Semyon make Maks for Illya?" I asked.

Beside me, still looking down at the skaters, Alena snorted softly, grinning, and muttered, "Say that ten times fast."

The joke caught Dan off guard, and he'd started to answer me, then did a double take, looking at Alena strangely. Then he said, "One of Semyon's boys—"

I interrupted. "He's got kids, too?"

"No, no, one of his crew, this one has a sister—Kiska, I think, is her name. Supposed to be a real beauty. Maks, a couple of the others, they're trying to get on Kiska's good side, trying to impress her. Talking about what they've done. And Maks, he tells her that he was with a crew out of Brighton Beach when he first came over. This gets back to Semyon, Semyon remembers me putting the word out, he contacts me, sends me a picture on the Internet, taken with camera phone. Looks like Illya. Vadim and I come out here, positive visual ID, like I say."

Dan put his big hands on the table between us, leaned forward.

"Are you happy now, Mr. Atticus? Please tell me you're happy now."

"I wouldn't go that far," I told him. "But for the moment I'm satisfied."

"So are we going to take care of this?"

"We're going to get some sleep," I said.

Alena and I checked into the Heathman Hotel in downtown, six blocks south of where Vadim and Dan were staying, at the Hotel Lucia. I used a credit card that said my name was Christopher Morse, and then showed the young woman who checked us in a

California driver's license to prove the fact. We got a two-room suite on the sixth floor with a view overlooking the street.

It was just after noon when we got into the room, and the jet lag was beginning to make itself known by then. I pulled the blinds and closed the curtains, hung the Do Not Disturb sign, then did five minutes of yoga to fight off the stiffness from the flight while Alena used the shower. When she was out, I took my turn, and then we both fell into bed, and fell asleep almost as quickly.

When I woke, the curtains and the blinds were once again open, and the gray sky of the day had turned into black night. I could hear Alena speaking to someone at the door, out of sight. Then I heard the door close, and a moment later she came into view, wearing one of the complimentary bathrobes and carrying a room service tray. She set the tray on the coffee table, saw that I was awake, and grinned.

"There's a fitness suite on the third floor," she told me. "Open twenty-four hours."

"Are you wearing anything under that robe?" I asked.

"No."

"I can think of a better workout."

"Cardio, maybe," she said.

"Muscle control, body awareness," I said. "With a little imagination, maybe even stretching and balance."

Alena looked down at the room service tray, and I watched the corners of her mouth curl up in a mischievous smile. She unfastened the belt holding her robe closed and let it fall away from her as she came back to the bed, sliding beneath the covers and beside me once more. We kissed, and despite the banter it was long and slow and tender, and when it was over I ran my fingers through her hair, looking at her, and deciding she was very beautiful.

"Dinner's going to get cold," I said, after a moment.

"It's yogurt and granola." She ran her fingers along my cheek, lightly traced the scar that had been left from a pistol-whipping I'd taken ages ago. "It'll keep."

"I think Dan's figured it out."

"You don't think Vadim told him?"

"I think Vadim told him, but Dan didn't believe it until today, not until you made that joke when we were at the mall."

"Joke?"

"Ten times fast."

She grinned, pleased with herself, then slid closer, pressing her body against mine. She kissed me again, still slowly, but this time with rising passion, and I responded in kind, moving my hands lightly over her body, delighting in the feel of her, the way I always did, the way it felt I always had. The first time or every time, it didn't matter; making love together was the only way she would tell me all the things she could never say, the only way I could answer her, saying that yes, I understood, and yes, I was here, and yes, I would stay, and I would forgive her for the sins she had committed and the sins she had yet to commit, just as she would do the same for me.

That yes, I loved her, too.

"One time slow," she said.

CHAPTER THREE

At seven minutes past four in the morning I went up and over the black iron security fence at the back of the condominium complex. It was still raining, or maybe it was raining again, and the bars were cold, but my hands were strong, and once I had a good grip at the top it was easy to use my hips and swing my lower body over, to follow my legs down. I missed a puddle, landed without a splash, and moved immediately to the carport, to shelter there from both the rain and the security lights that illuminated the lot.

There were two sets of stairs running up to the second-story condos, a main set of artificial-looking stone between the two buildings, and then a second, narrower flight on the south side of the building. I used that one, took it quickly up to the second floor. The stairwell was positioned to dump out facing the row of apartments on the floor, and I could stay low in it, hidden, and make a survey before proceeding. Not a single light burned in any of the residences.

I considered my options. A block and a half away, parked in an overlook, Alena and Dan were waiting in the Pathfinder for my call. The plan was for me to enter Illya's home, take a thorough look around, remove the potential of any surprises he might wish to spring on us. Once I was satisfied the condo was secure, I'd ring Dan on the rented cell phone he'd provided me. Then I'd wait for him and Alena to call up from the front gate, just like they were any other visitors. I'd buzz them in, they'd join me in Illya's home, and we'd get comfortable and wait until he came home from work. Vadim, currently staking out the Rose City Cab Co., would give us a call to alert us the target was on its way.

Then I'd take the answers I wanted from Illya, and when I was done, Dan could do whatever he damn well wanted. That what he wanted was most likely going to cause Illya a lot of suffering and misery before his final reward was of only minor discomfort to me; the way I saw it, if Illya hadn't sold us out, Natalie Trent would be alive and well and still a joy in the world.

My problem, at the moment, was finding a quick and quiet way into Illya's apartment. The quickest and quietest would be through the front door, so I checked it, and wasn't surprised to find it securely locked. There was a large window to the right of the door, blinds drawn but their slats parted enough that I could peek through into what appeared to be the main room. It was dark inside, but I could make out street light coming through another set of windows opposite, and I could see the door onto the balcony.

Rain was dripping off the edges of the rooftop above me, and I turned away from the window and back into cover, looking up. The rooftop extended about halfway across the walkway, another attempt to provide partial cover against the Portland weather.

Whoever had designed it had done so with at least a token nod to security, because even with the rake of the roof, its edge hung perhaps twelve feet from the floor at its lowest point. There was no way to reach it without a ladder.

Except that the walkway had a railing, four feet high, in all ways identical to the security fence surrounding the complex, but here it was meant to keep people from wandering over the edge and smashing themselves into the parking lot below. The security lights made the water that had collected on its surface shimmer, shining orange. The top of the fence couldn't have been more than half an inch wide, and it had to be slippery.

This is the reason you've been doing all that damn ballet, I told myself.

I moved to the railing, used my palm to sweep away the water, then checked the view around me once more, confirming again that no lights had come on, that no one was watching. The world was silent but for the sound of the rain hitting leaves and pavement. I swiped my hands dry on my sweatshirt, took hold of the railing, and then half vaulted, half stepped up onto the narrow strip of metal. The railing gave a disconcerting groan as it took my weight, vibrating, and below me the fall to the parking lot couldn't have been more than twenty-five feet or so.

More than enough to thoroughly fuck me up if I did this wrong.

I went up to fifth position *demi-pointes,* using both feet, opening my arms to the sides, then executed a half turn, a *soutenu en tourant.* The railing wobbled beneath me as I completed the move, lowering my arms to first position, but I was facing the edge of the roof now, still standing *demi-pointes* not because I liked the position or the style, but because there was nothing to rest my heels on. I paused long enough to check my breathing, pulled fresh air deep inside to keep the muscles well fed, then threw myself forward in something resembling a *grand jeté,* if the *grand jeté* in question were being performed from a rain-slicked railing at ten past four in the morning by a man trying to get onto a rooftop without killing himself, or making too much noise, in the process. The fact that I was starting in *demi-pointes* was really only adding insult to injury.

Somewhere, George Balanchine was spinning in his grave.

It was a good leap, and there was a lot of power behind it, and it did the trick. I put my hands out onto the composite shingles of the roof, landed without too much noise with most of my upper body resting against the surface. I used my hips, shifted, then swung them up and to the right, and they carried me over completely. The momentum of the move staved off gravity long enough for me to roll further onto the surface, by which time I was able to turn out of it and come up on one knee. I'd made myself good and wet, but that seemed to be the extent of any damage the jump had done me.

The rooftop rose to an awning eight feet or so ahead of me, hanging over a squat rectangle of a window, then continued on to its apex. I stayed low, hearing my sneakers squeaking on the shingles as I approached and tried to peer inside, but unlike on the ground floor, the view through this window was blocked by drawn curtains. I moved off, taking the rest of the ascent slowly, careful to keep from slipping. At the apex, I dropped low, to keep my silhouette down. The view was impressive, lights shining on Swan Island below; I heard the distant sound of trucks loading and unloading. Looking south, I could see where the Pathfinder was parked at the overlook.

The rooftop sloped downwards, now towards what was the front of the condo, and I went onto my belly when I reached the edge, peering over to see a balcony twelve feet beneath. The balcony was framed with more of the black metal railing, just large enough for two deck chairs and a small, glass-topped patio table to rest between them. Once again, there was no sign of light coming from inside.

This would be the second floor of the condo itself, roughly the equivalent of the fourth floor of the building. As it had on the walkway side, the rooftop overhung the balcony, providing shade in the summer and cover from the weather year-round, though on this side it didn't extend nearly as far, perhaps no more than a foot, maybe a foot and a half.

I took a closer look at the edge of the roof, where the shingles ended and the rain guard had been tacked into place along the lip. There wasn't a whole lot to grab onto; I was going to be asking a lot of my fingers, especially given the rain. It was cold, too, all of the day's meager heat already stolen away, and with my wet clothes, I was beginning to feel it.

Twisting so I was lying parallel with the end of the roof, I reached out, taking hold of the edge first with my right. The grip felt as secure as I'd thought it would, which is to say, it didn't feel secure at all. Carefully, keeping as much of my weight on the roof for as long as possible, I swung my legs out into the air and began lowering myself down, moving my left hand into position as I had my right. There was no place to set my thumbs, no positive hold, and I had to pinch the edge with both hands, hanging off the side of the building, arms fully extended. I could see more windows, these looking out onto the balcony, their curtains closed.

The strain of the hold was eating at my fingers and shoulders, I could feel the fatigue already building in my hands. If I didn't move soon, I'd lose the strength to move altogether.

I brought my legs together, again using my hips and abdomen to swing my legs back, away from the building. My grip started to go immediately, and I snapped my lower body forward as hard as I could before it went entirely, hoping the move had been enough to carry me onto the balcony. I arched my back and brought my arms down and in, trying to keep from smashing myself on the railing.

I landed between the railing and the glass-topped patio table, my shoes splashing down in a puddle of runoff, pulling my torso back into line as soon as I felt something solid beneath my feet. I got my hands out in front of me in time to keep from toppling forward, ending ultimately in a crouch, and for a moment I stayed exactly like that, catching my breath and hearing the rainfall beat a companion rhythm to my pulse. My fingers, all the way into my palms, throbbed, and I opened and closed my hands several times, trying to get the blood flowing properly through them once more.

On the street behind me I heard a car approaching, turned my head to see the lights coming along Willamette Boulevard, from the north. There was enough diffused illumination that I could make out the shape of a light bar at the top, a spot mounted on the driver's side, above the mirror. The police car continued past, without slowing. If it didn't turn off, it would pass the Pathfinder at the overlook.

Suddenly I was imagining a scenario with Alena and Dan and a dead police officer, and I didn't like that at all, and for an instant I thought about calling them, warning them, but the call wouldn't come in time anyway. It was an overreaction; they were keeping watch, certainly, and there were a dozen lies they could give the cop that would be a better solution than violence.

I put it out of my mind, pivoted in place, turning to face the door onto the balcony. It was narrower than the standard size, just as tall, its center clear glass. Looking through it I could make out a dresser, a small television resting atop it. Pulling my sleeve down over my hand, I reached out and slowly tried to turn the knob. There was no resistance, and it rotated almost a full one-eighty before stopping. When I pushed forward there was a slight squeak, the rubber seal at its base scraping the bottom of the door frame, but no real resistance. It opened easily, as I suspected it would.

This high up, this impossible to reach, why bother to lock the balcony door?

I slipped inside quickly, feeling carpet beneath my feet, still thick enough or new enough that it sank to receive my steps. Without light, I couldn't tell if I was leaving just damp impressions or something more as footprints. Hopefully, it wouldn't matter; I didn't see Illya entering his home in the same fashion I had done. I closed the door behind me, as quietly as I'd opened it.

Then I heard a rustle, a movement of bedclothes, and atop it the sound of a sleeper's breathing, broken for a moment.

The door to the balcony hadn't opened into the view of the whole room, rather just this end of it, and I had a corner to my right. I put myself against it, peering out. There was a bed, a queen, and there was someone in it, a shape just visible in the shadows, comforter and blankets heaped upon it. I drew breath slowly, waiting and listening.

There was another slight rustle from the bed, and I saw a hand appear for a moment, pulling the comforter back down. The breathing relaxed, resumed the rhythm of sleep. It had been the opening of the door that had done it, the shift in the air, just enough of the outside cold coming in to disturb the sleeper. That had been all.

There'd been no sign of Illya or his cab anywhere around the building that I'd seen, and I'd made a point of looking before climbing the fence. While Vadim didn't have Illya under surveillance at the moment, there was no reason to think that he'd come home and gone to bed. Which meant this was someone else under those covers, someone we hadn't anticipated.

Neither Vadim nor Dan had said anything about there being

another occupant in the condo. While their surveillance had been quick, I doubted it had been sloppy. So either this was a new arrival—someone who was sleeping here today—or it was someone who had been here but who hadn't gone out. Someone who Dan's friend Semyon either didn't know about, or had neglected to tell Dan about.

There was a faint scent in the air, and it was vaguely familiar, but I couldn't place it. Almost floral, but not quite.

The sleeper's breathing had become regular, steady and calm.

I stood up slowly, turned out from the cover of the wall, and stepped silently to the foot of the bed.

The sleeper was a woman, blond, maybe in her mid-to-late twenties. Almost all of her was buried beneath the bedclothes but for her head and her right arm. She was wearing flannel pajamas.

There was a red light glowing from something positioned on the nightstand nearest her side of the bed. It took me a half-second to realize what it was, and as soon as I did, I placed the scent I'd caught earlier, and that was all it took.

I left the room, entering a short hallway. Carpet continued to cover the floor, making silence easy to preserve. On my right, a flight of stairs ran past me down to the main floor of the condo. A folding door was set in the wall just past the head of the stairs, off the landing, open, and inside was a washer-dryer stack, both of them too small to be of much use. Another door, this one standard, was ahead of me, barely ajar, presumably the room I'd been unable to see into when I'd first climbed onto the roof. I knew what was inside it, now. I didn't need to see, but I wanted to.

Maybe I was hoping I would be wrong about what I'd find.

I wasn't.

The baby was asleep in her crib, butt in the air, blanket piled beside her. Stuffed animals surrounded her on all sides, Kermit the Frog and Elmo and a fluffy bunny rabbit and two Winnie the

Poohs, and one creature with one eye and no nose and a goofy grin. The odor of disposable diapers and scented wipes was heavy. She was breathing easy, the sound of an infant deep asleep, with one cheek mashed against the mattress, her mouth open. She didn't look happy and she didn't look sad; she just looked like a baby girl, finally letting her mother have a good night's sleep.

I made my way downstairs, and left using the front door, without making a sound.

CHAPTER FOUR

"You're sure it's his?" Alena asked me.

"I haven't the first fucking clue if it's his or not," I told her. "It's been three years, the baby can't be more than three months old, the math works. If it *is* his, and if he has been traveling around the way Dan suspects, then he must have hooked up with Mom someplace else, moved her and the baby here after he got settled. But it doesn't matter. The point is he's caring for the mother and the kid, so either it's his or he's taking responsibility for it."

We were seated outside of a Peet's Coffee perhaps a stone's throw from each of our hotels. Morning traffic was just beginning to trickle past us, heading west on a one-way street. The rain, for the moment, had stopped, and the sky was just beginning to lighten, hinting at daylight behind its gray mask. It was surprisingly warm, maybe in the low fifties. Looking past Alena, into the coffee shop, the baristas looked like ghosts as they moved at their counter, hidden behind the sheen of condensation that had formed on the windows.

I waited for Alena to say something more, and she didn't, and her expression didn't change. I wondered if she was seeing the same problem here that I was. She had a paper cup of herbal tea in her hand. They'd given her two bags for it, and their strings dangled over the side with their tags, and she was flicking them with her index finger lightly, but that was it.

"Fuck this," Dan growled, keeping his voice low. "Have you forgotten why we want this cumwhore? Have you forgotten what he did to us?"

I turned my head enough to meet his eyes, and hoped my expression gave him all the answer he needed. Then I checked my watch, and said, "I've got sixteen minutes past six. He gets off work in just under two hours. We've got maybe fifteen minutes to come up with a plan that gets us what we want without involving the woman or the kid."

"Fuck this!" Dan repeated, louder. "We go back there, we do what we were going to do!"

"It's not an option."

"He brought this on himself! He should never have taken a woman, brought her into this! It's his own fucking fault!"

Off the reflection on the window I saw Alena raise her head, focusing on Dan, and her expression still hadn't changed. In Russian, she said, "But it's not hers, nor the child's."

"What the hell is the matter with you?" he shot back at her, also in Russian. "Where the fuck's your head, Natasha?"

"The child and the mother stay out of it," she said icily.

In the past, the tone, the finality, would have been enough to shut Dan down completely. In the past, he would have pulled a face, then stopped it before it could take hold, either his fear or his respect for Alena getting the better of him. Not this time.

He shot me a glare that was full of naked hostility and accusation, then leaned across the table, moving his head closer to Alena.

"You're not thinking," Dan said in Russian. He said it calmly, as if trying to explain a mistake to a promising but stubborn student. "Your man here has goatfucked this, Natasha. Illya won't be in that apartment five minutes before he realizes someone was there, and as soon as he realizes that, he's going to run again. What happens if he takes the woman and the baby with him? We just give him a free pass for murdering Natalie?"

She didn't respond. Her index finger kept flicking the tags on their strings.

Dan shot me another glance, and I looked past him, watching the traffic on the street. If he was suspicious that maybe I understood what was being said, I couldn't blame him. He didn't know everywhere we'd lived for the past three years, only that we had started in Georgia, not that we'd ended there. But he'd have been a fool if he hadn't already considered the possibility that I'd learned more than just yoga, ballet, and some new hand-to-hand moves while we'd been away.

He frowned, clearly struggling with what he wanted to say next. He leaned further forward towards Alena, his hands resting palm up on the table, trying to appeal to her.

"You know what we have to do," Dan said gently, still speaking in Russian. "You know the best way to do it, and you know the tactics involved in something like this, the kind of pressure you're going to need to bring. Refusing to do this is weakness, it's the kind of thing that leads to mistakes that get you killed. You want information from Illya, the best way to get that will be to have the woman and the baby in the same room with him."

Her only answer was the quiet assault her finger was continuing against the tea tags. Dan waited to see if she would say anything, and he waited what seemed like a long time, maybe thirty seconds, but she didn't.

Abruptly, he straightened up in his chair, the frustration spilling from his voice into his posture and motion. "What the fuck is the matter with you? Natasha, seriously, and I say this with all the respect that is due to you, but you are seriously fucked up. I've known you, what, twenty years? Your man, here, he's got you twisted around, you don't know if you're going or coming anymore. I know you taught him, I know he's yours. But what he's taught you, he's changed you and it's not for the better."

Her index finger froze, and I felt as much as saw the subtle shift of her weight, the tensing of the muscles in her lower body, all the signatures of an upcoming attack. Dan saw it, too, or sensed it, maybe, and it didn't matter that we were on a public street at a quarter past six in the morning; it was in his eyes, the fear that he'd crossed one line too many, and that however much she might have been changed, she hadn't been changed enough to keep from killing him then and there.

"He has changed me," she told him. She said it quietly, but it had all the force of the physical attack he'd feared, each word precise and delivered with deliberation. "And I have changed him. And if one of us is the worse for it, it is not me. Do you know why you have always feared me, Danilov? Even twenty years ago, when you first saw me? Have you ever wondered why?"

Dan hesitated, as if uncertain that she wanted an answer, or perhaps afraid of giving the wrong one. "I didn't fear you, I respected you, you were a gifted girl, taught by the best, you were capable of—"

"You did, and you do," she cut in, softly. "You never saw a girl. You saw an empty thing. You saw a tool that could do everything you had been trained to do, but could do it better than you could ever dream of doing yourself. You saw a weapon, but you did not ever see a person. And that, Danilov, is what terrified you.

"The empty thing would agree with you, and think that using the woman and the child to put pressure on the target was logical and efficient. The empty thing would murder them afterwards, calling the act necessary and prudent. The empty thing wouldn't care.

"I am not that thing anymore. I would die before I became it again."

She paused, perhaps to collect herself, perhaps to let what she'd said take hold with Dan. It was the most I'd ever heard her say about herself, as the person she'd been before we'd met, the person the Soviets had designed her to be with their calculated abuse and refined instruction. From the expression on Dan's face, it was the most he'd ever heard her say on the subject, as well.

It couldn't have been lost on him just who, sitting at this table on a February dawn, she thought was an empty thing, and who she thought was not.

"Illya is the target," Alena concluded. "Not the woman. Not the child."

Dan swallowed, looked from her to me, then back to her.

"Then what do we do?" He was speaking Russian, just as she had been. "We can't let him go, Alena! What he did must be answered!"

I cleared my throat, and both of them looked at me.

"What kind of car is Illya driving?" I asked Dan.

His opinion of me was uncensored in his expression. "The fuck?"

"What kind of car? New? Old?"

"New, brand new. Ford Mustang, a black one. Vadim wants one, too. Why the fuck does it matter what car he's driving?"

"Air bags," Alena said.

"Vadim's got his own vehicle," I said. "Another rental?"

"Yeah, we rented on the same ID, same credit cards."

"We're going to need another two cars, then," I said. "Older ones. And a roll or two of duct tape, and something to keep Illya down, a good sleeping pill will do it, something like Ambien."

Dan looked at me as if he couldn't decide to be incredulous, outraged, or both.

"We can't let him go home," I explained. "And we can't let him get away."

"His car," Alena told Dan. "We'll take him at his car."

CHAPTER FIVE

The irony of springing an automotive ambush on Illya didn't hit me until I hit him, or more precisely, until the moment I smashed the front end of my stolen 1978 Lincoln Town Car into the back of his probably-not-stolen and brand-spanking-new black-and-silver Ford Mustang. The cars connected with the unique bang that only comes from automobile accidents, the almost-hollow sound of metal and fiberglass cracking together, the sudden tinkling of glass and plastic hitting asphalt.

It was a good hit, not too fast, eleven miles an hour. Enough to rattle the bones, to snap me against my seat belt and send me back hard into the driver's seat, and, more importantly, to send the Mustang forward. The new Mustangs have crap visibility out their rear, the window too small and set too high on the tail, and I couldn't see Illya behind the wheel, but I heard the second collision as his front end met the back of Vadim's Cadillac. The

Caddie, like the Town Car, was stolen, though a couple years younger, maybe an '82 or '83.

I lost a second getting the seat belt off, which isn't a long time in the concrete, but in the abstract was more than adequate for me to think about how slowly I was moving, and how badly this could turn out if I didn't speed things up. We were on a public street, and while the daylight wasn't broad due to the heavy cloud cover, it might as well have been. There was no place to hide, and certainly the sound of the crash would pull people from their beds or their breakfast tables, send them running to their windows to see what was happening on the street outside.

Then I was out of the car, the tire iron I'd found in the trunk in my hand, and running forward to the Mustang. Vadim was out of the Caddie, heading around its nose to come along the other side of the car, to the passenger side. I heard, then saw, the Pathfinder as it hopped up on the curb to my left, drawing even with the Mustang. Through the side window, I could see Illya still dazed, only now beginning to shake off the effects of three collisions in quick succession. While the first two—the Town Car and the Caddie—might have rattled his cage, it was the third, when his air bag had deployed, that had been the most crucial. For air bags to work, they have to work fast, and they have to be able to counter the force of the collision in their own right. Take one to the chest in a low-speed crash, and you'll feel it.

Illya was feeling it right now.

I reached his door and tried the handle, and wasn't at all surprised that it was locked. Inside, Illya was looking around, realizing what had happened and the trouble he was in. Opposite me, at the front passenger's door, Vadim was working with a tire iron of his own. We hit the windows almost simultaneously, and the glass shattered in concert, raining onto the wet street and into the car. In his seat, Illya started shouting at us, gabbling fear and outrage as he leaned forward, trying to reach with his right hand to the small of his back. I spun the tire iron around, jabbed the straight end hard through the now missing window and into his side, connecting with him just below the armpit.

Illya screamed in pain, jerking away from me and towards Vadim, who had the passenger's door open already. Seeing Vadim reaching in for him, Illya made another attempt to get at his gun, and I jabbed him with the tire iron a second time, just as hard, hitting him in the small of the back, above where he was wearing the weapon. Illya cried out again, lying down further across the seats, and Vadim grabbed hold of him by the back of his shirt and yanked.

Dan joined his son, and together the two of them pulled Illya free from the Mustang. Once they had him, they didn't let go, dragging him flailing to the door Dan had left open on the Pathfinder. I did a quick spin around in place, checking the street, catching Alena seated behind the Pathfinder's wheel as I did so. The traffic around us was light, not yet bloated with the morning commute, and only now really beginning to come to a stop. I didn't see any police, and I didn't see anyone who seemed to have witnessed the entirety of what we were doing, or at least, no one who had borne witness and therefore looked like they wanted to get involved.

"Let's go!" Dan shouted to me.

Tire iron still in hand, I came around the back of the Mustang, jumped onto the hood of the Town Car where the two vehicles had tried to become one, and came down again beside the Pathfinder. Inside, Vadim was holding Illya in a headlock while Dan forced him to swallow two of the Ambien we'd scored. I moved around to the front of the car, climbed in beside Alena, and we were moving before I had the door closed.

In the backseat, Illya emitted a muffled sob, finally succumbing to Dan's pressure.

"Ochen preyatna, cyka," I told him.

■ ■ ■

We caught Route 26 out of Portland, heading east, and by the time we'd hit Gresham, Illya was fast asleep, despite his best efforts. Given the dose, he'd stay down for at least the next eight hours, which would be enough to cover our transport time. As soon as he was out, Dan gave him a thorough search, coming up with a spring-action knife in addition to the pistol he'd been carrying at the small of his back. He had a couple hundred dollars in mixed bills, maybe his wages for the night's work, tucked into his pockets, as well.

We drove without speaking for most of the next hour, Alena at the wheel, myself beside her, Dan and Vadim in the back. The sky started to clear as we began climbing towards Mount Hood, and there was snow throughout the Cascade Range, and the trees were very green and very lush and very beautiful, and it reminded me of the little I'd seen of northern Georgia, where the Caucasus came down from the border with Russia. We stopped at a gas station in Welches to fill the tank, and Vadim and I took the opportunity to go inside to gather some supplies. He grabbed a six-pack of Budweiser and two bags of spicy Cheetos, and I made him put the Budweiser back.

"We do *not* want to be stopped for an open container in the car," I told him.

Vadim pulled a face that said that I absolutely needed to lighten up, then replaced the beer and got himself six cans of Red Bull instead. I went with two bottles of clearly-from-concentrate orange juice, and another two of water, and looked for something that wasn't purely high-fructose corn syrup. Failing that, I decided I wasn't hungry. I also grabbed a road atlas of Oregon.

Back in the car, now with Dan at the wheel and Alena seated beside him, and Vadim and I flanking the sleeping Illya at the back, we broke out the map and took a look at our options. Thus far, we'd done pretty well relying on our improvisational skills, but what we needed to do next would require seclusion and security. We had Illya; now we needed a place to button him up and do what needed to be done next.

"What are you thinking?" Dan asked. He asked it in Russian, maybe to see if I could keep up. "Take him out to the middle of the high desert, maybe?"

"It's the winter season," I said. "We want someplace quiet and discreet, and the further from Portland and the police the better."

"You think a vacation rental?" Alena asked.

"It worked for us in Georgia. We find a place that's not being used right now, maybe one that looks like it's only occupied during the summer. A fishing cabin, rather than skiing, say."

"So near a river," Vadim said. "Someplace near a river."

I checked the map. "Along the Deschutes would work. If we had access to a computer we could just do a quick search for vacation rentals, plug in the communities we like the looks of, see what's available, and see what's *not* being used at the moment."

"Hold on." Vadim handed me the can of Red Bull he'd been working on, then dug around in his pockets until he came out with one of the new Palm Treos, began fiddling with it. "Ah, it's going slow as shit, the coverage's no good out here. Hang on."

I looked to Dan, said, "Maybe we should keep moving while he does this."

Dan started the Pathfinder again, pulling us back onto the road. Vadim stayed bent over his Treo, occasionally muttering about how long it was taking for the pages to load.

"Okay," he said, after almost two minutes. "I've got a page here, it's got towns in Central Oregon with vacation rentals. Lots of towns. Bend, Eagle Crest, Sunriver—"

"Sunriver," I told him, checking the map.

There was another pause, this one perhaps half as long as the first, accompanied by more of his muttering about crappy connection speeds. "Got it. Lots of places. *Lots* of places, man, let me check availability, here... goddammit this is slow... yeah, okay, looks like about a dozen places we could use."

"Note the addresses," I told him. "We'll eyeball them when we get there, pick the one we like."

"This is amateur hour," Dan said, mostly to himself. "We should have had a location lined up before we grabbed him."

"We also should have known there was a woman and a child," I told him.

Dan didn't say anything else until we reached Sunriver.

CHAPTER SIX

The place we liked was the third one we looked at, number 18 Cluster Cabin Lane, not more than a mile east of where the Deschutes River flowed past Sunriver. It was snowing when we arrived, and it looked like it had been snowing a lot, and keeping the roads clear up to the area around the cabin wasn't a civic priority. We did the last part of the drive with Dan swearing, working the Pathfinder in four-wheel drive.

Then he stopped the car and Alena and I each hopped out, telling him and Vadim to stay put and keep an eye out. We'd seen absolutely no traffic coming in, and the nearest cabin was perhaps half a mile away, and it had looked as cold and empty as the one before us did now. With the car's engine off, the only sound was that of the snow coming down.

Without a word, Alena and I each headed for the cabin, taking opposite sides for the approach. It was ugly, late sixties style, two stories tall, and on the ground floor almost an entire wall was floor-to-ceiling windows, shutters closed behind them. Not the best design for a winter place, and not the best design for the summer, either; in the first, the glass would conduct all the cold outside; in the second, it would trap heat with the sunlight. Snow had slid from the rooftop recently, plopping in a great pile along the east side of the house. In some places it came up to my knees, and once, while trudging around, it reached my hips. But the only signs that the snow had been disturbed at all were ours.

We met up again at the foot of the porch, and again stopped to listen and look around, still not speaking. It was almost eerily silent, that pure winter quiet that comes upon a heavy snow. It made the world beautiful, and it made the world even colder. Snow was melting in my hair, running down the back of my neck, and I shivered, and I saw that Alena was trying to keep her teeth from chattering. Neither of us was carrying a lot of body fat, and the weather was working on us fast.

"It'll serve," she decided. "How do we want to get inside? I don't want to break any windows if we can help it."

"We shouldn't need to." I pointed to the small, rectangular metal box that had been screwed into the wall of the cabin beside the front door. "If we can get that open, we've got the keys."

She stepped up onto the porch, brushing snow off her shoulders, and I followed her. There were ten push buttons set into the box, each corresponding to a digit, zero to nine, running in two rows with a sliding switch set in the space between. She pushed four buttons, tried the switch, then pushed the same four, but in a different sequence, and tried the switch again. The third time, when she tried the switch, the box opened, and she removed the key.

"Eighteen eighteen?" I asked.

"Tried that first," she said with a grin, turning to fit the key in the lock. "Then eighty-one and eighty-one. It opened with eighty-one, eighteen."

"They should be more careful with their combinations."

"They should." She turned the key, gave the door a good push, and it swung open.

"Get inside and get warm," I told her. "I'll get the others."

There were three bedrooms, two with queens and one with two doubles, a full bathroom, a half bath, and a fireplace in the center of the main room on the ground floor. Vadim and I carried Illya inside while Alena set about trying to get a fire started and Dan headed back into town for groceries. We weren't going to need much; we weren't going to be here long.

We deposited Illya in one of the bedrooms with a queen, then duct-taped his wrists and his ankles. He was still out cold, though he mumbled when I pulled off his shoes and his pants. I covered him with a blanket to keep him from catching hypothermia before the heat could fill the cabin. Vadim began searching the rest of the building, less looking for danger than looking to see what he could find, and I joined Alena at the fireplace. She had a blaze already going, and smoke curled out over the mantle, spilling out into the room.

"Bad draw," she told me. "The chimney is cold. Soon as the fire heats the stone, the smoke will clear."

I nodded, crouched down on my haunches in front of the flames, feeling the heat work itself into my clothes. Steam was already rising from Alena's shirt and jeans.

She used a poker on the logs, repositioning them, saying, "Are you going to be able to do this?"

"We're already doing it," I said.

"You know what I mean."

The flames danced in the fireplace, famished, eating the logs. "He's going to give us what we want. He'll tell us what he knows."

"Without question." Alena turned the poker, nudging another of the logs. Sparks burst and then vanished. "I'm asking you how far you are willing to go to achieve that."

"He'll tell us what he knows," I repeated, after a moment. "One way or another."

She finished fiddling with the fire, replaced the poker in its stand, then turned her attention to me.

"Dan can do it," Alena told me. "You don't need to."

"It doesn't matter who does what, Alena. We're all guilty for what happens to Illya next."

"Just as he is guilty for what happened to Yasha and Tamryn and Natalie Trent."

"I haven't forgotten."

"I didn't think you had." I looked away from the fire to her. "The empty thing feels nothing," she said.

"And you are not an empty thing," I said.

"Neither are you."

"I know," I said.

I was just afraid of becoming one.

Dan and I were in the room when Illya finally woke up, each of us seated in chairs at either side of the bed. We'd been waiting with the lights off—my idea, not Dan's—and the only illumination came from the hall, a spear of gold that dug into the darkness. Outside, the snow was still falling steadily. If it didn't let up soon, we could find ourselves snowed in, and I didn't like that idea. I wanted to get this over with quickly, to get it done and then to get gone.

He came up slowly, as if he knew what was waiting for him when he was finally awake. I listened to his breathing change, the regular and gentle cadence becoming more rapid, more broken, and then the bed creaked, and creaked again. I knew he was moving, that his eyes were now open, that he'd realized he couldn't move his hands or his feet. Then the memory hit him, what had happened, and the panic followed, and he cried out, inarticulate, and the bed creaked again, louder, and knocked back against the wall as he began thrashing about.

The lights came on, and I'd been ready for it, but Illya hadn't, and he cried out again, wincing and trying to shield his eyes with his bound hands. He wasn't a big man, perhaps four inches or so shorter than me, not handsome so much as pleasant-looking, with a broad face that seemed more inclined to laughter than to curses. His hair was black, and his brown eyes were so dark they might as well have been, too.

Then his vision returned enough to see Dan, and then he saw me, and Illya froze, and the look of fear and despair that flared in his face was heartbreaking.

It made me furious. It made me want to get out of my chair and take hold of his throat in one hand, and to punch him again and again with my other, and to ask how fucking dare he try to make me feel for him, care for him. It made me wish I could open my mind, that I could dump the memory of Natalie into his, that last vision of her, with bone and brain and blood on a New England dawn. To scream at him that he had done this, and in so doing had killed any hope of sympathy or mercy from me.

Dan, still seated as before, said, "Hello, Illya."

Maybe because the words were so very innocuous they seemed to terrify Illya all the more.

"Dan..." he said, in Russian. His voice was hoarse, whether from fear or disuse, I didn't know. "Oh God, Dan, please—"

"You don't want to be talking to me," Dan told him, switching to English and looking at the pistol he was holding in his right hand, as if noticing it for the first time. It was the same gun we'd taken from Illya when we'd made the snatch ten hours ago, a cheap Taurus semiauto. "You want to talk to him."

Illya twisted his head back towards me, much the same way the Next Victim turns to look over her shoulder in horror films.

"Depending on what you say to him and how hard he has to work to get you to say it, then you'll want to talk to me," Dan told him. "So you better tell him what he wants to know, Illya. If you want anything from me at all, you better fucking well tell him what he wants to know."

Illya swallowed, then nodded. "I... I didn't know what they would do."

I stared at him, doing my damnedest at keeping anything that I was thinking, anything that I was feeling, from my face. No fury, no sympathy, no hatred, nothing. Trying to let him supply all of those things, instead, to put on me what he feared and what he hoped.

"You don't... you don't believe me," Illya said to me. His English was only mildly accented, as if he'd been working on perfecting it at the same time I'd been trying to master Russian and Georgian. "I know you don't, I can tell you don't. But I didn't know, I swear."

I looked at Dan. Dan sighed, then leaned across the bed towards me, handing over the Taurus as Illya eyed it with visible alarm. I took the pistol and nodded to Dan, and Dan got out of his chair and left the room. Illya didn't know where to look, bouncing his eyes from the pistol to Dan to me, and it was obvious that the panic he was struggling to keep at bay was gaining ground, and quickly.

It gained more ground when I racked the slide on the Taurus. I didn't point the gun at him; I didn't need to. I pointed it at the floor.

"Oh God," Illya said, switching to Russian. "Oh God oh my God please don't kill me."

Alena entered the room, moving around to stand behind me in my chair. Then Dan returned and took his seat once more, Vadim following him, picking a place at the foot of the bed. Illya struggled to sit up straighter in the bed, backing further against the headboard, as if hoping he could melt himself through the wood and the wall to freedom.

None of us said a word, all of us staring at him.

Illya began to tremble. Tears started filling his eyes, then began to spill down each cheek.

"I didn't mean to, oh God, I didn't mean to," he said, and he was unable to look at any of us, so instead he studied his hands, the duct tape wrapped thick around his wrists. "They picked me up, I was at Millat's, I was just doing some shopping and they grabbed me when I came outside, they said I had to go with them. I didn't have a choice! They showed me—they showed me IDs, like that, not . . . not badges, but cards. They knew who I was, Dan! They knew who I was, everything, they said I was an illegal, that I was a criminal, that they were going to arrest me!"

He twisted in the bed, focusing on Dan. His hands came up, as if to implore him.

"I didn't have a fucking choice, you understand, don't you? You have to understand, I would never have betrayed you for anything, but they had me, they had me, they were going to put me away, send me back!"

Behind me, I felt Alena resting her hands on my shoulders. It was a subtle movement, but Illya was strung out on his fear and his adrenaline, and he caught it, twisting back in our direction, terrified.

"This is what they said, okay? This is what they said, what they wanted, they didn't want me, they said they didn't care about me, they wanted my help, that's what they wanted. They just wanted to know where the two of you were, that was all. They just wanted me to tell them where you were, when you would be there, then they wanted me to go away. They gave me money, they told me fifty thousand dollars if I did this.

"I tried to tell them I didn't know what they were talking about, I tried to tell them they had made a mistake, but they knew! You understand? They knew about you and about her, that she was somewhere around New York, that you two were together, working together, that Dan was helping. They said that was all they wanted, only the two of you, they said Kodiak and Drama, that's what they called Natasha, they said that was it, just the two of you, that was all I had to do, just tell them where you would be, where and when you would be there. If I did that, they said that would be all, they would take care of it. I swear to God I didn't know they wanted to kill you!"

He stopped speaking abruptly, clamping his mouth closed, breathing noisily through his nose. He was still shaking, and I could see the muscles in his jaw working as he clenched his teeth.

I looked pointedly at the pistol in my hand, then back at Illya. He was lying, at least about the last part. Maybe whoever had grabbed him had never said, yes, we want Kodiak and the woman, Drama, dead, but he had been brought in by Dan as one of the bodyguards for Alena, and that should have been more than enough to explain the stakes. It was justification, that's all it was, lies to absolve himself from his guilt.

"I'm telling you the truth!" Illya cried. "They never told me what they wanted to do! They never told me!"

I pointed the Taurus at the headboard by his right shoulder and put a round into it. Wood splintered and popped, and the report in the bedroom was explosive. Illya screamed.

"Stop lying to me," I said, softly. "You're smart enough to have stayed hidden for three years. You're smart enough to know better than to lie to me."

"I'm not—"

"I was never supposed to go to the house in Cold Spring, Illya," I said. "You had to have contacted them and told them I was going to be there as soon as you found out, probably when Dan sent you to find me a car. So what did you think they were going to do to me when they told you to tap the tank? What did you think it meant when they told you to leave your post at the door, to run as soon as you saw them?"

"I didn't, I didn't think—"

I handed the pistol to Alena, who took it and fired a second round, this into the headboard on the opposite side of Illya from where I'd put my shot. He screamed again, cringing.

"Fifty thousand dollars," I said. "You sold us out for fifty fucking thousand dollars."

Illya had tucked his chin to his chest, raising his bound arms to cover his face. He was sobbing.

"I want a name," I told him. "And I want it now."

He lifted his head, his look pleading, his eyes shining with tears. "I didn't . . . they never told me—"

Alena handed the pistol to Vadim.

"—I don't remember!" Illya screamed, and he tried again to push himself backwards, through the headboard and the wall, watching Vadim with alarm. When he ran out of room for his retreat, he started off the bed, instead, flopping to my right, and Dan lurched forward, grabbing hold of Illya by the upper arms, and gripping him tightly, forced him back into position. I half expected Dan to follow it up with a free shot, a punch to the gut or the side, but he didn't. He just shoved Illya back into place on the bed and then resumed his seat.

Illya remained motionless for a second, staring at Vadim, now holding the pistol, then cried out and threw himself in the opposite direction he'd gone before, this time towards me. Unlike Dan, I didn't move, just let him topple from the bed and onto the cold wood floor. He landed hard, no way to catch himself or, at least, no consideration in his fear to do so, and took the impact on his right shoulder. He sobbed, bound feet working, scrabbling against the wood floor, trying to drive himself into the corner, alternately pleading and whimpering.

I felt like I was going to be sick.

"Alena," I said.

"Atticus?"

"Leave us alone for a couple of minutes."

She put her hand back on my shoulder, resting lightly just for a moment, then turned and headed out without a word. Dan followed her, more slowly and much more reluctantly. Vadim started to follow, then turned back. He offered me the pistol.

"I don't need it," I told him.

Vadim's brow creased, as if he wasn't sure what to make of me, or at least, as if he wasn't sure what I was up to. Then he shrugged, cast a last glance at Illya, and followed after the others, taking the Taurus with him.

I waited until Vadim had closed the door, then rose from where I'd been sitting. Illya had wedged himself into the corner, and his bladder had emptied, and the smell of urine was ripe and tragic. I put my hands on his shoulders, gently, but all the same he cringed when I did it, and I don't blame him at all for that.

"Come on," I said. "Let me help you up."

I felt him shudder, exhaustion and surrender together, and he let me lift him back to the bed. I didn't have anything for his wet underpants, but I put the blanket back around him all the same, trying to keep the chill away. He watched me with confusion and with fear.

Once he was propped up once more, I resumed my seat in the chair.

"Dan's going to kill you," I told him. "There's nothing to be done for it. You're going to die, and you don't want to, but you and I already know that's the way it's going to be."

"You . . . you could stop him."

"I could," I agreed. "I'm not going to stop him."

The despair seemed to flood his entire body.

"No one is going to," I said. "This is where it ends for you. This is where the choices you've made have brought you. Do you understand that?"

"It wasn't my fault." He said it softly. "They were government men, don't you understand? What was I supposed to do?"

"You didn't have to call them, Illya. No one had a gun at your head. They'd cut you loose. You could have waited until it was all said and done and vanished. But you did it for the money. Or you did it because Dan treated you badly. Or you did it because you thought when it was over you'd come out on top in Brighton Beach, or any other reason that only you can know. But you're not going to convince me you're a victim, here. It's been three years, and you're selling meth and you're still trying to be a big-time Russian hood. So it doesn't matter why you did it. It only matters *that* you did it."

Illya closed his eyes, his upper teeth working on his lower lip. After several seconds, he nodded, slightly.

"Tell me about these men, the ones who paid you."

"There was only one," Illya said, after a second. "The others, the ones who took me, they were working for him. But there was only one in charge. Bowles. His name was Matt . . . Matthew Bowles."

I nodded, just barely. Matthew Bowles had held the strings on Oxford. One of the middlemen, and it was logical that Bowles had been responsible for setting up what had happened in Cold Spring the same way he had set things up for Oxford, at least until Scott Fowler and I forced a stop to that. Bowles was a facilitator, a fixer, but he wasn't the shot-caller. Natalie Trent had died because of what Bowles had put into motion, and he would taste his own blood for that, I would see to it.

But that wasn't going to be enough.

"Did Bowles say who he worked for? What part of the government?"

"He didn't... he didn't say." Illya shook his head. "I thought at first he was FBI, or maybe CIA, but it wasn't that."

"How do you know?"

"When he offered me the money, I told him... I told him it was a good offer, but he could offer me anything, why should I believe him? How could I know he would do what he said, that he even had the money to give me? And the man, he gave me his business card, it had his cell number on it and his name and all of that."

"You're a fool, Illya, but you're not an idiot. We've been over that already. You can't expect me to believe you did what you did on the strength of a business card anyone could have created."

"No, no, not like that," he said hastily. "You misunderstand, he gave me the card, but he showed me this ID, this pass. It was the real thing, it had to be. Hologram, microchip, picture, everything. It was real, Atticus. I knew he wasn't lying."

"What place?" I asked, and when he didn't answer immediately, I repeated myself, turning the words harsh. "What place? Who'd he work for?"

Illya met my eyes, and even through his defeat and fear, I could read something else. A dawning realization, perhaps, that he and I weren't so far apart in our circumstances as the moment might lead one to believe. There was almost humor in it, almost glee, but not quite.

"You're fucked," he said, softly. "You and Natasha and Dan and his shit of a kid, you're all fucked now. You don't even realize it."

"Who did Bowles work for, Illya?"

"It doesn't matter." Realization was creeping into his voice, and with it, new strength. "It doesn't matter what I say. It doesn't matter what you do to me. You can't win. You're going to die. Just like me, you're all going to die."

I shot from my chair to where he lay on the bed, pushed the middle and index fingers of my right hand into the side of his trachea while holding his head back against the headboard with my other. I pressed down, and I pressed hard, because I was angry. Illya's eyes bulged.

"Maybe," I said. "But you'll die first. Who did Bowles work for, Illya? Where was the ID from?"

He croaked, his lips pulling apart in a smile.

With a rasp, Illya said, "The White House, motherfucker."

I held my fingers against his skin, didn't move. Illya's eyes seemed to fill with laughter as much as tears. For a long moment, I thought about finishing him then, about twisting his head around or crushing his trachea or using any of the other dozen ways that I knew to end his life.

"Dan!" I called out.

He was at the door within a breath. "Atticus?"

I released Illya.

"Make him pay," I told Dan.

"We all do," Dan told me.

PART THREE

CHAPTER ONE

The woman who took my passport application at the post office in Whitefish, Montana, was in her mid-fifties, shaped like a dumpling, and chatty.

"Oh, travel," she said. "Where you heading, then?"

"I'm thinking about visiting South America," I lied. "Rio, maybe, someplace warm."

She clucked, checking to see that my two headshots had been properly affixed. The photographs were new, taken that morning at a copy shop a couple blocks south of Whitefish Lake. I'd worn my glasses for the photos, and the young man working the camera had needed to remind me that I wasn't supposed to smile.

"That'd be nice, someplace warm," the dumpling said. "All this snow, can you believe it? The winters, they're just getting colder. Global warming."

"Global warming," I agreed.

"Oh, you're on Iron Horse Road," she said, looking at the address I'd put on the application. "Bought one of the new places up by the lake?"

"It's about a mile from the lake."

"So you're a resident, or is it just a vacation home?"

"Resident," I said. "Just arrived."

She stopped reviewing my application long enough to offer me a doughy hand to shake. "Well, then, welcome to Whitefish. I'm Laura."

"Atticus," I said.

Laura checked my application. "Atticus... Kodiak? Like the bear?"

"Like the bear."

"Atticus Kodiak. Odd name, you don't mind me saying."

"I don't mind you saying it at all, Laura," I said.

She laughed, either pleased with my generous spirit or still wildly amused by my name, then moved my application to a tray beside her scale. "Well, everything looks just fine to me, Atticus. You should have a response in the next six to eight weeks."

"Sooner, I hope," I said, with a smile.

It was still snowing when I stepped back outside onto Baker Avenue, and I put my watch cap back atop my head and got my gloves back on my hands, then started walking north, in the direction of the lake. Snow, clean and white and wet, coated almost everything the eye could see. The temperature was below freezing, and there were a few people about, but no one paid me any attention. Whitefish billed itself as a resort community more than anything else, golfing, hunting, and fishing in the summer, skiing and sledding and skating in the winter, and a variety of festivals and events to fill in the gaps between. Resident population wasn't more than 7,000, and while the income divide between those who visited and those who remained was dramatic, the cost of living wasn't so high as to make it intolerable.

I walked in the cold and the snow, following Baker north over the short bridge that spanned where the Whitefish River flowed through town, then a couple blocks later crossed the railroad tracks on Viaduct. Whitefish had begun as a fur-trading town in the 1800s, and then the Great Northern Railway had come in the early 1900s, and fur turned to logging, and now, a hundred years later, logging had given way to leisure. All along the shores of the lake, resort homes were cropping up as fast as the hammers could raise them.

It took me most of an hour to get back to the house, partially because of the snow, but mostly because I was taking my time. If I was being watched or followed, I saw no signs of it, and I suspected that was because there was nobody watching or following me. It had been exactly a week since Alena and I had left the unpleasantness of Sunriver, Oregon, behind us. To our knowledge, Illya's body hadn't been found yet.

The way Dan and Vadim worked, I doubted it ever would.

Still, Alena and I had kept our movements discreet since then, doing our damnedest to stay beneath the radar. We were still hunted, and with the information Illya had given us, there was no question that the hunters had the power of the federal government at their disposal, at least in some part. That we'd been back in the U.S. for ten days without attracting attention could only mean that we'd managed a good job of it, that we'd kept any alarms regarding our whereabouts from being tripped.

Not anymore. Not after my passport application—submitted in my real name, and with the photographs to prove it—reached the State Department. There wasn't a doubt in my mind that my name had been flagged, that I was on a watch-list someplace. Whoever it was giving Matthew Bowles his orders would learn of it, and he or she or they would learn that I had listed an address on Iron Horse Road in Whitefish, Montana, as my place of residence.

There would be a response; there would have to be. Whoever wanted us dead didn't have a choice.

The same way that, because of what had happened in Cold Spring, I didn't have one, either.

"It's done?" Alena asked as I moved past her into the faux flagstone entryway of the house. She had a pistol in her hand, practically an afterthought, and by the time I'd turned back from shutting and locking the door, she'd made it disappear. I removed my hat, knocked snow from my shoulders and stamped it off my boots. Spatter caught her bare feet, and she hissed at me, dancing back onto the safer warmth of the carpet.

"Signed, sealed, and delivered," I told her. "You should put some shoes on, you might need to move fast."

"It will be the end of the day before your application is sent to the offices in Bozeman, and tomorrow morning—at the earliest—before it's processed." She headed away from me, towards the kitchen, adding over her shoulder, "We have time."

I removed my coat, and the sweatshirt I was wearing beneath it, and hung both from the row of pegs on the wall. When I'd told Laura the Dumpling that I was a resident I'd been lying, inasmuch as the house was a rental. It was, like many of the homes in the vicinity of Whitefish Lake, a recent construction, not more than five years old, and everything in it and about it still felt new, from the spring in the carpet to the smell in the bedrooms. Architecturally, it was of that same open-plan, high-ceilinged family that seemed to be the modern equivalent of posh-log-cabin, and in an odd way, it reminded me of Alena's home in Bequia before I'd burnt it to the ground.

Alena was at the counter in the kitchen when I caught up, the kettle on the gas stove spewing forth a column of steam. On the table was a MacBook, the Web browser open. We'd bought the laptop at the Apple Store in Seattle after clearing the cache in Burien, just south of the city. Alena had established the Burien cache years earlier, along with dozens of others around the world, when she'd worked as one of The Ten. Most were in Western Europe or the United States, since those were the places she'd most often visited in pursuit of her targets, and each was designed to be used once and never again, and each held the same things: weapons, cash, alternate identities. The Burien cache had contained sixty-three thousand in American dollars, two sets of false identities, including driver's licenses (one for the state of Washington, one for the state of Idaho), companion credit cards (Visa and American Express), and passports, four pistols (all of them semiautos), ammunition for the same, and two sets of clothes. Everything had been tailored for Alena's use, which meant the IDs and clothes were useless to me, since I suffered the obvious gender disadvantage.

Seattle had been our last real stop before Whitefish, an overnight that had followed our leaving Vadim and Dan in Sunriver. Given what Illya had told us, taking airplanes seemed an unnecessary risk.

Alena turned off the flame beneath the kettle. She used a dish towel decorated with leaping fish to take the handle, then proceeded to fill the two mugs she'd prepared. When she'd finished, I indicated the laptop with my head. "No joy?"

She glanced to the computer, her expression flickering sour. "Nothing. No one I recognize, no one I recollect."

I took my mug and sniffed at the liquid within. The tea she'd made had a citrus, floral scent, and for the first time in a long while, I wished I was drinking coffee, instead.

"Not to insult your vanity, but it is possible that whoever wants us dead is someone *I've* offended, and not you," I said.

"I find that unlikely." She was watching my examination of the tea. "You are not, and were not, ever counted as one of The Ten. If it is someone in the White House, someone in the current administration, who pursues us, then the odds are far greater that it is someone I have had dealings with, either directly or indirectly. Someone I did a job for. That is the only plausible explanation for this vendetta."

I used two fingers to pluck the tea bag from the mug, dropped it into the sink. The splash it made on impact was the color of ketchup. "Vendetta makes it sound like it's personal."

Alena shook her head, opened her mouth, then closed it, looking at me with the mug still in my hand. I sighed and took a sip, and was profoundly relieved to find the tea tasted nothing like ketchup. If it tasted like oranges and hibiscus, however, I couldn't tell.

"That was not my intent. Only that the strike in Cold Spring indicated a certain . . . zealotry, perhaps."

"Assuming you're correct, that this goes back to work you did as one of The Ten, work you did for the CIA or the Pentagon, we're talking about a job you did four years ago, at least."

"It would be six, I think."

"You *think*?"

"The contracts are always initiated through cutouts, Atticus, you know that."

"Yeah, but you vet the source on each job, that's just common sense."

She nodded her agreement, almost absently. "But it is possible

I missed something. That the person, the people, I was working for in one or more instances were not the people I thought they were. Mistakes happen. Governments subcontract the work. It is possible that someone discovered the contact procedures for me, the ones used by your government, and employed that method for their own ends."

"There's our answer," I said.

She nodded slightly. "I did consider that. That someone in the White House is someone I did a job for might be motive enough. Before he died, Agent Fowler, you, and I had a long conversation about what I did and who I did it for. If he reported that information back to his superiors, if he was, perhaps, not as discreet as he should have been, it is possible that whoever our adversary is took alarm, saw that potentially his or her relationship with me was in danger of being exposed. Wishing to protect himself or herself, they have taken steps to silence both of us."

"Don't say that," I said.

"What?"

"It's not Scott's fault," I said. "Don't blame the dead man."

"I'm not insulting the memory of your friend," Alena said, carefully. "Simply stating a fact, however unpleasant it may be to hear. What matters is not how the information reached our adversary in the White House; what matters is that once it did, he or she deemed us a threat that needed to be addressed, immediately and completely."

"Which means we're being hunted for something you know that you don't know you know."

"Yes."

"Maybe you should try to remember."

"I have been."

"Maybe you should try harder."

Alena took another sip of her tea, then set the mug down and moved the two steps required to stand in front of me. She put her hands on my forearms, her expression serious, meeting my eyes.

"There are other ways to do this, Atticus," she said, gently. "We can leave here right now, and the passport application will have done no more harm than has been done already with the death of Illya. We can withdraw, try to find another way."

"No," I said. "We really can't."

"It is a big planet. There are many places to hide."

"I don't want to hide anymore."

Her grip on my arms tightened slightly, almost imperceptibly. "And what if they do not wish to question you? What if we are mistaken, and their desire to find me is not more powerful than their desire to silence you?"

"Then you'll keep me alive," I said.

The fear was easy to miss, just a flash in her eyes, hinting at her doubt and the pain that it brought. It wasn't much at all. In Kobuleti, when I'd angered her or annoyed her or delighted her, she'd been willing to show it, though it was still something she was learning to allow herself. Since our return to the U.S., that had begun to fade. The professional emerging to subsume the personal.

Except the problem here, the problem for both of us, was that they were the same. Nothing was personal, and everything was. Every move we made had to be as professionals, and yet the motives behind them were anything but. We could have argued that what we were doing was for self-defense and survival, nothing more, and maybe for Alena, that would even have been true. But it wasn't for me, and we both understood that; it was about the future as much as the past, about the home we had made for ourselves in Kobuleti as much as about what had happened three years earlier in Cold Spring on a New England autumn's dawn.

"It has to be answered," I told her. "And if the way to find out who needs to answer is by bringing them to me, then that's what I'll do."

Her hands moved up my arms, then stopped, fell away, and I could read the conflict in each movement, the struggle she was having. Then she stepped past me, leaving the kitchen to disappear further into the house.

"I have to pack," Alena said.

We made love that night, and it was all need, cathartic and hungry, and when we were finished we clung to each other as we had during our passion. The night was utterly silent, the quiet of the snow broken only by the hiss of the forced air trying vainly to keep the chill from the house.

Her lips against my cheek, Alena said, "They will hurt you."

"I know."

"I will come as soon as I can."

"I know."

"I will come for you."

I kissed her.

"I know," I told her.

She was gone in the morning.

I made the surveillance four days later.

Two days after that, as the last of the sunlight slid away from Big Mountain to the north and the valley was turning to darkness, there was a knock at the door. I'd built a fire in the fireplace, half to stave off the chill, half to stave off the apprehension and loneliness I was feeling. I'd been reading a book of Kurt Vonnegut essays that I'd bought in town, and they had done nothing to improve my mood.

Then the knock at the door, three quick raps, no doorbell to follow, and I knew it was time. I marked the book and set it on the coffee table beside one of the guns from the Burien cache, a Walther that was resting there. For a moment, I considered taking the weapon up, carrying it with me, but then I thought that the last thing I really wanted to do was give them another reason to shoot first and ask questions later.

If they were knocking on the front door, it meant that there was a team already in position at the back. I hadn't heard any glass breaking, hadn't felt a shift in the air inside the house in answer to a sudden draught. So no penetration, not yet, which meant they were covering the perimeter; they'd wait to enter until they were certain I wasn't going to try to bolt in their direction.

Assuming, of course, that the object of their exercise was to capture and not to kill.

There was a second set of raps on the front door, this a little brisker.

I left the gun where it was, and went to answer the door.

Three men stood waiting for me on the porch outside, none of them obviously presenting weapons, but if two of them hadn't come heavy, it was because they'd been ordered not to. Those two wore blue jeans, boots, and bulky down parkas, flanking the third on either side. The third one broke the mold, in a suit and overcoat and gloves.

Of the three, I recognized two, one of them immediately. One took a second to place, and it wasn't his appearance so much as the shared recognition that came from his eyes when they met mine. The last time I'd seen him, he'd worn a black watch cap and been flat on his back in a Citgo lot.

"Sean," I said, surprising myself that I could recall his name so easily, and he started, possibly just as stunned by my use of it. "How's the shoulder?"

Then Matthew Bowles, in his navy blue suit and black overcoat, stepped forward and looked me up and down, as if checking stock in a back room.

"Son of a bitch," Bowles said. "It really is you."

"It really is," I said.

Bowles smiled at me, and it was the same strained, thin-lipped smile I remembered him using when Scott Fowler and I had seen him last, three and a half years earlier. It was the smile he'd produced while listening to us explain everything we knew about Oxford. It was the same smile he'd used when he'd picked up the phone, and given the order to cut Oxford loose. It was the kind of smile smug in its assurance that he knew more than you, that all of your assumptions were incorrect, and that he'd be there to see it when you learned so yourself.

I hated that fucking smile.

I hated it all the more when Bowles said, "Take him."

Sean and the other one came forward, and I heard a crack, then a crash, from inside the house, and I didn't resist, just raised my arms to my sides. I thought they'd go for cuffs, but it turned out that was naïve of me, and Sean eagerly set me straight with a punch to my left side, just beneath my ribs. It came hard and mean, but I'd like to think I could have shaken it off if I'd wanted to.

Then the other one got in on the act, and I went down on my knees on the porch. From behind me I could hear movement, voices, the perimeter team reaching us. Someone put a boot in, and then a second one followed the first, and another fist, or maybe a baton, and my vision flared and the familiar taste of my own blood came into my mouth, and then there was nothing else but the cold of the snow that had settled in drifts on my front porch.

CHAPTER TWO

"Patriot," Bowles said. "How's that for a fucking irony?"

I used my tongue to probe the inside of my mouth. All of my teeth seemed to be intact and in place, though blood still leaked from what felt like a good-sized tear on the inside of my right cheek. I spat what had gathered onto the floor, and discovered in the process that my lower lip was numb, and consequently it wasn't so much a spit as a dribble. The floor was wood, finished planks, rustic and shiny. My blood and saliva shone where it landed.

Matthew Bowles moved into the seat opposite where I'd been positioned at the table, unloading his laptop from its black nylon case and setting the machine beside him. He always had a laptop; it was his security blanket. It chimed as he switched it on, began to hum into the boot cycle.

I looked around the room. My vision was clear, and I was

mildly surprised to discover that my contacts hadn't been knocked free in the beat down. The beat down, as much as I could recall of it, had been sincere, and I suspected there'd been a few extra free shots added as a bonus after I'd lost consciousness. Most of me ached, and I was pretty sure that the parts of me that didn't only declined to do so because, like my lower lip, they'd gone numb. That said, I didn't think anything had been broken. At least, not yet.

The room itself wasn't much to look at, ill furnished, walls finished with knotted pine planks and a floor that hadn't known care. Not much in the way of furniture, a couch with upholstery that had started as red and had since faded to a pinkish brown, a couple of wooden craftsman chairs, and the rickety table I was seated at now. Sconces were set irregularly on the wall, their dusty glass in the shape of large candle flames, the wattage of the bulbs weak. To my left were two small windows, curtains drawn, and through the gaps in the fabric I could see nothing beyond. Presumably it was night outside, though I supposed the windows could have been painted over. Opposite me, to the right of the couch, what was either the front or back door to the cabin.

Sitting on the couch were the two who'd been with Bowles when I'd answered the door, Sean and the other one. Both had their jackets off, and each wore a holster with a pistol at his hip, and against Sean's side of the couch had been propped a shotgun. Of them, Sean had the clean seniority, both in age and manner. When my eyes ran over them, the eyefucking I received from each in return was severe.

I continued to look around as Bowles continued to tap on his keyboard. A moth-eaten Indian rug hung on the wall over the fireplace, its colors faded. There were no tools for the fire, and I wondered if that was because they'd been moved, or because they'd simply never been. That was it for the décor.

Off to my right ran a short hallway, carpeted in a thick orange and brown shag, doors along either side. There was a kitchen down that way; I could make out the sounds of movement, the scrape of a pan on a stove. The scent of frying bacon reached me, mixing with the weaker scent of dust and disuse. Behind it all lurked the cloying musk of mold, probably from the carpet.

The cabin was, in its own way, oddly reminiscent of the one to which we'd taken Illya in Sunriver, and that made sense to me. Far easier to keep me in Montana, perhaps to move south, further from the Canadian border. Certainly deeper into the woods, to someplace secluded, and God knew there were plenty enough places like that to be found. In the steady throb of pain, I couldn't discern anything that felt like a narcotic trying to wash out of me. So I hadn't been drugged, which made it more likely that we hadn't left Whitefish that far behind.

"So," said Bowles, still focused on the laptop. "Are you? Are you a patriot?"

One of the doors on the hall opened, and two men emerged, both apparently acquired from the same supplier who had delivered the two on the couch. The variations were cosmetic. They were zipping closed their down parkas, and one already had a watch cap on his head. Both were armed, another shotgun and an AR-15. They passed the table without sparing me a glance, moving straight to Sean, who was getting to his feet. There was a brief exchange, kept to whispering so I couldn't overhear, and then Sean led them to the door. When he opened it, a puff of snow blew inside, driven by the icy air. He let the two out, closed the door once more, and resumed his seat.

Bowles, who had turned to watch, brought his attention back to me, explaining, "Perimeter."

I didn't say anything.

He slid the laptop aside and set an elbow on the table,

leaning forward and resting his chin in his hand, grinning. He'd removed his overcoat and suit jacket, but the knot on his necktie was as tight and perfectly centered as ever. He was roughly my age, perhaps a year or two older, with straight black hair combed neatly back, and a pale face that was so smooth as to appear almost prepubescent. His eyes were so dark I could barely discern his pupils against the irises.

"Nothing to say for yourself?"

My hands were in my lap, and I brought them up slowly, felt pain stabbing through my fingers. They'd been bound with black Flexi-Cuffs, and whoever had done the binding had pulled them tighter than they needed to be; I could see the plastic biting into my skin, slowly killing my circulation. When my hands were at eye level, I showed them to him.

"You're kidding, right?" he asked.

I set my hands on the table, sighed, then said, "How about something to drink?" When I spoke, I could feel the dried blood at my mouth and lips crack.

He considered. "Water."

"That would be fine," I said.

Bowles half turned in his seat to the two on the couch, and the one who wasn't Sean got to his feet with a grunt. I watched him go, disappearing into the kitchen out of sight. There was murmured conversation, the words lost to the distance, but I was making out at least three voices.

So seven of them, then, including Bowles and his buddy Sean and the two on patrol. Maybe a couple more lurking someplace, but I doubted it; the cabin didn't look like it could hold many more people.

Still, seven, and if I was correct in assuming that Bowles had limited combat experience, that still left six of them who knew what they were about, and probably knew it quite well. If these were contractors—and Sean's presence all but confirmed that they were—they'd come with a pedigree, with years in the Army or Marines backing them up, maybe even some time with Special Forces. An awful lot for Alena to handle alone and in the cold and with a leg that, despite everything, still wasn't what it should be.

"So, where you been hiding?" Bowles asked me.

"Oh, you know," I said, turning my attention back to him. "Here and there."

"I'm guessing Eastern Europe. Maybe some time in Africa."

I shrugged.

He checked the laptop screen, clicking one of the keys a few times. "You have gotten around, though. Jakarta, São Paulo, Tokyo. Quito . . . huh. What were you doing in Ecuador, Atticus?"

"Someone's got to pick all those coffee beans."

Bowles smirked, nodded, tapped, and I wondered if he knew that, in fact, I'd never been to any of the four cities he'd just listed. If he did, this was gamesmanship, but to what end, I didn't know. If he didn't, I had no desire to correct him.

The one who wasn't Sean returned from the kitchen, setting a paper cup of water on the table by my hands. I took the cup in both hands, sipped at the water. It was so cold it hurt my teeth.

"Patriot," Bowles said for the third time, and I felt a flicker of annoyance. "You never answered my question. Are you a patriot, Atticus?"

"Probably not the way you or Sean, there, would define it."

On the couch, Sean's eyefuck dialed up to eleven.

"Don't you love your country?" Bowles asked.

I met his eyes with a look that, hopefully, told him just what I thought of people who asked that kind of question. It was a stupid question, it was a rhetorical question, it was the kind of question asked by people trying to establish their moral superiority. It was a question used to identify enemies, not to make friends. It was an all-or-nothing question, and there was never a right answer. It was a question that had nothing to do with place or history or current affairs or society. It was a question that asked only one thing: Are you with us or against us?—and us were always the people posing the question in the first place.

It was a question that, from the first time it had ever been uttered outside the Garden of Eden, was a justification to violence. Cain, I was sure, had asked Abel if he loved his country.

Bowles held the look, and his smile grew, and then he made a soft laugh and said, "Patriot," once more. Then he turned the laptop so I could see what he'd been looking at on its screen.

It was the Interpol file on Alena, except in it she was called Drama. The header dated the file from the winter of the last year, only four months earlier, identified the document as a law enforcement briefing-slash-update. According to the same header, it contained the latest intelligence for distribution on The Ten. It put "The Ten" in quotations.

With a gentle nudge, Bowles moved the laptop closer, so I could have access to the trackpad and keyboard. I scrolled down. There was a small file photograph, grainy and ill-focused. I'd seen the photo many times before, and it was now well out-of-date, almost five years old, taken when she'd been spotted in New York, trying to kill a man that I'd been trying to protect. I was only vaguely surprised that, since then, no one had managed to acquire a better one.

There were lines for her vitals: gender, height, weight, hair color, eye color. Country of origin. Aliases. Distinguishing marks. Characteristics. Methodology. Where the information was known, it had been filled in, which meant more lines about her had been left blank than had been completed, and much of what was there was incorrect. They'd gotten her gender right, that was about all.

I scanned the document, careful to limit the curiosity on my face to that alone and nothing else. There was a section on group affiliations, another on contacts, another for her known associates. Scant and theoretical biographical information followed, mostly surmising that she had been trained by the Soviets, specifically the GRU, prior to the end of the Cold War. Several pages were devoted to cataloguing her list of crimes, either those that had been definitively attributed to her, or those she was suspected of committing. The section ended with an analysis of the quality of this intelligence, and what could be reasonably concluded from it.

The list of aliases attributed to her numbered seventeen, and of them, I recognized only two. One of them was "Natasha." Nowhere was the name "Alena."

Under contacts was listed Danilov "Dan" Korckeva.

The list of murders was presented by date, from earliest attributed to most recent. It stretched back a little over ten years, and racked up thirty-three bodies. Seven of them had been killed in the last three years, which pretty much threw that section of the file into question. I'd been with her night and day for the last three years, and if she'd murdered anybody during that time, I'd like to think I would have noticed. Of the murders she was accused of committing prior to our association, only two of the crimes matched what she herself had told me, and, in the main, I was more inclined to believe her than anything Matthew Bowles put in front of me.

The analysis, at the end, concluded that Drama was still considered to be active, and had taken on a partner. There was a hyperlink embedded in the document, to a new entry on "Patriot."

"Oh, c'mon," Bowles said. "You know you want to."

The link jumped the file to a new page, with a new heading and a new photo. The photo was of me, excellent quality, though a little small, and, as with Alena's, nearly four years out-of-date. My entry followed the same format as hers, though this time many of the lines had been filled in, most of the time correctly. My distinguishing characteristics included the thin scar along my left cheek, and the fact that I required the use of corrective lenses.

According to the file, I'd done a lot of traveling in the last three years. I'd visited São Paulo and Jakarta and Tokyo and Glasgow. I'd been in Vienna and Stockholm and Brussels and Cairo. I'd apparently stopped briefly in Quito. According to the file, I'd never stayed long in any of the locations.

Just long enough each time to commit a murder, before moving on.

"They call you Patriot because you're one of the only members of The Ten they've actually pulled a full bio on," Bowles told me. "Date of birth and education and, of course, your military service. The honorable discharge, that was the thing that did it. That's why they call you Patriot."

"I don't know that anyone is calling me anything," I said.

"Sure you do. You're on the list, Atticus. You're one of The Ten. Congratulations."

I stared at him, trying to find the angle. There was no reason to believe that the document was legitimate. It could have easily been manufactured by Bowles, or more likely, by someone working for Bowles. Just a tool to put me off balance, prepared solely to be used in this interrogation, to provide him with a psychological edge.

It was also just barely possible that the document was legitimate. That, through one machination or another, Atticus Kodiak had been presented to Interpol as an assassin-for-hire. I had no doubt that the crimes listed had actually occurred, and in that case, it would have been a small matter to manufacture the evidence that linked me to these murders. We were talking about The Ten, after all; we were talking about people like Alena and Oxford. When they did their work, they left little behind in the way of evidence. For them, supposition and rumor were often all that existed to tie their presence to the crime.

Bowles arched his left eyebrow in amusement. "You think I made this up?"

"No," I said.

"Good."

"I think you're too busy being someone else's errand boy," I said. "You probably had a lackey do it back at the White House."

"I'm in the private sector now, Atticus."

"You weren't when you recruited Illya."

"Having trouble recalling that name, actually."

"So who are you working for?" I asked. "Who is it who's pulling your strings, giving you your orders? Someone in the administration? Someone connected to it?"

He rocked back in his chair in mock surprise. "*You've* got questions?"

"Bushels of them. I want to know who, and I want to know where, and I might even go after the why, if I feel like it."

"Why?"

"Cold Spring." I looked past Bowles, to Sean, still seated on the couch. If he'd moved at all, I couldn't tell. "Why this guy and his gun-buddies Grant and Mark tried to kill me. Why the second team went after the safe house. Questions like that. After the thing with Oxford, it was supposed to be finished, Matt. You'd pulled the plug. You said that was that."

At the mention of the gunfight, Sean's right hand moved slightly, started up towards his shoulder. He arrested it, dropped it back into his lap. The eyefuck that had been at an eleven stayed steady and straight, and it struck me that it was his act, his part in these proceedings. Whether or not he actually hated my guts for shooting him, I couldn't tell, but I wouldn't have blamed him if he did.

"Does it ache?" I asked him. "Because of the cold?"

"There was a lot of blood on the ground," Sean remarked. "Some of it was yours."

"Some of it was. But none of it was because of you."

Bowles moved his right hand, waving it slightly back in Sean's direction, keeping him from retorting. He needn't have bothered. Sean didn't seem at all inclined to take the bait.

"You've got so many questions," Bowles told me. "I have only one: Where is she?"

I creased my brow. "Drama?"

"Yes. Where is she, Patriot?"

"Fuck if I know," I said. "Haven't seen her since that cluster-fuck of yours three years ago."

"You expect me to believe that?"

"Not really, no."

"Where is she?"

"I don't know," I said, and it sounded honest because it was honest.

"We need to talk to her," Bowles said. "You bring her in, we can do a deal for the two of you."

"A deal?"

Bowles nodded.

"I'm trying to guess what that would be," I said. "All I can come up with is two head shots for the price of one."

"What happened in Cold Spring was a mistake. Let's move past that. It was fallout from Oxford, that's all it was. An over-zealous mistake. Orders got confused, wires got crossed. It was a mistake."

"You're right," I agreed. "It was."

He missed my meaning entirely, continuing. "We're trying to correct that. We've been trying to correct that for the last few years, here. But you and Drama, the two of you up and vanished. How were we going to make it right when we couldn't even find you guys to do it?"

"So you make it right by beating me, cuffing me, and then dragging me into the middle of the woods to ask some questions?"

"If I'd just come knocking on your door back in Whitefish all alone, you'd have been happy to talk? With you blaming me for what happened in Cold Spring, like you just said?"

"I put in the passport application for a reason."

"You wanted us to find you, I get that. What you don't seem to get is that you're one of The Ten, Atticus. You're one of the motherfucking *Ten,* you're one of the most lethal, most dangerous, most skilled professional assassins working in the world today. You're Oxford, Atticus. You're Drama. You've become the person that—back when your head was on straight and you protected people for a living instead of whacking them—scared you so bad you would pee yourself."

"Flatterer," I said.

"So you can understand why I might be suspicious of your motives, how I might think going to meet you by myself would be a good way to end up quickly dead."

"I put the application in for a reason," I repeated.

"Because you have questions."

I moved my cuffed hands up and touched my nose with an index finger.

"Back where we started," Bowles said. "Where is Drama?"

"I told you, I don't know. Who wants us dead? Who was it who put Sean here and his Soldier of Fortune buddies on us?"

Bowles shook his head, growing aggravated. "Not going to work like that."

"If it's someone in the current administration, it's someone pretty high up but not high-profile. Someone with enough influence to shut down any media attention about what happened that morning in Cold Spring, at the least. How many dead? Two at the Citgo and another six or so at the safe house? That really should have made the news, don't you think? Someone had to dance pretty damn quick to hush it all up."

Bowles shook his head again. "Where is she, Atticus?"

"You want something for nothing," I said. "You've got me cuffed and beaten here, you think I'm going to just give up the only bargaining chip I have?"

"Yes," he said. "I think you will."

Sean and his buddy on the couch got to their feet.

"You're not going to beat it out of me," I told Bowles.

"You are an arrogant son of a bitch," he snapped, suddenly furious. "You're standing on *nothing*, you realize that? You're standing on fucking thin air, you're the goddamn coyote in those cartoons the second before he realizes he's off the cliff, you're just too damn stupid or stubborn to realize that gravity's got you by the balls. You cannot beat this thing, don't you get it? You're one of The Ten, now, you've got no friends, you've got nothing. I make one call, every cop in five hundred miles comes hunting for you. I make a second one, the FBI joins the chase."

The one who wasn't Sean moved to the hall, called out a "hey." Almost instantly, the two he'd been speaking with when he went to fetch the water emerged from the kitchen. Like the others, they were Caucasians, mid-to-late thirties, wearing more denim and flannel. The one who wasn't Sean motioned them to join us.

Bowles got out of his chair, closing the lid of his laptop.

"You're going to give her up. You can save yourself a lot of discomfort if you do it now."

"Who gave the order?" I asked. "Who sent you here?"

"Take him outside," Bowles told Sean.

"A name," I told him. "Just give me the name, I'll give you what you want."

Bowles shot a glance at me, ripe with disgust.

"Even if I gave it to you, Atticus, you wouldn't be able to do a damn thing with it," Matthew Bowles said.

CHAPTER THREE

When he said, "Take him outside," what Bowles actually meant was take him outside, strip him down, and then beat the living shit out of him, preferably by knocking him down in the snow over and over again. It meant don't speak to him, and it meant don't do anything that will keep him from talking when he eventually decides to, and it meant take your time, because the cold is frankly more effective than your feet or your fists will be, but all three in concert, that should do the trick quite nicely.

It meant that bringing a bucket of water from the bathroom and throwing it on him might also be a good idea, just to help things along.

When they moved to grab me, I went for Bowles's laptop and broke the nose of the guy who'd brought me water with it. Then I tried to kill one of the others by ramming the corner of the computer into his trachea. He moved, and I missed, and hit him high on the sternum instead, and since I was having to deal with the three others at the same time, I don't fault myself for failing. I got a kick into the side of someone's knee, and had the gratification of hearing him cry out before Sean tackled me, and then I lost the laptop.

There followed a dog-pile, and it took all four of them to lift me up and get me out into the night and the cold and the snow, and they dropped me twice because, unlike back in Whitefish, I felt no need to be nice about it. I got a glimpse of thick trees and a clear, star-filled sky when they finally hauled me outside, and there wasn't a hint of light pollution, and wherever we were, I knew I could make a lot of noise and no one who cared would hear it.

I hoped to God that Alena knew where I was, that she was out there, somewhere, armed and ready and waiting and with a plan that could pit her against seven and bring her out on top. It was the walking patrol she'd have to worry about first; once she targeted the house, she wouldn't want anyone at her back.

Sean and the others pinned me in the snow, knees on my neck and back, forcing me facedown. The snow was deep, maybe three to four feet in places, and it stole the heat out of me immediately. One of the heavies had demonstrated the foresight to bring some clothing shears, and they used those to cut my shirt and pants off me. It was better than using a knife, at least, and they didn't break any skin. They left me my underwear, that was all. Adrenaline and fear notwithstanding, I was shivering before they actually started in to work.

Then they used the bucket, and the bastards filled it with hot water before dumping it on me, which made the cold all the worse. The water in it probably hadn't been that hot, but it didn't need to be. It felt scalding all the same.

They worked me over one at a time. They stayed away from my face for the most part, not out of concern for my rakish good looks, but more out of desire to protect their hands, even though they all wore gloves. When I tried to stand they were quick to put me down again, on my back or my knees or my face. Mostly, they used their fists, though the one who wasn't Sean threw a couple of kicks at the start, one of which caught me hard on the hip, almost exactly where I'd been shot. Remembered pain lanced my middle and down my legs, and the one who did it liked the reaction he got so much, he got ready to do it again, but Sean put a stop to that. I couldn't tell if that was because Sean was playing the good cop in this routine, or because he was afraid a kick would do too much damage and might keep me from talking, or because he had less of a taste for the affair than the others.

Whatever the reason, it didn't keep him from delivering a savage jab to my kidneys when his turn came.

What they did to me hurt.

It hurt a lot, and in many different ways.

It made me angry, and it humiliated me, and it was, of course, just plain old painful as hell.

None of that was the worst thing.

The worst thing was the doubt that began to creep in as the beating seemed to go on and on, as the time stretched and contracted all at once. As their gloved fists beat me again and again, as my skin, raw with cold, stung and split and broke.

She wasn't coming.

Either she couldn't or she wouldn't, and it was the *wouldn't* that had the hooks, that dug into my mind and my thoughts, tangling itself until I couldn't silence it or ignore it. Nothing else had weight in its face, nothing else mattered; not everything we had between us, not all of the things we had shared and said. I was seeing the display on Bowles's laptop, the file less than five months old, telling me all the things I'd been a fool to let myself forget.

She was a professional, she was one of The Ten, she was Drama, and couldn't it have been an act all along? Why should she care about what happened to me? Why would she care about what had happened to a woman who was my friend, not hers?

Why would she risk her life and her liberty for these things?

She had warned me. She had tried to convince me not to do this, not to draw them out, not to give myself to them. She wasn't coming, that was what she'd been trying to tell me. I was on my own.

She wasn't coming.

They made me doubt her.

For that, I hated them more than anything else.

After a while, I don't know how long, they quit, and Bowles emerged from the house with a cup of something that steamed invitingly in his hands. He'd put his overcoat and his gloves back on, as if to demonstrate all the more to me that he was warm and I was not. He crunched through the disturbed snow to where I was shivering and bleeding, dropped down to his haunches, and waited for me to meet his eyes. It took some will to do it, because mostly I was considering passing out, but also because I was having a hard time focusing. The ambient light had turned the snow a blue that seemed to rise up around where I rested. Where my blood had spilled it had turned black.

"Where is she, Atticus?"

My teeth were chattering so much it was hard to say the words.

"Who gave the order?" I asked.

He shook his head sadly, then poured out half of his hot coffee on my still-bound hands. The heat exploded through the numbness, sent sparks and shards into the bone, and I screamed, tried to lunge for him. He'd expected it, backing up, and I went down face-first, my hands still burning with the cold, with the heat.

I lifted my head from the snow, seeing him standing a foot away, seeing the four others gathered outside the front door of the cabin, the warm light spilling from within.

Bowles moved his mug so that he held it over my head, tilted it slightly, as if readying to dump the remaining contents onto my neck and back.

"In a few more minutes, we're going to take you back inside," he told me. "We're going to let you warm up. We're going to clean you up. We might even let you nod off, go unconscious.

"Then we're going to take you back out here, and we'll do all of this again. Except this time, I won't bring a mug of coffee. I'll bring a fucking kettle hot off the stove, do you understand me, you stupid piece of shit?"

My chattering teeth wouldn't let me respond, so I nodded.

"You tell me right now, you tell me where Drama is, where I can find her, and this is over, it's finished, we'll be done. That's all you have to do, Atticus, that's all you have to tell me. Where is she?"

"Why?" I asked. It took effort just to get that much out.

He looked honestly disgusted by the question.

I shook my head, realizing he'd misunderstood me. They needed us both, yes, I'd gotten that much, I understood that much. It was why they'd hit the safe house at the same time they'd ambushed me. They were trying to kill us, that wasn't news, not to him, not to me.

It was harder to say it the second time. "Why us?"

Bowles wavered in my vision, then shook his head, declining to answer. This time, I was sure he'd understood what I was asking, but even now, he wasn't willing to give me the motive. Whatever crime Alena or I or we together had committed, whatever the threat was that either of us alone or together might pose, he wasn't about to explain it.

He moved the mug, let another dribble of his coffee spatter out onto my back. I heard a scream, and I thought that it might be mine.

Then I heard it a second time, and I knew it wasn't.

It rolled out of the trees and the darkness from somewhere behind me, awful with fear and pain. Bowles, Sean, all of them froze in place.

"Son of a bitch," Bowles murmured.

I blinked several times, trying to convince at least one of my eyes to focus on him. I wondered if, this time, I had lost a contact.

"Okay," I said. "You win. I'll tell you where she is."

Bowles threw down his mug, reaching into his overcoat with his other hand, spinning in place all at once even as he brought out his pistol. He did not look at me.

"It's Drama, it's fucking her, that fucking cunt is here, she's come to get him," he said quickly to the others. "She's fucking out there and she's taken the overwatch and you are going to find her and you are going to kill her."

They started moving all at once, Sean directing them. Two ran back to the house, the third staying close by. Bowles pivoted back towards me, kicking up snow as he did so. He grabbed hold of me by the Flexi-Cuffs around my wrists, shoved the gun against my temple.

"Get up," he told me. "Get on your knees!"

I struggled with it, and not only to buy time, but because most everything hurt, and those parts that didn't were silent only because they'd gone numb with the cold. I'd be dealing with frostbite in another few minutes, if I wasn't having to deal with it already. While Bowles muscled me to my knees, the two who had gone for the house reemerged, carrying three long guns and three sets of NVG between them. Everyone but Sean and Bowles got a long gun and the goggles.

Bowles rammed the pistol into the side of my neck.

"You don't want to do that," I told him.

"Shut up," Bowles snapped. "Shut the fuck up, call her, call—"

A third scream, more broken than the two that had come before, the voice issuing it already threading with strain. It sounded awful and piteous. It sounded like someone not only in agony, but in terror, and all of them heard it, and none of them liked it.

"Jesus Christ," one of them whispered. "That's Ryan. What the fuck is she doing to Ryan?"

Sean ran his free hand in a cutting motion across his throat, angry, indicating to all that he wanted them to shut the fuck up. They gave him his silence, and in it he flashed out a sequence of hand signals, deploying the three men. They began making towards the line of trees surrounding the cabin, and I'd been right about their pedigree. They moved well, spreading out to keep from bunching up while still keeping each other in sight enough to provide backup. Hand signals flashed between them, and maybe they had a line on the screams, where their friend Ryan was, because they seemed to know where they should go.

"Drop the gun," I told Bowles. "Listen to me."

He glanced down at me, then dug the barrel harder into the side of my neck. I was so cold it didn't feel like much other than pressure against my skin. "Call to her. Tell her to come out."

If I'd been able to, I would have laughed. As it was, I coughed and snorted all at once, ejecting more blood and mucus.

To my right, just at the edge of the cabin, one of Sean's men staggered at the same moment that the wooden wall behind him splintered, sprayed with a coat of gore and blood. The sound of the shot came at almost the exact same moment, the concussion of a Magnum round rattling the trees. The man fell to his knees, then dropped face-first into the snow.

"Seven o'clock!" one of the others shouted. "Muzzle flash, seven—"

The top of his head shredded before he could finish the sentence. The report chased after the echoes of the first.

Both Sean and the last of his men dove to the ground. Sean was smarter about it, staying clear of the cabin, using the deep snow. It was a good move; unless Alena had taken a position with elevation, and I knew that she hadn't, the snow would keep him out of her line of sight.

The last one wasn't as lucky, and when he went for cover, he tried to use the cabin, to get around the corner. He almost made it; if he'd been a little faster, or Alena had been a little slower, he would have.

But he didn't.

Bowles balked, then dug his pistol deeper against my neck. The thought of taking it from him, freeing myself, flicked through my mind, but I ignored it. The condition I was in, the posture I was holding, I'd never be able to manage it.

"I'll kill you, she doesn't come out." Bowles still wasn't looking at me. "I'll kill you."

"Then she's gone," I said. "If you get the shot off, she's gone. And you want us both, remember?"

He swore softly.

"Drop the gun," I said again. "Please, Matthew."

"Shut up! Sean! Sean, do you see her?"

"I need answers," I told him. "You can give them to me. Drop the gun, don't do this."

The pistol left the side of my neck, and for an instant I thought he'd seen reason, that he'd let it go. He backed away from me a step.

"I know you're there!" he shouted into the trees. "I know you're there, I'll kill him if you don't come out! Give yourself up!"

"Don't!" I shouted, as much to Alena as to Bowles, and I tried to get to my feet, tried to rise up and block the shot that I knew would come, because I knew what Bowles would do next.

He raised the pistol on me, leveling it with both hands at my head.

"You've got five!" Bowles shouted.

"Just put it down!"

"Four!"

"Dammit, Bowles–"

"Three!"

Then the hole opened in his chest, high on the sternum, and Matthew Bowles dropped like a marionette whose lines had been cut. Foamy blood blew out from his mouth, dripped over his lips, into the snow.

He rattled out the last of his air, and died.

"You stupid son of a bitch," I told him. "All we wanted was an answer."

CHAPTER FOUR

While you were always, in your way, alone, you were never on your own.

Always there were others, the people giving the orders or the people teaching the lessons or the people in support of the operation. At every stage, there was a network.

You may have been plucked from an orphanage in Magadan at the age of eight, or seconded from the SAS, or recruited from Detachment Delta. When it began is irrelevant. You were chosen, or you volunteered, or you fell into it by circumstance, but at some point a decision was made, and you went from soldier or guardian or child to assassin, and that was when the divorce took place. Partially, this was a psychological transformation, a necessary stage in your education as dictated by those who instructed you, a need to remove you from the herd. The wolf doesn't run with the sheep, after all, and even were it in the wolf's mind to do so, the sheep would have none of it.

It is a survival mechanism. What you do now, at the behest of your government or group or cause, is dangerous in the extreme. It must be performed in secrecy and anonymity, and the best way to be anonymous, to keep a secret, is to keep the number of people involved to one. You work alone.

Or you pretend that you do, because, in truth, you have support. Be it from your government or group or cause, there are people who stand behind you, people to secure the things that you need to do your job. They do this not because they like you or because they care about you. They do it because you are a tool, and you must be directed, and you must be properly employed. If you are their hammer, they don't simply point you at the board and say start pounding; they must provide you with the nails. That they pay you a wage—if they pay you at all—is incidental, just another means of directing the tool.

It cannot be stressed how vital this network is. They give you purpose, for without them, you would not be used. They designate your target. They provide the intelligence, the means, the wherewithal to reach it. Plane tickets and weapons, identification and money, maps and photographs, everything you require to perform your task. And should you complete the job they have given you successfully, they are there at the end, to tend your wounds, to continue honing your skills, to, in fact, maintain the tool so that it may be used again and again and again either until it is so worn as to be useless, or until it is lost to damage or circumstance.

You are alone, perhaps, but never on your own.

Until you decide, for whatever the reason, that what you do for government or group or cause is best done for yourself and yourself alone. Until the day that you find that the world has changed, that your usefulness is coming to an end, and that you are soon to become a liability. Until the day you discover that the wage you are paid for the task you perform is not commensurate with the risk you undertake. Until the day that you realize the only pleasure in your life lies in taking the life of another.

It is unlikely that your decision is based on any moral argument, on a question of right or wrong, or good or evil. You are what you are, what they made you to be, and one of the first things they did upon removing you from the rest of the herd was make it clear that such concerns no longer matter to you. Tools are not concerned with how they are used; it isn't the gun that kills, it is the person who pointed it at the victim's head and then pulled the trigger who does. The gun is the mechanism. The shooter is the killer.

They have worked very, very hard indeed to convince you that you are the mechanism, nothing more.

And even if such arguments have failed to completely wash away your questions or to utterly still your conscience, you have discovered that it is better not to press the subject. Not with your masters, nor with yourself.

So, be it for survival or fear or greed or kink, you take what they have given you, you take what they have made you, and you leave. And because you are a tool that has cost tens of millions of dollars to create, and because to make you what you are you have learned things that are dangerous to others, that threaten their security and their position and their futures, they are, shall we say, loath to let you go. It would be different if you maintained your loyalty, but for whatever the reason, that time is passed, all loyalty is dead.

So you cannot simply leave.

You must run.

■ ■ ■

For the first time, now, you are truly alone. There is no one to help you, no one to turn to. There is no network; there is no support.

You stand in the world with a handful of secrets and a set of skills that are, putting it mildly, highly specialized. Marketable skills, when marketed to the right people, of course, but therein is another problem; how do you find those "right" people without revealing yourself to the government or group or cause you have—in their eyes, at least—now betrayed?

If you are smart, if you are at all wise, you have money. Perhaps you even have a lot of it, acquired during those jobs performed for your masters. If you were very smart, if you prepared for this day, some of that money might even still be safe. But regardless of how much or how little you have, it will not last, because the things you need to continue to survive are expensive. Much that you require is illegal, and that brings with it a tremendous surcharge. You are a person without an identity, because every identity you have ever been known by is known also to the people you have just betrayed. And so you must create a new shell, a new name. This is crucial, because without that foundation, you can acquire nothing you need to survive. How can you rent an apartment if you cannot prove you are who you pretend to be?

Your money will not last for long, if at all.

It is possible, now, that you may decide to turn your back on what you know, what you can do. If your departure was a decision of self-preservation, rather than, say, greed, you might now consider trying to adopt what is called a "normal life." After all, you know many things, you have many skills.

But they are skills that cannot be sold legitimately. You have no references, no recommendations. Your military service, if you have one, cannot be revealed. You have no identity, and thus, no history. Thirty years old, and on the job application in front of you, under "prior experience," you find yourself forced to write the word "none."

Certainly, there is work to be found that is not contingent on a well-rounded résumé. You can find yourself waiting tables, perhaps, or working in a garage, or cleaning an office in the middle of the night, but, honestly, how long will that last before your money runs out entirely?

This is further complicated by the fact that you are now hunted. Those you betrayed by departing are certainly keeping one eye open for you, at least for the moment. You have evaded them thus far, and a stalemate of a sort has descended; but they can be very patient, for their resources are nearly limitless; they are waiting to see where you appear next, to see what you have become.

In the end, you make your decision. You will put your marketable skills to use. You will do the thing that you have been made to do. You will sell the only thing you have to sell. You will make yourself available, because you know that somewhere there is a man or a woman who, for whatever the reason, wishes another man or woman dead, and all they lack is the means to make it happen.

You are that means. You are that mechanism.

That is the service you can provide.

And now you come to the problem: You cannot, absolutely cannot, do by yourself what is required.

It is simply impossible; there are not enough hours in the day. What you sell is illegal, which means that anyone looking to buy your services must be investigated thoroughly before you even begin to consider taking the job they offer. What you sell is illegal, which means that you must insulate yourself in such a way that the law cannot find you. What you sell is illegal, which means the tools you most often use must be acquired illegally. What you sell is illegal, which means you must never be the same person for long, so identity after identity must be prepared.

Every one of these things takes time, and you have yet to even approach your first target.

You cannot do it alone. You need help. You need the services of someone who can provide the support you once enjoyed, or at least something approximating it. Someone to handle the details, while you handle the work.

Like it or not, eventually, you are going to have to trust somebody.

You need a lawyer.

Switzerland is too obvious. Certainly, the Swiss reputation for discretion and financial wizardry is well earned, but as a result it has begun to draw unwanted attention. What you need is a location that sees a lot of money passing through, as well as a lot of people. A place that, ideally, has more resident aliens than actual residents. Someplace where your erratic comings and goings will be entirely beneath notice.

Monaco is ideal.

The place decided, the right person must now be selected. This must be done delicately, with great care. The wrong approach to the wrong person could end your new career before it even begins. Research is required. Your ideal representation would be male, in his late fifties, and single. Someone working in their own firm, or in a firm of adequate pedigree and prestige, meaning a firm that represents clients the world never knows. You do *not* want the firm that represents, for instance, Paris Hilton; you want the firm that represents the rest of the Hilton family.

You comb through newspapers and online archives. You search for names that you have come across in your work, the powerful men and women who surface only once in a great while, buried deep inside the *Financial Times* or *Le Monde.* People associated with the Carlyle or Blackstone groups, perhaps.

You make a list of candidates, learning everything you can about them as quickly and discreetly as possible. This person at that firm is married with three small children. That person at this firm was arrested for possession of narcotics. This one appears time and time again in photographs at social events, parties and the like. That one has taken three privately operated trips to Thailand in the last two years.

All of these you dismiss as too risky.

If you are lucky, you may find yourself with as many as three or even four names.

Now you must make your approach.

The meeting takes place in the attorney's office, by appointment. The appointment has been made with some urgency, a day or two earlier. If your research was productive, you may even have dropped the name of another client to the firm as the source of the referral. You have dressed for the part. If you're female, perhaps you've chosen something a little more flattering than normal, not because you wish to seduce the candidate, but to establish a type of personality. If you're male, perhaps you arrive a minute or two late for the meeting, apologetic, blaming the delay on a business call.

You are met at the office, offered a seat, asked if you would like some refreshment. You accept, taking water. The most cursory small talk takes place, and then the door closes and you and the candidate are left alone.

The candidate addresses you by name, asking how he can be of service to you.

You tell him you wish to secure title to an object of some expense. What you choose depends on the state of your resources, of course, because you will have to outlay this cash (though you will also recoup the expense later, if all goes well). Whatever you choose, it must be something appropriately expensive, to indicate that the monies involved will be worth the candidate's time, yet it cannot be so outlandish that it will bankrupt you. If your finances were not everything they should have been before reaching Monaco, it is possible that you may have detoured in the South of France, and taken the opportunity to secure more funds by robbing a bank, or better, by taking down a narcotics sale. It may even have been necessary to do this multiple times, though, of course, each crime you commit brings greater risk.

An expensive car would work, a top-of-the-line Ferrari, perhaps, or an Aston Martin. A small yacht might be acceptable. Real estate, however, is best.

In this instance, you tell the candidate that you're interested in purchasing a small villa here in Monaco. Nothing fancy, you say, perhaps five, six million dollars. You travel quite a lot, as it happens, but you do love it here, and are interested in setting down, say, some shallow roots.

This I can help you with, the candidate says.

Wonderful, you say. I have the place picked out already.

The candidate smiles.

As for the issue of title, you say, my ex is a gold-digging piece of excrement—pardon my language—and I'd rather the purchase remain off the books, so to speak. Would it be possible to have the title placed in some sort of shell company, some way to keep my name out of it? That I could own the property without there being a paper trail that says as much? Is that possible?

And you smile, just enough so the candidate doesn't know if you're being naïve, or something more.

One of two things happens.

In the first instance, the candidate frowns slightly, embarrassed, and perhaps sits back in his seat. After a moment, with regret, he explains to you that the laws in Monaco—the banking laws—are under the French system, and doing such a thing would be illegal. He's extremely sorry, but he cannot help you.

At which point you look mildly surprised, apologize for taking his time, and depart.

Scratch one candidate.

In the second instance, the candidate appraises you for a moment or two, then nods and says that such a thing can be done, but not without some legal maneuvering. He may mention additional cost, though, in all likelihood, will not, as that would be gauche in the extreme.

You respond by saying that you suspected as much, and would appreciate any assistance he can offer.

The transaction then takes place. You remain in Monaco long enough to see it to conclusion, and at its end, you thank the candidate, and ask if he might be available to you in the future.

There is a chance here that he will say no, that this is the extent of the illegalities he is willing to undertake. But, if all has gone well, if you and he have managed a rapport of some sort, he will say yes, certainly.

You thank him, and part company.

■ ■ ■

Perhaps two or three weeks later, you call to make another appointment. The sooner the better; you only need a few minutes of his time. If your last transaction was as successful as it seemed, he will accommodate you.

You come to the office with a briefcase. Not one of the metal-sided aluminum Halliburton cases, because those positively scream "ill-gotten gains" at the top of their lungs. Something elegant, leather, preferably.

The candidate greets you warmly, ushering you into his office. He offers, once again, refreshment, but this time you decline. You have a train to catch, you apologize.

Then you set the briefcase on his desk, opening it as you speak. You say that you have some business to attend to in South Africa, and you would be very grateful if he could hold this for you, just in his office safe, perhaps, until you get back at the end of the week. You show him the contents, stacks and stacks of currency, preferably in dollars. Half a million dollars, you tell him, and you of course will pay him for the service.

Again, this may prove to be too much, and he may refuse. In such a case, it is best to apologize and depart with no further fuss.

If he agrees, you do much the same thing, with gratitude in the place of apology, before leaving to catch your train.

You are not going to South Africa.

You are staying in Monaco, and putting the candidate under the microscope, or at least the best microscope you can manage while working alone. First, you must ascertain that he has not told anyone of his dealings with you, especially the authorities. This can be determined in relatively short order. Next, you begin tracking his movements, his activities, devoting multiple days to this task. You mark his social habits, his associates, any friends, any lovers. You follow him in his off hours, to and from work. You watch him about town, and at home.

You're looking for things you might have missed, anything that might become a liability. Soon, now, you and the candidate will be entering a very long-term, very permanent partnership. Once the next step is taken, there will be little opportunity to correct any errors of judgment. Now is the best time to put the brakes on, before things progress.

So you follow the candidate, and you learn everything you can. One morning, after tailing him to his office, you double back and return to his home. You break in and perform a comprehensive search, taking most of the day to do it, going about it carefully, so as to leave no signs of your presence. You examine his clothing, noting the labels, discovering the name of the tailor he uses. You read the old love letters kept in the back of the bottom desk drawer. You find his collection of art-porn DVDs. You discover that he has a taste for very expensive whiskey. You take note of it all.

Once all of this is done, you withdraw to consider what you have learned. You must make your decision. Can you trust this person, this man? Is his greed enough to be of service to you, and yet not so great as to be a liability? Is his willingness to break the law pathological, or considered?

No matter what you do, however, you cannot eliminate the risk you are about to take. The best you can make is an educated guess. Do you bring the candidate in, or abandon the pursuit?

Eventually, you are going to have to trust somebody.

Eleven days after leaving the briefcase with the candidate, you call again. This time, you speak to him personally. You tell him that you'll be in town that evening, and that you'd like to come by and collect your case, settle up, and speak about other business. It is a given, at this point, that the candidate is happy to accommodate you.

You arrive that evening, just as the offices are closing, and the candidate greets you, asks how your trip went. You tell him that it went well. He invites you into his office, and returns your case to you. You do not bother to open it and check the contents—you are trusting him, as he has trusted you—but instead produce an envelope from your bag or your coat, and hand it to him in turn.

For your help, you say.

He resists the urge to examine the envelope, to count the money. He can tell by the feel of it that it is substantial, and in cash. He tucks the envelope away, then offers you a drink, as he has on each visit. This time you accept, a glass of Scotch or brandy, perhaps, if he is willing to join you in it.

He is, and now, each of you seated in the office, you relax. Perhaps you light a cigarette, perhaps you loosen your tie, but by your manner and your look, you make it apparent that you are off the clock, and you are inviting him to act in the same manner. You exchange more small talk; maybe you steer the conversation to one of the hobbies or interests you learned of while examining his life. You keep it subtle; the ideal is that he does not realize until days later that the reason you spoke of the air show you saw in Paris is because you know of his fascination with vintage biplanes.

Finally, you set aside your drink and say to the candidate that you appreciate everything he's done for you. He's been very helpful, you say, to such an extent that you'd be interested in expanding upon your business relationship.

He indicates his interest, his curiosity. He asks you to please continue.

I'm a consultant, you tell him, in the risk business. I've clients all around the world, and most of them are very, very sensitive about their privacy, about having their identities known. For that reason, even I need to be able to distance myself from the people who hire me.

The candidate looks at you, listening closely. His expression tells you that he is trying to determine just what, exactly, the "risk business" is.

Go on, he says.

Look, you say, I realize this sounds very cloak-and-dagger, but in my profession, absolute privacy of the client is the paramount concern. I'm certain you understand the need for that kind of discretion.

Absolutely.

You nod, as if to confirm that his words and your thought are entirely as one. You lean forward, making eye contact, and then continue. I need someone who has proven himself to be both responsible and resourceful to act as my intermediary, you say. Someone who can retrieve business propositions for me from a variety of sources, and then forward them to me in a timely and secure manner. This is something that, at least in terms of contacting me, may only occur a handful of times a year, not including the one or two meetings we would have face-to-face.

You sit back, giving him a moment to consider what you have said.

If you are interested in helping me out like this, you then say, I can tell you the following. My annual income is projected to be in the tens of millions of dollars. Now, I understand that what I'm asking you to undertake for me will require a significant amount of your time and resources. Acting as my agent, so to speak, you'd of course be entitled to a generous portion of my earnings.

Do you think this would be something that might interest you?

There is a silence while the candidate considers. He is trying to determine what he knows, trying to balance that against the prospect of a generous portion of millions of dollars a year. Certainly, he has concluded that what you are doing for a living is illegal, though precisely how illegal, he is unsure. He is considering the risk to himself, not because he has reason to fear you—although, if he is the man you want, he will have realized by this juncture that you are certainly dangerous—but because money is of no worth to him if he cannot spend it.

Yes, he says, before the pause stretches too long. Yes, I am interested.

You smile, making your pleasure with his decision apparent. Wonderful, you tell him, I'm very pleased. I think we're going to work very well together, and I think you're going to find our association to be a lucrative one.

It certainly sounds that way, he agrees.

I do have a project I am working on now, you tell him, as a matter of fact. What I need is a driver's license for the U.K. with my picture on it, but in another name.

The pause this time is very brief. Perhaps he hesitates because he has realized the first thing you are asking of him, now that you have made your relationship formal, is to break the law. Or perhaps he is merely wondering how best to accomplish the goal.

I can arrange that, he tells you with a smile of his own. Yes, I can arrange that.

The name of Alena's lawyer was Nicolas Sargenti.

CHAPTER FIVE

"I don't know what you want me to tell you, Elizavet," Nicolas Sargenti said. "Even if you had done work for Gorman-North, there would be no way to prove it. The entire nature of the transaction, from its beginning to its end, is perfect in its anonymity. That is how *you* have always desired it, for both of our sakes, I must add."

Alena growled from the back of her throat, and spun away from where the attorney sat in the reading chair by the window of our hotel room. "It would have been American, an American job."

"A job on American soil?" Sargenti asked. When he spoke, his accent was more Italian than French. "Or a job bought by an American?"

"The latter, it would be the latter."

"The same problem. Impossible to say." Nicolas Sargenti

released a pained sigh, looking to where I was lying on the bed, back against the headboard. "Michael, what is this about, please?"

"We're having some trouble," I told him, and indicated the bruises that covered my torso. They were glorious in their color, and while Alena had massaged most of the swelling down, their array of green, yellow, red, and blue remained spectacular, and covered me in strips and splashes from my shoulders on down, disappearing beneath the waistband of my pants.

The damage could have been much worse, and as it was, it was relatively minor. I was stiff and I was sore, but the frostbite hadn't taken, and my fingers and toes had feeling and motion. Given another day or three of rest, I'd be back to fighting speed, so to speak.

Nicolas Sargenti managed a courtesy chuckle. "Dare I ask what has placed you in such an ignoble position?"

"I fell," I told him. "In the snow."

Alena filled a glass with orange juice from the glass pitcher on the room service cart, left over from our yogurt-and-muesli breakfast. The cart also held a pot of tea and some rapidly fading fresh fruit.

"All right," she said to Sargenti, handing me the glass and a handful of ibuprofen. "You are still checking inquiries?"

"Not as frequently as I once did." Sargenti adjusted his glasses and refocused his attention on her, his voice as mild and soft as ever. "But I do check them, yes. I add that you did tell me that you were retired, Elizavet, so if this has been a shortcoming on my part, I think you will understand. For the last several years I have not thought it necessary to stay atop them as I once did." An almost hopeful gleam came to his eye. "Though I still field requests for your services. Would you be reconsidering your decision?"

"No, I am not. I am retired. I intend to stay that way."

Sargenti nodded slightly, letting his eyes go about the room again, taking it in. He didn't speak, but he didn't need to. If she wanted to maintain that she was retired, that was fine with him. She still required his services, as I now did, and he still took a hefty annual stipend to provide what we needed.

This was the third time I'd met Nicolas Sargenti in person. The first time had come some two and half years earlier, in Warsaw, at the Radisson Hotel off Grzybowska Street and Jana Pawla II Avenue, near the business center of the city. It had served as both Alena's annual meeting with her attorney, as well as my introduction to him. At that point, Alena had explained that I was now her partner, and she was hopeful Sargenti would be willing to provide for me the same services he provided for her, for an increased percentage, of course. He had been willing; his only question had been whether or not she was still retired, and if so, did that mean that I would be taking on the clients she now declined. He had seemed entirely ambivalent when I'd explained that, no, I was not, at the present, looking for work.

The second meeting had been almost thirteen months prior to today's, in Moscow, at the Rossiya Hotel, near the Kremlin. The Rossiya had closed its doors the following month, though I doubted our business there had played any part in that. Sargenti had supplied Alena and me with a new battery of identities, and then gone over the books with her. He had noted that her expenses were outstripping her earnings, but had then assured her that her investments were still performing quite well, and that there was more than enough money left in the account. Her investments, I learned, were primarily in real estate owned around the world. At the Moscow meeting, she had directed him to sell two of her properties, one of them in Hong Kong, the other in California. Together, the two sales had netted over thirty million dollars.

Considering that Nicolas Sargenti now took forty percent for his services—an increase from the thirty he'd earned when representing her alone—the fact that she was retired didn't seem to bother him in the slightest. And no wonder, then, that when she'd e-mailed him from Bozeman the day before yesterday with the sentence "Tuesday morning grove," he had dropped everything to meet us at the Grove Hotel in Boise this morning.

He hadn't traveled to us out of greed alone. He'd come because he had to. It was the nature of the relationship. He would come, because if he didn't, he believed either Alena or I would kill him. The only way out of his dealings with her and me was in death.

He certainly knew it as much as Alena or I did. That it didn't bother him in the least said volumes. It wasn't something he ever considered, I don't think; the idea of betraying her was absolutely alien to him, and probably had been so even before he had discerned exactly what she was doing to command such enormous fees. Sargenti was in his late sixties, now, retired from private practice. He had everything he could want, and more money than he could ever spend.

I found him fascinating, and had from the first time we'd met in Warsaw. From what Alena had told me, I'd expected someone in his forties, perhaps approaching fifty, but Sargenti was nearly twenty years older than that. His hair, worn flat on his scalp as if glued there, had gone entirely to gray where hair remained, and not much of it did, and his head itself was shaped almost exactly like an eggshell. He was an ugly man, genuinely so, as if genetics had conspired to intentionally mismatch his features to optimal effect. His eyes were hazel, muddy, widely spaced, and heavily lidded, and each seemed to protrude from its orbit enough that I thought they must surely brush against the inside of his spectacles. His nose managed to be both narrow, high, and flat at the same time, leading with the nostrils, and his mouth was small, as if to compensate for the real estate taken by everything above it. Pockmarks finished the ensemble, old scars from a childhood illness.

But where nature had failed him, money had come to the rescue. His winter suit was perfectly tailored, and he wore it well, from the silk tie to the braces to the fine leather shoes. The attaché he always seemed to carry with him gleamed with the warmth that only superb leather has, and the Zenith watch on his wrist was never the same one twice, and always unpretentious in its elegance. There was nothing ostentatious in how he presented his wealth. He had it, he was comfortable with it, and that was all he wanted from it.

I understood greed, or thought I did, but Nicolas Sargenti gave me a whole new perspective on it. For him, this wasn't about acquiring wealth; it was about his right to have it in the first place, and to keep it. Perhaps it was entitlement, or a sense thereof, born from some psychological need or trauma. But whatever the reason, he was greedy because he wanted to be, and in that I also understood why, in him, Alena had made a perfect choice. She indulged his desire, satisfied it. She did so in a way that allowed Sargenti to feel everything he had was well earned.

Alena moved to the window, parting the privacy veil with her hand enough to look out, thinking. Sargenti waited, taking a sip from his cup of tea, then replacing the cup carefully on its saucer.

"The requests for my services," she said. "You do not respond to them, I assume?"

"I have seen no point in it," Sargenti admitted.

"But they've come, these requests, they've come through the established channels?"

"I am unaware of any other way to retain your services than those protocols we established to do so. Your anonymity—and Michael's, for that matter—is entirely intact. I have done nothing to compromise that, Elizavet, I assure you," he added. "For your sake as much as my own."

Alena let the curtain fall back. She smiled down at Sargenti, in his chair. "No, Nicolas. That is not my concern."

"I am relieved. I have always, as you know, treated my work for you with the utmost care."

I spoke up from where I was on the bed. "Do you know if it's been the same person or people trying to contact her?"

Sargenti cocked his head, perhaps trying to parse the question. "I'm not certain I understand your meaning, Michael."

"It's an insulated process, right? It starts the same way, say, uses the same initial point, but it's the cutouts that change, the steps necessary for the initial inquiry to reach you?"

"Ah, yes. Yes, though there are several possible points of initiation."

"And when you've received these, when you've checked, you've simply ignored them, right?"

"Disregarded, I would rather say."

"Disregarded, then. No response."

"Correct."

"But you're still receiving requests. So someone isn't getting the message, or is ignoring it."

Sargenti frowned. "Perhaps so. I had presumed that the requests were being made by different individuals, not by the same individual again and again. But it is possible."

"How many points of contact are there?" I asked. "How many starts to the chain?"

"Five," both Alena and Sargenti said, together.

I looked at her. "Is it likely they know more than one point of contact?"

She shook her head.

"So we're looking for multiple attempts stemming from the same point of contact."

"Possibly."

In his chair, Nicolas Sargenti closed his eyes, combing his memory. "A moment," he murmured.

Alena moved back to where I was on the bed, taking a seat beside me. Her right hand moved to find mine, simply to rest her fingers against my own. She looked tired, and she looked worried, and she looked guilty, and none were states I was used to seeing on her.

Our experience at the cabin in the Montana woods had, in its way, been far worse on her. While Bowles and the others had worked over my body, what Alena had done to secure my freedom had worked over her soul, fragile as it was. It had forced her to step backwards to what she once had been, and it made her doubt she could ever change.

Sitting on the side of the bed, not looking at me, afraid to even hold my hand, I knew what she was thinking. It didn't matter what changes the last three years had wrought upon her; she now believed it was only an illusion.

She was still an instrument of killing, still an empty thing, and she always would be.

Bowles died, and I went for the pistol he dropped, my fingers too numb to manage the task easily. It took me too long to do it, I was too slow, and all I was thinking was that if Sean wanted to finish what Bowles had put into motion, I wasn't going to be able to stop him. I didn't know where he was, and that meant that Alena most likely didn't, either.

With the pistol in my swollen, useless hands, I fought myself to my feet, slipping in the snow. My teeth had stopped chattering, and I was beginning to feel warm again, and I still had enough wherewithal to recognize that was a very bad thing; it meant I was turning hypothermic, and that I wouldn't last for much longer in the cold.

Then I saw Sean, standing at the door to the cabin, and I brought the gun up much too slowly, but he didn't move, and I realized why. He'd disarmed, dropping his weapon, standing with his hands raised to either side. Between two of his fingers something sparkled.

"Just a job," Sean said. Slowly, he moved his hand, showing me what he was holding. "I've got the key for the cuffs. It's yours."

I lurched forward a couple of steps. "You speak Russian?"

The confusion lasted only an instant. "No."

In Russian, as loud as I could, I shouted for Alena not to shoot him, that we were going into the cabin, that I had to get warm. Sean flinched slightly at the abruptness of my voice, but that was it for movement until I reached him.

"Inside," I told him.

We went into the wreckage of the front room. The table had busted during the fight, as had one of the two chairs. I all but fell onto the couch, not feeling the room's warmth at all. Sean turned to close the door.

"Bad idea," I said.

"The heat's going out."

"She'll kill you."

He stopped, watched me as I held out my hands, still holding the pistol. I doubted I could actually get my finger to contract on the trigger if I needed to, and I suspect he doubted it, too. He put the key in the small lock on the Flexi-Cuffs and twisted.

"Take them off me."

When he dug his fingers between my skin and the plastic, I

didn't feel it. He pulled the cuffs free, careful to draw them over the pistol without touching it, then threw them aside onto the floor. As soon as he'd finished, he unzipped his parka, then draped it around my shoulders.

"Thanks," I said.

"There are blankets in the bedroom. If I go and get them will she kill me?"

I shook my head.

He went to get the blankets, returning with three dark wool ones that smelled of mothballs and must. He was wrapping the second one around my legs, tucking its end beneath my feet, when Alena entered. He didn't hear her come inside, and the only reason I knew she was there was because I'd been watching the door.

She'd dressed for the work and the weather, winter camouflage in the form of overwhites. Her hair was hidden beneath a black watch cap, and that was barely visible beneath the drawn hood of her white parka. Grime and mud peppered her clothes, and the blood that soaked her right arm and spattered her right side was bright in contrast. The rifle across her back was a monster, a Winchester, the kind the locals used for hunting big buck, and in her hands she held one of the guns we'd taken from the Burien cache, a modified Ruger with an integrated suppressor.

She had the pistol pointed at the back of Sean's head before she'd finished crossing the threshold, and the look on her face made it clear that shooting him was not only what she intended to do, it was what she needed to do. If she was seeing me at all, I couldn't tell.

"No," I told her. "Friendly."

Alena didn't move and neither did Sean, and it was a struggle for each of them, because each of them wanted to. Yet neither did, Alena keeping the gun and her vision fixed on the back of Sean's head, and Sean, perfectly still with the last blanket in his hand.

"He's helping," I said to her. "You can close the door."

Sean brought his eyes up to mine, and that was the extent of his motion. His eyes were so brown they might as well have been black. He didn't seem afraid, but he wasn't happy.

"The door," I said again.

Without shifting her aim or looking away from Sean, Alena stepped back, extended her right foot, and used her boot to close the door.

"Who is he?" she asked in Georgian.

It took me a moment to parse the switch in languages. I was beginning to feel drowsy, another symptom of the hypothermia. "Sean. I shot him back in Cold Spring."

She thought about that. "We will have to kill him."

"I'm hoping we won't."

She thought about that, too. Then she lowered her aim, still with the gun in both hands, just no longer pointing it at Sean's head.

"Move away from him," she said to him, switching back to English.

With the caution reserved for handling poisonous snakes, Sean raised his hands and got up, stepping carefully away from me. He went to the side, avoiding the debris on the floor, giving Alena space. She watched him move, staring at him like he was a window and she wanted only the view beyond. For nearly thirty seconds more, none of us moved.

Then she came to my side at the couch, and looked down at me.

"I'm sorry I made you wait," she said.

"You're here now," I said. "I'm going to pass out, okay?"

I didn't hear her response, and when Alena woke me some time later, I found that I was still on the couch, but somehow I'd been dressed in dry clothes. The pain that surged in rising clamor throughout my extremities told me that I was going to recover.

"It will be dawn soon," she said, speaking in Georgian. "We must go."

I blinked the world back into focus, saw that Sean was seated on the chair, the Flexi-Cuffs now around his wrists. He was watching us impassively. As far as I could tell she hadn't actually harmed him, but there were ways she could have done it that I wouldn't have been able to see.

I sat up, and Alena pushed a mug of something hot into my hands. She'd stripped off the overwhites and cleaned off any of the blood that might have reached her skin. "Why'd you do that?"

She didn't bother looking at him. "To be safe."

"Well, I'm awake now," I said, switching to English. "Uncuff him."

Alena's lips compressed, the taste of my words unpleasant. She did it anyway, though, brusquely working the lock on the cuffs and then whipping them away from his wrists, then moving back to stand by me at the couch.

I sipped at the mug, discovered that it was warm water sweetened with sugar, nothing more, and nothing had ever tasted quite as good. I tried to drink it slowly, downing about half of it before attempting to move. The soreness and the stiffness that had settled into me made me wince.

"So, Sean," I said. "What do we do with you."

"You either kill me or let me go," he said. He glanced for a second to Alena before coming back to me. He was flexing his hands, working his fingers, and I wondered how tight Alena had fit the cuffs on him.

"Who does—did—Bowles work for?"

"I thought he was DoD, but the way you were talking to him I'm guessing I was wrong about that, that he's with the White House. I don't know, he never told us."

"That was the first you'd heard of a connection with the White House?"

"I'm with Gorman-North, Mr. Kodiak. I'm a contractor. I get the job, I do the job, I take my money, and I wait for the next job. It's mission-specific; I know you understand that."

"What was the mission?"

"To apprehend you. If possible, to apprehend the woman. To secure your cooperation in locating the woman if she couldn't be found."

"And then?"

"We were to drop you."

I admired the way he said it; he said it the same way he'd said everything else about the job so far, without opinion, merely reporting the facts.

"So Bowles was your contractor, that's what you're saying?" I asked him.

"I don't know if Bowles was the one paying Gorman-North for our services," Sean said. "But he's definitely the contact guy. This time and that thing in New York, he was management."

"Just your luck to be on both jobs?"

"It's a small community. You know that."

I took some more of my sugar water. "Getting smaller every day."

Sean looked at Alena again, clearly trying to compose his next words, then went back to me. "I don't know what you were into, or why they want you. I don't give a damn. It's not my job to give a damn. You cut me loose, I'll tell them what happened, that you overwhelmed us."

"So why should we let you do that?" Alena demanded.

"It'll come out either way. You're not going out there to dispose of the bodies, not in the snow and the daylight, at least. Whoever it is that wants you, they're going to know we blew the job, that you're still on the loose. You kill me or you let me go, that won't change."

"Unless this gets covered up. The way Cold Spring was covered up," I said.

Sean considered that. "Yeah, that's a possibility. Not sure how much it alters, though. They'll still know what happened."

I finished the sugar water, thinking that Sean was right. "What's your name, your full name?"

"Sean Baron."

"What were you before? Delta?"

He looked a little indignant. "Force Recon."

"Marine."

"Semper Fi."

I chose not to remark on the irony of that, used the arm of the couch to get to my feet. "We're leaving, Sean Baron. If you could give us a couple of hours before you call Gorman-North and tell them that the job's gone tango uniform, I'd appreciate it."

His surprise was minor, and quickly concealed. "I can hold off on it until this evening, say that's how long it took me to get clear."

"You won't take it the wrong way if I say I hope never to see you again," I told him.

"Honest to God," Sean Baron said, "I have it my way, I wouldn't have seen you in the first place."

In his chair in our room at the Grove Hotel, Nicolas Sargenti opened his eyes.

"The man in Cape Fear," he told us. "He has passed on a message for Mr. Collins four times in the last two and a half years."

"You're certain?" Alena asked.

"Of course."

"The man in Cape Fear?" I asked.

"Nicolas can explain," Alena said, dropping back into her thoughts.

"The man in Cape Fear is named Louis Woodburn," the lawyer told me. "He sells yachts. For the last decade or so, he has received, every Christmas, an annual gift in the form of a porcelain doll of the kind that is popular in France. Upon breaking apart the doll, he has discovered ten thousand dollars for him to spend as he might choose, and a telephone number. The number changes each year, of course. Currently, it is for a private voice mail box run by a singles-matching service in London.

"In return for this annual gift, Louis Woodburn takes a message should anyone ever call his business, asking to speak to Mr. Jacob Collins. Mr. Collins is the name of a schoolmate of Mr. Woodburn's, one he has not had any contact with since he was twelve years old. The caller asks if Mr. Woodburn knows where Mr. Collins might be reached. Mr. Woodburn explains that he has not had any dealings with Mr. Collins since they were in school together, but should he run into him, he can take a name and a number to pass along. Whatever name and number he takes is then forwarded to the voice mail box to be collected by me."

"At which point you do what?"

Sargenti checked on Alena, who gave no indication that she was even hearing us. Taking that as permission, he continued. "Were Elizavet still seeking new clients, I would then call the number that had been left. In every case it is another cutout, and I would leave a message in turn, with a name and a number to be contacted at, and a time. Assuming that I was then contacted as described, Elizavet would direct me to arrange a personal meeting, at the time and place of her choosing. The client would then be collected at the stated time and place, and taken to a location not unlike this one, for a personal interview to be conducted by me. In some cases, Elizavet would attend, though her presence would be concealed or otherwise obfuscated."

I nodded my understanding. If each of the five initial contacts led to procedures as convoluted and insulated as this, there was almost no chance of the communication being traced back to either Sargenti or Alena until they were certain it was legitimate. Whichever of them established the initial contact point certainly had done so under an assumed name, so even should that be discovered, it would lead only to a dead end.

Much like where we were now.

Alena abruptly rose, saying, "Thank you for coming, Nicolas. You have the paper?"

Sargenti straightened in his seat, and if he was bothered by the abruptness with which she was terminating the meeting, he did not, like everything else, reveal it. He took his attaché from where it stood beside the chair, moving it onto his lap, then worked the combination on each latch with deliberation before snapping them open. From inside the case he produced a slate-gray mailer, slightly smaller than the standard American business size, bulging with its contents. He offered it to Alena, then closed his case and got to his feet and reached for his overcoat.

"Do you wish me to look into Mr. Collins?" he asked us.

"No," she told him, then added, "You're flying back tonight?"

"I spend tonight in Montreal. I should be home the day after tomorrow."

"We need reservations for a hotel in Wilmington, North Carolina." Alena gestured with the mailer, then tossed it to me on the bed. "In one of these names, please."

"For how long?"

"Three weeks."

"You shall have it before I leave for Montreal," he assured her, then leaned forward and gave Alena a kiss on each cheek, which she returned. He nodded good-bye to me, then went with her to the door. I listened for the sound of the locks falling back into place, then dumped out the contents of the mailer beside me on the bed. There were four identities, two for each of us, and in each set we were husband and wife, and it was the full battery, from driver's licenses to credit and library cards. One set said we were Canadian, from Toronto; the other identified us as Americans, from St. Louis. Passports for each identity had been provided.

Alena returned, stopping at the room service cart to pour herself the last of the orange juice.

"Wilmington?"

"I do not know what else to do, Atticus." She turned to me, draining the glass and setting it back on the cart. Frustration was evident in her voice. "It is a very long shot that the person or persons who has been trying to reach Mr. Collins is the same person or persons who is trying to kill us. But I do not know what else to do."

"Gorman-North uses the Mr. Collins contact?" I asked her.

"I do not believe I have ever done any work for Gorman-North. Of course, I could be mistaken in that. I believe the two jobs I did for the CIA before my retirement came through the Collins contact. Given the relationship between the government and its civilian contractors, the people who move between those two sectors, it is reasonable to believe that someone at Gorman-North knows of it. But that is incidental, perhaps."

"Because it doesn't go back to the White House?"

"It presumes that Gorman-North is the connection with the White House, yes, and we have no evidence of that."

"No reason to think there isn't."

"But no reason to think that there is, either."

"So we go to Cape Fear, and we watch Mr. Woodburn, and we

hope that whoever has been trying to reach you through him pays him a call?"

"Or is watching him already, and we can make the surveillance, double back on it."

"And then try to get out of whoever might be watching him what we hoped we'd get from Bowles."

She looked almost stricken. "I didn't have a choice, Atticus."

"I'm not blaming you."

"He was going to kill you, I had to—"

"I'm not blaming you, Alena."

Her mouth closed tightly, and I saw her hands ball into fists. Her expression contracted, filling with her anger and her frustration and her fears.

"Come here," I said.

She shook her head, almost childlike.

I thought for a moment, then said, "You're not who you were. Don't think that you are."

The anger in her voice matched the anger in her eyes, still directed more at herself than anyone or anything else. "You can't say that. You don't know. You can't say that."

"If it had been you," I said. "If it had been you in the snow, half naked and taking that beating, if it had been your head that Bowles was pointing the gun at, I would have done the same thing."

She shook her head, refusing me, saying, "No, no, I *cut* him, Atticus, do you hear me? I needed to announce myself, I needed to draw them away from you. The two men on patrol—I killed the first one, but the second, I kept him alive so I could cut him, so I could make him scream, so they would know that I was there. I cut him so it would hurt, so they could all hear."

Her voice trailed off. She wasn't looking at me, perhaps she felt she couldn't, and maybe if I was someone else, she'd have been right in that.

I brought myself forward on the bed, wincing as I swung my legs onto the floor. She refused to look at me still, even when I put my hands on her shoulders, brought her around to face me. There were things I could say, things I could offer to try to make her feel better about what she had done, what she once was, what she was afraid she always would be. I could have told her that her guilt was the thing that declared she had changed, that her self-loathing at this moment was the mark of her relearned humanity, that what she had told Dan in Portland had been true, that what she once was wouldn't have batted an eye.

There were a lot of things I could have said to try and help her through it, to try to make her feel better, but I didn't say any of them. I just took her in my arms and I held her, and she let me do it.

I certainly didn't tell her that what she'd told me didn't change anything I'd said.

Had the positions been reversed, I would have done exactly the same thing.

Including cutting strips off a man to make him scream.

CHAPTER SIX

We were on I-84 heading east by ten the next morning, Alena driving the Subaru Outback she'd bought off a used-car lot the previous evening. The Outback was five years old, dark green, ran fine, and smelled faintly of cat's urine, which explained why she'd gotten it for a steal. She'd bought it on the same ID we'd used to get from Portland to Whitefish, the same ID we used to settle up before checking out of the Grove. Before leaving Boise, we'd destroyed each of our sets. For the trip cross-country, we'd use the St. Louis ones that Sargenti had provided. Once in Wilmington, we'd switch to the Canadian, since that had been the name Sargenti had used for the reservations we'd requested.

Aside from the smell, the drive went just fine, and we didn't push it, because neither of us saw an immediate need to. We were driving cross-country on a long shot, and neither of us had much hope that it would play out. Driving gave us both time to think, to try to come up with a better plan. I'm sure that's what Alena did, at least; mostly, I tried to sleep and convince my body to speed along in its recovery.

It was late afternoon when we reached Lynch, Wyoming, and that seemed a fine time to call it a day. There was a Best Western not far from the Interstate, called the Outlaw Inn, and that was too good to pass up, so we pulled into the lot and parked. It was typical Best Western, long and two-storied. A minimall was across the street, replete with dry cleaner, video rental, and convenience store. It was cold, the air dry and sharp, and a crust of ice had filmed over everything, including the snow.

I was getting very tired of snow.

We pulled our bags from the car, anxious to get fresh air in our lungs and more importantly, our nostrils, then picked our way carefully across the lot to the office. The bags weren't holding much—Alena's laptop, the new clothes she'd bought for us after acquiring the car, toiletries, vitamins, and the spare IDs. Each of us had a gun, taken from the bodies we'd left outside the cabin in Montana. The contractors had all carried extra clips, so between us we had somewhere in the neighborhood of sixty rounds if we encountered anything that required that much dissuasion.

The office had a cowboy motif going, from the wood carving of a bucking bronco to the laminated lariat that hung on the wall beside the front desk. There was a coffeemaker with complimentary coffee, stained with the dregs it had spilled over the years, and a couch that wasn't leather but wanted to be. Behind the counter was a display of travel-sized amenities—aspirin, toothpaste, shampoo, everything you might need if you'd forgotten to pack before meeting your mistress. A television hung nearby on the wall, burbling news softly, but instead of aiming out so the guests could enjoy it, it had been turned the other way, to service the management.

The management, such as we could see, consisted of an overweight man who could have been anywhere from early twenties to late thirties. He watched us come through the door with an absolute lack of interest, perhaps even the hope that we would change our minds at the last minute and maybe try to find another place to rest our heads. His interest perked up a bit when we actually made it inside and he saw Alena, but then diminished when he realized that, yes, I was probably sleeping with her.

We took a room on the second floor, settled our things and ourselves, and then talked about what we would do for dinner.

"Wyoming," I said. "Beef."

"There must be another choice."

"You want to try the fish they're serving in Lynch, be my guest," I said. "I'm thinking there's got to be someplace with a salad bar."

"Salad bars are worse." She looked honestly horrified. "They're breeding grounds for bacteria and disease."

I looked at the clock by the bed, digital and frail. If it was to be believed, it wasn't yet five. "I'll see if I can find a grocery store," I told her, and headed back down to the office.

The same man was behind the counter when I came in, speaking on the phone, but as soon as he saw me he cut off whatever it was he was saying and hung up. He hung up hard, the handset clattering into the base.

"There a grocery store nearby?" I asked.

"There's the Get N Go," he said, then pointed past me, out the windows and to the lot across the street. "That's nearby."

I followed the direction of his finger, nodded, then looked back at him.

"Yes," I agreed. "It is, though it's not really what I had in mind. I was hoping for something with a wider selection."

"There's Boschetto's, down Elk a ways. Imported stuff, if you like that kind of thing."

I wasn't sure what he meant by that, but it seemed that he meant something.

"And there's a Smith's, out on Foothill, but you probably don't want to go that far," he added.

"Thanks," I said, and walked out of the office, making sure to clear his line of sight through the windows. I looked up at the sky, the darkening gray, and began counting off slowly in my head.

When I reached thirty, I turned and went back into the office.

This time, the handset was back in its cradle before I was through the door.

"What time's checkout again?" I asked.

"Eleven," he said. "It's eleven."

"Right, thanks," I said, and left the office a last time, climbing the stairs back up to our room. I knocked on the door before using my key to enter, found that Alena had moved the furniture around, and was now in the corner by the closet, doing yoga.

"I think we've got a problem," I told her.

She was in an abdominal stretch, her back arched and her head on the floor, her feet folded back beneath her buttocks, looking at me upside down. "What kind of problem?"

"I'm not sure yet," I said. There was a remote control for the television on the bed stand, and I picked it up, switching on the set that was bolted to the bureau at the foot of the bed. It came on with genuine reluctance. I began searching for a cable news channel.

Alena exhaled, then flipped out of her position, to her feet, and I thought that was maybe just maybe showing off for my benefit. I found a twenty-four-hour news channel as she came to my side.

"What happened?" she asked.

I started to answer, then stopped myself, staring at the television. On the screen was footage of the cabin in Montana or, at least, what the cabin in Montana looked like when graced with daylight. There were police and state troopers and men wearing parkas that had letters like "DHS" and "FBI" stenciled on their backs. There were crime-scene people taking photographs, and more people moving body bags.

Then the picture cut to a talking head behind his desk, and he said the words, *"terrorist cell"* and then, on the screen, appeared two pictures, side by side.

The same two pictures Bowles had shown me in his Interpol file four nights before, the file photos of Alena and myself.

". . . considered armed and extremely dangerous," the talking head was saying. *"It is unknown, at this time, if they still have any quantity of ricin in their possession. . . ."*

"Oh," said Alena softly. "That kind of trouble."

CHAPTER SEVEN

There were sirens, and they were most definitely headed our way.

Alena and I looked at each other, thinking the same things. Running was out of the question; every cop, sheriff's deputy, and reserve officer in a hundred square miles was currently converging on our position. Getting onto the open road would lead to a high-speed pursuit, and that was a game we would lose. Once on the Interstate, there was only one direction we could go, and that was whatever direction we started in. Too easy to drop spikes on the asphalt, to roadblock us, to force us to a stop. Factor in the weather, that with night falling the roads would be that much more treacherous, and it just wasn't an option. If we were going to die, I didn't want it to be because we'd lost control of our car on a patch of black ice.

Shooting our way out was an option, but I didn't like it, for a number of reasons. With the contractors in Cold Spring and again in Montana, the situation had been different. They'd come to the game with violence, their intentions plain; for lack of a better phrase, they'd known what they were getting into. But the idea of shooting some poor S.O.B. cop who was doing his job, that didn't sit well with me. There were a lot of things I already had on my conscience, and many more that I would have to learn to live with. Bringing about the death of a police officer in the line of his duty wasn't going to be one of them.

I said as much to Alena.

"Agreed," she said, then went for her bag, pulling the MacBook from within. "Curtains."

I went to the windows. Our view wasn't bad, given that there wasn't much to it, at least, not yet. It was almost full dark outside now, the overcast sky helping the night's approach, and streetlamps had already come on. I could see the expanse of the parking lot, see the Outback parked where we had left it, and then, across Elk, the lot of the minimall, likewise illuminated. As I watched, the first car arrived, cutting its siren as it pulled in across the street. Red and blue flashed off the sheen of ice on the ground, bounced from the glass of nearby windows.

I closed the curtains, then moved to the bathroom. There was no window, not even a tiny one. I came back to find Alena at the desk, searching the drawers furiously.

"No way out the back," I told her. "Which, I suppose, means no way in, either. And we sure as hell aren't leaving by the front door, not unless we're in custody, at least."

"The Ethernet cable," she told me. "I can't get a wireless signal. There should be a cable in the closet or somewhere."

I snapped back the bifold doors on the closet, came eye-to-eye with a small clear plastic bag dangling from the clothes rod. I didn't bother to unhook it, just tore the bag loose and tossed it to

Alena. She freed the cable, plugged it into the cable modem on the desk, and opened the Web browser.

"Do we have a plan?" I asked her.

"I'm working on one. The response—what are we facing?"

I moved past her at the desk, back to the window, and parted the curtains enough to peek out. The lot across the street was filling with emergency vehicles, and as I watched, a SWAT van pulled in to join the others. I wasn't hearing any helicopters, but that didn't mean there weren't going to be any; only that they hadn't arrived on-scene yet.

"SWAT just pulled up," I told her. "I'd guess at ten minutes before they cut the power."

"The news showed the Department of Homeland Security and the FBI."

"They'll have been notified," I agreed. "The Feds will want to run the show, which means they'll put the brakes on the locals, keep them from rushing us, even if they were inclined to do that, which I doubt. How many people in Lynch, you think?"

"Twenty thousand? Perhaps thirty?"

"Not a big SWAT team, then, and probably not a lot of experience on it, either. They'll do it by the book, all the more so because they think we're so damn dangerous. SWAT tactics are universally the same. They evacuate the immediate area, form a perimeter, and then wait. They'll try to negotiate us out, especially if they believe we're in possession of a chemical or biological agent."

"Don't forget the federal response."

"I don't know DHS's reach," I said. "Figure they'll scramble a major unit on us, maybe a Delta Squad, maybe the Hostage Rescue Team out of Quantico. So four hours, maybe five before they can reach us."

"Longer, I'd think. Closer to eight. They have to deploy, then transport, then arrive on site, then redeploy."

"Speaking of which," I said. The SWAT team in the lot outside the Get N Go was scrambling, men with rifles running beneath the lights in several directions at once. I tried to get a count of what I was seeing, and it confirmed what I had suspected. It wasn't a large team. On the basis of that, then, they'd secure the perimeter before trying to convince us to come out. Whatever they had for the breaching team, if they decided to come in and take us by force, I didn't know. Before I pulled back from the window, I caught sight of a news van approaching.

"Local media's arrived."

"Good for them. The SWAT team, did they have night-vision?"

"Couldn't tell."

"We'll need to know," she said.

I considered, then reached for the remote control and showed it to her. She actually grinned.

"Very clever," she told me.

I shoved the remote into my back pocket, moving to look over her shoulder at what she'd been doing with the laptop. Apparently, she'd been Googling Wyoming airports.

"We're going to need an airport," she explained to me. "Preferably an international one."

"The idea being to convince them that we're still here while we're actually on a plane to parts unknown?"

"If we are quick, it will work. They will not breach the room unless provoked or until they have no other choice."

I was at the bureau beneath the television, now, yanking open the drawers. The television was still rambling news, and for the time being, it seemed, wasn't talking about us. That wouldn't last much longer. If the initial story was national, then the addition to it currently playing out in Lynch sure as hell would be, too. I kept searching, and in the lower right-hand drawer found the phone book for Lynch, as well as a copy of *Hustler*.

"Remind me to have a word with housekeeping," I said.

"What? Why?"

"Never mind." I started flipping through the listings. "Lynch has an airport, the Sweetsprings County Airport."

"International?"

"Are you kidding me?"

She was typing quickly. "If we check in for international flights, we only have to clear security once before arriving at our destination."

"Fine, but we were going to Wilmington."

Alena glanced from the laptop to me, and she actually looked annoyed. "We don't *go* to the destination. We get on a flight routing to Paris, say, but that requires changing planes somewhere on the East Coast—Dulles would be ideal. Then we simply walk out of the airport, rent a vehicle, proceed from there."

"There's an international airport in Casper," I said, discarding the phone book and taking a look at the ceiling. It wasn't terribly high, just out of my reach. I tried to remember the grade of the roof, how severely it had been raked. "Probably one in Cheyenne, as well."

"Denver is closer," she said. "Here, the local airport has connections to Denver. Also a flight school. That will be useful."

She snapped the laptop closed, then reached around and pulled the cord from the jack. While she did that, I pulled myself up on the dresser, began pushing at the ceiling. It gave with pressure, and as soon as I verified that, I punched at it. My angle on it was bad, and I couldn't get much force behind my blows, and all of the bruises on my torso came back to life when I did it. It took three tries before I broke through with my fist. Debris and dust floated down, coating my arm and face.

"They'll be looking for a man and a woman traveling together," Alena said.

I began tearing a hole in the ceiling. "We're going to have to split up."

"Once we're clear, yes. We will rejoin one another at the hotel in Wilmington, but each of us will have to travel by a different route to get there. The longer we can convince them we are still here, still trapped in this room, the more time we will have to escape, to get further away."

The phone started ringing.

"You take it," Alena told me. "You must convince them to wait, that they do not need to storm the room."

I hopped down from the bureau. Alena had risen, replacing her laptop in her bag, and I gave her a lift up to where I had just been standing. She resumed widening the hole I'd made in the ceiling, working slowly to keep her efforts silent as I went to answer the phone.

"What?"

"Mr. Morse? This is Bobby Galloway with the Lynch Police Department. I'm here to help you."

"You're what?" I asked.

"I'm here to help you."

"What makes you think I need your help, Mr. Galloway?"

"Well, Chris, it seems there are some people who think that there was this incident in Montana a few days ago involving some law enforcement officials," Bobby Galloway told me, using his best hostage-negotiation voice. It wasn't bad, pleasant and with a definite promise of friendship. "We'd really like to get that sorted out. There's a lot of confusion about what happened back there."

"Not from where I'm standing."

"That's the thing, there are always two sides to every story."

"You want to help me so much, why do I think that if I open my curtains and look out the window I'm going to be seeing the SWAT team surrounding this hotel?"

"Well, Chris, unfortunately things have gone beyond where I can just come over there and chat with you. We're going to need to bring you down to the station, try to sort this out there."

"You're going to arrest me?"

"I'm not going to lie to you, we do have a warrant for your arrest, Chris. We also have a warrant for Danielle's arrest. We've been told that she may have been wounded, is she doing okay, does she need any medical attention, anything like that?"

I took a second, trying to get my thoughts ordered as quickly as possible. So far, Bobby Galloway was proving himself to be a very good negotiator, better than I'd expected given the circumstance and the location, and that meant I was going to have to be very careful in what I said to him. Asking about Alena was mining, trying to gather intelligence.

Galloway had the potential to become our greatest ally, *if* I could convince him that he had control of the conversation, that he could keep me talking, and more, keep me willing to talk to him. That would be ideal, because it would allow him to turn to his superior, his chief of police or whoever, and say the same, that he could keep us from being a danger to ourselves and the community, that he could keep us stable until HRT or whoever arrived. That maybe he could get this resolved peaceably, without needing to storm the room.

He could buy us the time we needed to get away.

"Chris? Is Danielle doing okay?" Galloway asked.

"She's fine," I told him. "She's more than fine, she's never been better."

"How about you? Are you injured at all? Do you need any medical assistance?"

"I'm doing fine," I said. Then I added, "I've got everything I need right here with me."

It was a deliberate opening, and he took it, but he took his time. A worse negotiator would have jumped on the line like a politician on a vote, but Bobby Galloway waited almost three seconds before speaking.

"Yeah? What do you have in there that's so helpful, Chris?"

"Don't you worry about what I have or what I don't," I snapped. "I've got everything I need, that's all you need to know."

"All right."

I let a pause start, then, trying to sound pissy, said, "Can I ask you a question? Am I allowed to ask questions, here?"

It was as calculated on my part as anything he had said on his, because I was giving him exactly what every good negotiator wants to hear: I was giving him power. Three minutes into the conversation at the most, and psychologically—at least from where Galloway was standing with his headset and his paper cup of coffee at the mobile command post across the street—I'd turned the first corner he wanted me to take. I had asked his permission, and that meant that I'd put him in control.

"Sure, Chris," Galloway said. "Go ahead."

"You guys want to arrest me, why don't you just come up to the door and come and get me?"

"Thing is, the information I've been given says that you two have some dangerous stuff up there. That you've got some firearms and ammunition, like that, maybe even something that could make a lot of people really sick."

"Yeah," I said. "Yeah, coming up here would probably be a bad idea, Bobby. It would probably make a whole lot of people a whole lot more than just sick."

"There you go, that's what's got us where we are, here," Bobby Galloway said. "You want to tell me about what happened in Montana? You want to talk about that?"

"No."

"This is a good opportunity, Chris, this is a good chance for you to tell your side of things, you hear what I'm saying? There are always two sides, it's like I said, and from where we're sitting out here, I mean, it looks like you're the bad guy, so it would be good to hear your side. You sure you don't want to talk about it?"

"I'm sure," I told him. "I've got nothing to say about Montana."

To my side, Alena had finished clearing the hole in the ceiling, just wide enough now that I could fit through it. She quietly dropped from the bureau, took the last chunk of debris and set it on the floor, then began clearing off the other pieces she'd pulled from where they rested on the bed.

"All right, Chris," Galloway said, after a moment. "I'm going to take a couple minutes here and consult with my superiors, maybe use the bathroom, get another cup of coffee. You should think about what I've said, see if we can't work this out."

"Sure," I said, but it went into dead air, he'd already disconnected. I did likewise.

"He hung up?" Alena asked.

I nodded. "He's pretty good."

She motioned to the remote control. "Shall we?"

"Yeah, let's see if that brings him back."

I handed Alena the remote and she moved to the window, crouching down to one side before sliding it between the fabric and the glass. She pressed several of the buttons together, as if trying to control some distant television.

The phone began ringing again.

"Guess they're wearing night-vision," I said.

"I guess they are." She came off her haunches and set the remote back on the dresser beside the television. Remote controls use infrared light to send their commands to whatever it is they're commanding. By its nature, it's outside the visible spectrum, but not when using night-vision. When using night-vision, it shows up like what it is—a nice, bright pulse of light. Multiple buttons meant that there had been multiple pulses at multiple frequencies.

Seen by someone on the perimeter, maybe by several someones, it had made an unexpected and potentially alarming light show, because there was a very good chance they had no idea of its source. Galloway, maybe getting himself his cup of coffee, but just as likely reviewing his notes and consulting with his bosses, had been urged to get back on the phone and find out just what the hell we were doing in there.

"Goddammit," I said when I answered. "What?"

"Just checking that everything's all right in there," Galloway said. "You two still okay? Something happen?"

"Why wouldn't we be?" I demanded. "This is bullshit. I want to talk to somebody in charge. That's what I want. You put your boss on. I want to talk to him."

Over the phone I could make out voices speaking in the background. None of them sounded like Galloway.

"Don't ignore me, Bobby," I said sharply. "Don't ignore me, man, you don't want to do that."

"I'm not ignoring you," he said. "I'm afraid you're stuck with me, Chris, there's no one else available. You're sure everything's all right in there?"

"Everything's just fine. Everything's just great, why are you asking, you think everything's not fine and great?"

"Just checking with you, that's all."

"We've got everything we need in here, I told you that. Don't play games with me, Bobby, I don't like it. I don't want you playing games with me."

"I'm dealing with you straight, Chris. No games."

"No games."

"So how are we going to get you out of this, Chris? You and

Danielle, how are we going to get you to come on out so nobody gets hurt?"

"We're not going to hurt anybody. That's not why we're here."

"You know, I think that you mean that, I really do. Maybe you can do something to demonstrate that to us. Maybe you can hand over some of your weapons, or some of the powder you have up there—"

"And how am I supposed to do that? I just open the door and drop it out front? I don't want you guys coming up here, I don't want you coming near here. I want you to go away, that's what I want."

"That's not going to happen, Chris. We can talk about anything else you want, but we're not leaving, that's not even on the table, it's not even in consideration, you get me?"

"Fuck you," I said, and hung up on him, then moved over to Alena, who was once more back atop the dresser. I braced myself against the furniture, and she put a foot on my shoulder, then stepped up and pulled herself into the crawl space between the ceiling and the roof.

"How's it look?" I asked.

Her voice came back soft, a little muffled. "Cold. There's insulation. The shingles look like composite."

The phone started ringing again.

"We're going to need more time," she told me.

"I don't want to talk to you right now," I said.

"Listen, I've got to tell you something." Galloway sounded concerned. "You're not going to like this, but I think you need to hear it, and I'm hoping you'll take it well."

"You don't want to come up here," I said.

"The guys that are running this show out here, they're getting some grief, Chris. It's twenty degrees out here, it's dark, we've got the media watching this play out. You got your television on? You can see it, we're on the television. And my bosses, they're saying they're going to cut your power. No reason you should be comfortable and warm and have light in there when we don't. So we're going to put you and Danielle in the dark, and it's going to get cold up there pretty fast."

"You do what you have to do," I said. "You do what you have to do, but I got over being afraid of the dark a long time ago. I'm hanging up now, I don't want to hear from you right now. You can call me back in an hour, maybe we can talk then."

I hung up, then turned to the gap in the ceiling and said, "They're killing the power."

"About time," Alena said.

The lights went out. So did the television.

"Keep your voice low," she warned.

The phone started ringing again. I checked my watch, saw that it was seven minutes past six. I let it ring. It stopped after three minutes, and silence flowed into the void it had made. I could make out the slight sound of Alena above me, in the crawl space between the ceiling and the roof, trying to remove the shingles one by one. From her bag, I found a sweatshirt she'd picked up in her shopping, sent it up through the hole to her, but she sent it right down again.

"I don't want to sweat," she said. "It'll be cold outside."

I stowed the sweatshirt back in her bag, then went through my bag and put on a couple of extra layers myself. I zipped the bags closed, moved them to the dresser, beside the television, so they would be easy to hand up. Then I went to the door and gave it a listen. No outside noise penetrated, no sounds of traffic, no squawks of radios.

They were waiting, just like we were waiting. In the main,

hostage negotiations follow the same patterns as SWAT deployments and the like. Once negotiations have been opened, the guiding principle is to continue them for as long as possible, unless a further development changes the situation. Even though I was refusing to answer the phone, the negotiations were still considered open. Closing them would require a command decision—most likely not to be made until the federal forces arrived—or an act of violence on our part that forced an escalation. If we became an immediate threat to life and limb, they'd have to take us.

But otherwise, they would continue to try to wait us out. With the cold and the darkness and the promise of a very long night ahead of us, they could afford to.

After another fifteen minutes, the phone started ringing again. It rang until a little after half past six, then stopped.

At a minute past seven, Alena stuck her head down through the hole in the ceiling. "It's done."

I moved to help her down, and she slid out of the gap headfirst, into my arms, and it was almost like dancing the way I flipped her onto her feet.

"You get a look outside?" I whispered back.

"There's no one on our roof. The grade is severe, and the ice makes it treacherous. We will have to be very careful. But because of the ice, they will think we won't try the roof."

"Anything to secure to, to lower ourselves down?"

She shook her head, then pointed to the queen bed.

We stripped the bed, including the pillowcases and the bedsheet. We tore the linens down to roughly five-inch strips, working as fast as we could. The phone started jangling again, and I stopped my shredding to check my watch. It was six minutes past seven. I waited until the second hand had swept past the twelve, then answered.

"I told you I'd talk to you in an hour, I meant an hour," I said. "Did you not understand me?"

"Just wanted to make sure you knew I was still here for you, Chris. You two still doing all right?"

"It's getting a little cold," I admitted.

"Yeah, nights like this, it can get down in single digits, sometimes even lower. Gets too cold to snow, even."

"I'll take your word for it."

We shared a companionable pause, or a pause that, at least, we both hoped the other thought was companionable. Alena had all our strips piled on the bed now, was beginning to secure the ends one to the other in knots.

"You sure you don't want to talk about Montana?" Galloway asked. "Give me your side of it?"

"You keep asking about that."

"It's confusing, it's not really clear."

I fumbled around for something to say, something that would suit the part, and finally found myself parroting Bowles. "I'm a patriot, I love my country, you understand me?"

"Sure, I understand."

"But part of that, part of being an American is fearing my government. That's my job as a citizen, right? That's what we're supposed to do, to keep them honest, to keep an eye on them."

"I know what you mean."

"Everyone's got their hand out," I said. "I mean everyone, it's out of control, it's greed, it's just pure greed. Everything is about how much they can get from you and me, and the hell with the rest of it."

"Tell me about it."

"I am, okay? I am telling you about it. It's all greed, it's all these government types just taking and taking and robbing us, robbing us of our future and our promise."

"Sure. I mean, utility companies, look at that. That's just another secret tax, right? They're just another arm of the government."

"That's right, that's right exactly."

Out of the corner of my eye, I saw Alena pause in her knot tying, shaking her head in mild amusement at my performance. I shrugged.

"You're making a lot of sense, Chris," Galloway said. "I think there are a lot of people who feel the way you do."

"There are. A lot of us, there sure are."

"But I guess you'll agree that, you know, how things look now, people aren't getting that message. How things look now, you understand, that message isn't coming across."

"What?"

"You and Danielle, you're in that room, the lights are out and the heat's off and we're all out here, and the cameras are out here with us, you understand. And nobody's going to let those cameras go in there, we just can't do that. You're a smart guy, I can tell you know why we can't do that."

"Let me talk to one of them," I said. "One of the reporters."

"My superiors won't allow that, Chris, c'mon. You want to talk to these people, you're going to have to come out of there, that's the only way it'll work. You come out, nobody gets hurt, that's better for you in the long run, don't you think?"

"Don't talk to me like that, don't do that," I said, getting angry. "You're pissing me off again, Bobby, don't do that."

"I didn't mean—"

"No, no, I'll tell you what, I'll talk to you in the morning," I said. "I need to think, I need some time to think."

And I hung up, then moved to where Alena was coiling our

makeshift rope on the bureau. I hoisted her up again, this time just lifting her from the hips, and she pulled herself the rest of the way into the crawl space. I climbed atop the bureau, handed up the two bags, then the rope, then took hold of her outstretched arm and followed her into the cold and musty darkness.

Leaving the phone to ring in the room alone.

CHAPTER EIGHT

It was bitingly cold and it was treacherously icy and the drop from the edge of the roof to the shadows along the rear of the hotel was easily thirty feet. As Alena worked quickly to conceal the hole she'd made in the roof, I scanned the sky above us. I'd heard the distinctive sound of a helicopter doing fly-over while I'd been talking to Galloway, but now there was no sign of the bird. It was possible it had been ordered down for the night, maybe to preserve fuel or to give the pilot a rest so he'd be ready when really needed. Whatever the reason, it was luck, and dawdling on the roof would be a good way to squander it.

We stayed on our bellies, sliding as much as crawling along the shingles. Now that we were outside, the sounds of the siege became audible, the distant crackle of radios, the sound of the occasional vehicle coming along the road. There wasn't much noise coming from Lynch, and not a hell of a lot of light, either. Either it was a sleepy little town on a late winter's night, or, more likely, everyone was at home watching what was happening in their backyard on their televisions.

We moved carefully, sliding ourselves towards one of the many vents that had been cut into the roof. I had to clear some of the snow away to make room for our rope, and it was so hard it cut my hands. Once again, I felt the ache of the cold. If I got frost-bite a second time so soon after the first, I'd end up losing my fingers. While I readied the improvised rope, Alena took the opportunity to eyeball the surroundings, using the elevation to our advantage.

"It's not deep," Alena murmured in my ear. "The perimeter seems confined to the hotel lot, patrol cars running out the next couple of blocks. The streets have been closed."

I nodded, finished looping the rope around the vent, then handed it off to Alena. She took the two ends, rolling onto her back and then back onto her belly to stay low, wrapping them together rappelling style around her waist and crotch. Then she let gravity slide her towards the edge of the roof, and, without any hesitation or pause, simply continued over the edge. I waited to hear the sound of her impact, the smack of a body landing wrong on the ground, but it didn't come, and as soon as I saw the rope turn from taut to slack, I followed her.

We were at the rear of the hotel, the side furthest from Elk, in a narrower and shallower extension of the parking lot that dominated the front side. Most of the light had been coming from the other side of the street, and the shadows were adequate enough to be comforting. A fence, wooden, perhaps seven feet high, marked the edge of the lot on this side. From above, I had seen that it butted up against the lot for a fast-food restaurant on the other side, then another street that seemed to run parallel to Elk.

That would be the edge of the perimeter, then. Over the fence, through the lot, across the street, and we'd have broken the ring. All we had to do was manage that without being seen or heard.

Alena edged out of the shadows, checking to the right and the left, as I turned back to the building and took hold of one of the ends of the linked sheets. It came free easily, and I drew it down quickly, pulling it hand over hand. Once it was down I gathered it together and looked for a place to hide it. I didn't see one that wouldn't be discovered immediately upon daylight, so I shoved it into my bag, instead.

Alena stepped back silently, crouching down, motioning for me to join her. I dropped, and for the better part of another minute, neither of us moved, listening and letting our eyes adjust. There was more light than I'd realized at first, and while it made our concealment less effective, it was going to hurt anybody wearing NVG worse. Night-vision can be a terrific tool, but it has to be used in the right environment. In near-total darkness conditions, it's ideal.

In an illuminated urban setting, not so much.

This was why Alena had been so insistent that we know if they were using NVG or not, because it gave us both an idea of their spotting distance, both actual and imagined. Wearing their goggles, the team members would believe they were seeing farther, and seeing more, than they actually were. Given the lighting conditions as a result of the streetlamps, the refraction from all the snow and ice, the signposts for the various services offered this close to the interstate, and the general urban light dome, anyone wearing the goggles was actually seeing far less.

She put her mouth to my ear, so close that I could feel her lips brush my skin. "Patrol car right, under the streetlamp. No motion."

I looked, saw the car she was speaking of. The streetlamp nearby was dropping glare almost precisely on its windshield.

"Left, rooftop, countersniper and spotter," she whispered.

They were harder to spot, but I found them after a moment. About three hundred feet away, set up on the flat roof of a service station. They'd focused on the door that led to our room, and with good reason: As far as the Lynch PD was concerned, it was our only way in or out. Given that the SWAT team had very clearly shifted to a waiting posture, I wasn't surprised they'd missed us. They had to be bored and miserably cold, and if the spotter was wearing NVG, half blind as well without even realizing it.

"On three, to the fence together," she said. "Put me up and over, then follow. Don't stop."

I nodded.

She used her fingers, showing me three fingers, then two, then one.

We ran for the fence, low and light. I was faster, and that let me get into position before her, dropping my bag as I went down on one knee, turning to face her approach. She didn't break stride, just put her right foot into my hands, and I lifted with my arms as much as my hips, heard the fence behind me groan for an instant as she made contact with it, and then her weight was gone. An instant later, I heard her landing on the other side, and it sounded like she'd come down hard, and badly, because she couldn't keep from making a noise.

I looped my arms through the straps of my tiny duffel, pressing it against my chest, then reached for the top of the fence and pulled, swinging my legs to the side, to bring them up and over with me. I wanted to be quick, and I wanted to be quiet, and that meant letting my arms, once again, do most of the work until my legs had the momentum to lead. Once they had cleared the top of the fence, though, I twisted with them, turning and following them over.

My landing, like Alena's, was bad, and I discovered why the

second I came down. The crust of snow against this side of the fence was deceptive, and thin, and it concealed a layer of ice as slick as oiled glass. My feet went out from beneath me the moment I came down, and I tried to readjust, and instead landed hard, on my left hip.

The urge to curse was almost overpowering.

Alena offered me her hand, and I used it to get back to my feet, then almost immediately went down again for precisely the same reason I had the first time. She caught me, started to slip, and then I had to catch her. It would have been pure Buster Keaton if it wasn't so damn deadly.

There was a Dumpster off to the back, and even in the winter cold, it stank of spoiled milk and rotting meat. We got into its cover, facing the direction we had come, looking back at the fence. The night maintained its relative silence; nothing in it seemed to spike, nothing in it seemed to indicate that anyone knew we had moved.

To the left, the drive-through lane of the restaurant was staggeringly illuminated. Behind us, the light increased until reaching the shelter of the building itself, where it diminished in its awning. From the rooftop of the hotel, I hadn't been able to see if the restaurant was still actually open, or if the lights it had on were a security precaution. Whichever way we went from here, though, we risked greater exposure.

And there was still the problem of getting across the street and past whoever was almost certainly posted there to contend with.

I checked my watch. According to its luminous hands, it was twenty-three minutes past seven. We'd been outside for all of six minutes.

"We use the drive-through lane," Alena said in my ear.

I needed a second to follow her logic, but then I saw it. The drive-through lane was well lit, true, but it was also blocked from view on each side. On the left was the restaurant itself; to the right was a cinder-block wall bordering that side of the property. If we hurried through it, staying to the restaurant side, we'd have cover at least until we reached the edge of the building.

"You go first," she said.

I shook my head. She was slower, and I wasn't about to risk leaving her behind.

Her eyes narrowed, and she was going to argue with me, but then decided that would be an even greater waste of our time. She showed me the three fingers again, counted them down to one, then went into motion. I followed after her, as close as I dared.

It was very bright in the drive-through lane. Glancing past the giant-sized decals of burgers and two-for-one deals in the windows, I could see the restaurant was empty inside.

The building ended at a children's play structure, encrusted in snow and ice, and looking very much the worse for it as a result. It threw shadows down for our benefit, and we took to them eagerly, hunkering down, now with a view of the street ahead of us. Just as I dropped onto my haunches behind Alena the sound of engine noise reached us, a car approaching, and each of us dropped flat.

A patrol car rolled slowly into view, the driver's floodlight on, splashing light towards the building. I wrapped my arms around Alena's middle, pinning her against the duffel still on my chest, then rolled onto my back, wedging us beneath the last few feet of a slide. She didn't move, and together we watched as the light from the flood flowed in our direction, daylight bright.

Then the light hit the slide, and the shadows concealing us bloomed deeper. I rolled us back the way we'd come as the car continued past.

We waited until the silence returned, the red glow of its taillights marking its passage, and then we sprinted for the street, the edge of the perimeter, and yet another extension to our diminishing freedom.

CHAPTER NINE

The lipstick was hot pink and called "cotton candy" and Alena applied it quickly, checking herself in the sun visor's mirror. Then she drew herself up in the seat beside me, unfastened the top two buttons of the black-and-red flannel she was wearing, and pulled the shirt taut down her front, tucking it hard into her pants. She settled the cowboy hat atop her head, then gave her reflection a final appraisal before turning to me, still sitting behind the wheel of the Ford pickup truck we'd stolen from the parking lot of a bar some five blocks away from the Outlaw Inn.

When in Rome and all that.

We'd found the lipstick in the glove box, the flannel on the floor, and the hat behind the seat. We'd also found a box of triple-ought shotgun shells and the shotgun it went with, two empty cans of Rock Star energy drink, and a silver hip flask engraved with a picture of a bucking bronco and the words "Ride 'em, Cowgirl!" The flask had been empty.

"Well?" Alena asked.

"You're going to think less of me for saying this," I said. "But I'd definitely do you."

It didn't earn a smile, just a curt nod, and then she looked out the front window, to the warm lights of the Sweetspring County Airport's flight school. From where we sat in the truck, I could make out a handful of people inside, bathing in the glow of a television screen somewhere out of sight. I knew what they were watching, the same as Alena did. They were watching the same thing the people at the bar where we'd stolen the truck were watching.

Alena and I had to split up. I knew that, and I knew the reason for it, the logic behind it, and I knew both were solid and good. It had been forty-two minutes since we'd managed to sneak out of the hotel and the siege we'd been put under. As far as the world was concerned, we were still trapped in our room, not out and running free. At least, if everything was going according to plan.

But that wouldn't last for long. Maybe another four or five or six hours, if we were exceptionally lucky. Then time would run out, and Bobby Galloway would give way to HRT or a squad of Deltas, and the door would come down, and the people with guns would find our room empty and a hole in the ceiling. The APBs would issue forth like threats of damnation from a Southern Baptist pulpit.

Those APBs would be for a man and a woman, traveling together.

We *had* to split up.

But I didn't want to. This wasn't going to be like Whitefish, where the cold and the pain had brought me to doubt, because then, doubt had been all it was. This was different. This was each of us traveling alone.

For the first time in over three years, we wouldn't be able to protect each other.

That scared me. Looking at Alena, still staring out the windshield at the flight school, I knew it scared her, too.

"We can find another way," I said.

She shook her head, then shook it again, more vehemently, resolving herself. "We're wasting time. I'll see you in Wilmington tomorrow."

She slipped out of the truck cab, letting a gust of cold in to take her place.

"Be smart," I told her.

"Be smart," she agreed.

Then she slammed the door shut and started for the terminal, and I turned the truck towards the Interstate, and tried not to believe that I would never see her again.

Here's what she did:

There were five people in the flight school office, all of them gathered around the television, still watching the live play-by-play of the siege, and all of them past the point of boredom with it. One was a woman, working behind the counter, but the other four were men, the youngest in his early twenties, the oldest perhaps in his mid-fifties. Two were wearing coveralls, clearly maintenance, and so it was the remaining two that Alena focused on even as every eye turned to mark her entrance, and it was the younger of those that she directed her words to, because he would be the most likely to need the opportunity she was about to provide.

"Please," Alena said, and she said it like a local, and not like a woman who was born six thousand miles away. She said it earnestly, and she said it with just enough emotion that everyone could hear it, with the thinness that comes from speaking out of the throat rather than the chest, and that says tears are only a heartbeat away. "Please—are you a pilot?"

"Yes, ma'am," the man said. "Well, almost. Not certified yet. Can I help you?"

"I need to get to Omaha," Alena said, and the tremor in her voice increased, and the tears began to well in her eyes so much that the man looked away, embarrassed for her obvious distress. "I have to get to Omaha tonight, my mamma got hit by a car, I have to get to the hospital to see her. There aren't no flights out of Lynch, I can't get a flight. I asked Sarah, my friend, Sarah, she said I should go to the flight school, she said that if I offered to pay for fuel and the rental and all of that, someone might be able to fly me, someone might need hours and be able to fly me. She says there are always people who need hours and that someone could fly me. Can you fly me?"

"Calm down," the man said. "Just... why don't you sit down, catch your breath."

She snuffled, wiping at her nose with the back of her hand. "Do you need hours? I'll pay for the rental, I will, please. I have to get to Omaha, I have to go tonight."

"Do a good deed, Brian," the woman behind the counter said, her attention already back on the television. "Fly her to Omaha. Get yourself another five hours, at least. Not like you're going to miss anything—they're still waiting for the Feds to show."

"Go on, son, do it," the older man said. "The damsel's in distress."

"Please?" Alena said. "Please, I'm so scared she's going to die. I have to see her, I have to be there for her."

The man, Brian, hesitated for a moment longer, and Alena saw his eyes sweep over her face, and she saw there was no recognition of her in them at all.

"Sure," he said. "I'd be glad to help you, ma'am."

They landed in Omaha just past midnight, local time, taxiing into the charter terminal, and just like at the charter terminal in Lynch, there was no security to speak of, only a bored guard at the door to the tarmac whose job it was to keep unauthorized people out. As with all charter terminals, there was no passenger or baggage screening either going or coming. Alena passed the security guard without earning a second glance, caught the first cab she could, and took it straight to the nearest hotel, where she checked in using her half of the St. Louis identity that Sargenti had provided us.

Once in her room, she used her MacBook to purchase a ticket from Omaha to London that required a change of planes at Washington-Dulles. The flight was scheduled to depart at ten past six that morning. She spent the next three and a half hours watching television coverage of what was happening in Lynch, and determined that what was happening was nothing. As predicted, the authorities in Lynch were playing out the siege by the book, and that meant waiting us out through the long, cold night. The Feds would assume command in the morning, and shortly thereafter determine the rooms were empty.

Alena watched until she had to leave for the airport, checking out at twenty past four. She was in her economy-class seat at forty minutes past five. She was still wearing the cowboy hat.

She reached the Wilmingtonian Hotel in Wilmington, North Carolina, shortly after one that afternoon, driving the rental car she had picked up at the airport outside of Washington, D.C. She parked in the lot, entered the lobby, and found that Sargenti had done as she had asked and as she had expected, and that there was a room waiting for herself and her husband.

She also found that the man listed as her husband had yet to check in.

Here's what I did:

It took me until just past eleven to reach a truck stop that I liked the looks of, outside of Casper. I parked the pickup at the far end of the lot, out of the lights. In exchange for the flannel shirt, cowboy hat, and lipstick that Alena had taken, I left behind our makeshift bed linen rope and the pistols we'd been carrying, hiding them in one bundle wedged beneath the seat bench. I took a couple of minutes to give the interior a wipe-down before abandoning the pickup.

The drive had been unpleasant, filled with a rare fear, physically intense, that seemed to rise from the groin and race along the spine. I didn't want to lose Alena, and I couldn't help but sense that, somehow, someway, I already had. I kept the radio on the entire drive, bouncing from AM station to AM station in search of news, and even though the situation in Lynch seemed to remain the same, it gave me no comfort.

Once inside the truck stop, I rented myself a shower and a rack, and bought myself a pack of disposable razors and a can of Gillette shaving cream. Under the water, I shaved my head, but left the stubble that had been growing on my face alone. It took me three of the razors and a lot of time, mostly because, on top of everything else, I was afraid of taking a slice out of my scalp.

After I'd finished, I dressed in the last of the clean clothes from my bag, then found one of the multiple banks of pay phones and started calling airlines. Twenty-two minutes later, I was booked on a flight from Casper to Amsterdam, via Minneapolis and then Dulles. I got myself a bite of something that tasted remarkably like wood, then spent a couple minutes going through the offerings in the gift shop, where I purchased a cowboy hat of my own and a new jacket. The jacket was blue denim, with a bald eagle flying against an American flag embroidered brightly on the back.

Then I hit my rented rack and tried to get some sleep, and instead proceeded to have one of the worst nights of my life.

Every noise outside was a threat. Time and again I started awake at the sound of a laugh, or a voice, or a door slamming closed, or a horn sounding at the pumps. My mind wandered, refusing to focus, refusing to surrender to sleep. Over and over again, I found myself wondering what the hell I thought I was doing. Over and over again, I found myself doubting my commitment to the course I'd chosen. Over and over again, I worried about Alena, about her progress and her safety.

And over and over, I would close my eyes, and I would see Natalie Trent, lying on her blanket of leaves.

At six that morning I called myself a cab to the airport then wandered through the gift shop again while waiting for it to arrive, trying to get a look at the television there and the latest news. What I saw surprised me. Apparently, there had been no change in the standoff in Lynch.

That was no longer the case by the time I reached the airport, and I was on my way to the security checkpoint when I caught sight of yet another ubiquitous television, this one in a food court. On the screen, men in tactical gear and full body armor were finally storming the hotel. I glanced at my watch, and realized it had been just over twelve hours since I'd hung up on Bobby Galloway for the last time.

They'd played it by the book.

I was showing my St. Louis ID and my ticket to the TSA agent at the security checkpoint while, one hundred and sixty miles away, the door to our hotel room was being smashed down. While they were clearing the hotel room and securing the perimeter around the Outlaw Inn, I was settling into my seat. Somewhere, somebody with a badge was putting two plus two together, and coming up with a stolen pickup truck.

By the time I was changing planes in Minneapolis, the news was reporting that the truck had been found in a lot outside of Casper. Someone on the screen speculated that Danielle and Christopher Morse could be almost anywhere by now, and asked the audience to be vigilant, and report any possible sightings. If I'd been anywhere else, I might have abandoned my track then and there, gone for an alternate route. But I'd made the first connection, and the way airports work, I was already behind the security screen. I walked from my arrival to my departure gate without incident, the only attention drawn due to my spectacularly embroidered jacket.

It was twenty-seven hours and fourteen minutes after I'd left Alena at the airport in Lynch before I saw her again. When she opened the door to the suite at the Wilmingtonian, I saw in her expression that she'd felt the time as acutely as I had. I came through the door, dropping my bag as she threw the locks, and when she turned back to me I was ready for her, and I took her in my arms without a word.

I was content just to hold onto her for a very long time, then.

She was content to let me.

PART FOUR

CHAPTER ONE

I slept late into the next morning, my body greedy to make up for the rest I'd denied it over the last day and a half. By the time I got up it was working towards noon, the sun was shining, and there was no snow to be seen anywhere when I stepped out onto the balcony of our suite at the Wilmingtonian Hotel.

I was profoundly grateful for that.

Alena had already gone out, leaving a note asking that I stay put, and adding that she would return no later than one that afternoon. There was plenty of room in the suite, so I did yoga for half an hour before climbing into the shower to the accompaniment of the television. The yoga served as a self-diagnostic of a sort, and I was pleased to see that everything on me appeared to be in working order. The bruises were still lingering, and there was a new one on my hip from the fall I'd taken on the ice in Lynch, but that was all. Alena, I had noted the previous evening, had a companion bruise of her own, but on the right hip, not the left.

The television was a different education altogether. After some hunting, I settled it onto CNN, and waited for the Montana Terrorists story to come back for an update as I worked through my poses. It was taking a while, and that struck me as odd, and I didn't think it was because I was being vain. Two fugitives with an unspecified amount of ricin in their possession should have ranked pretty high in the Top Stories list; instead, we were buried halfway through the cycle. When they did finally get to talking about us, what they had to say surprised me, and I turned in the pose I was holding to give the screen my full attention.

There had been developments, but not the developments I'd expected. Given Lynch, I'd have thought the media play would have been pure hyperbolic fear, insistent and foreboding, with plenty of informative pieces about how to protect yourself from exposure to ricin and the like. Instead, there was confusion and frustration, and an odd lack of anxiety, and it took the anchor cutting to a new talking head before I began to get an explanation.

"According to sources at the Pentagon," the anchor said, "the search for the Montana Two has now been suspended."

"That's what we're hearing, though federal authorities are refusing to confirm."

"How could they make a mistake like this, Jim?"

"Well, it's important to remember, Laura, there's a lot that goes on that the general public simply isn't privy to. Remember, one of the nine-eleven hijackers had his visa renewed fully three weeks after the plane he'd been on went down—that's three weeks *after* his body had been identified. So it's difficult to say. This may be a simple matter of a misidentification, or something else entirely. But it happens more often than you might think. I could regale you with story after story of this kind of thing. The real tragedy here is what it does to the people involved—"

"Danielle and Christopher Morse, in this case."

"—yes, the alleged suspects. This has to have turned their lives completely upside down. We're now hearing that they were never even in Lynch, that law enforcement there responded to a tip that later proved to be entirely unsubstantiated."

"No word, then, that the Morses are in custody at this time?"

"Again, Laura, the Feds are saying no, but what we're hearing unofficially from the Pentagon is yes. Take your pick."

"And meanwhile, there's news of this new cell—"

"Yes, Al-Qaeda of North America, apparently. This emerged last night, that intelligence agency officials believe that what happened outside of Glacier National Park in Montana was actually the work of four Syrian nationals who had come over the border from Canada. And that it's actually this group that may be in possession of the ricin. Obviously, every effort is being made to find and apprehend these men."

"Really is extraordinary," Laura the anchor said, turning back to address the camera and shaking her head with bemusement.

She wasn't the only one, though I was more troubled than amused.

Alena returned as I was running the razor over my face, trimming my stubble in an attempt to shape what was growing into a beard that would, hopefully, do something to conceal my features. I didn't like growing the beard; in another couple of days it would start to itch, I knew that from experience, and I'd have to fight myself to keep from scratching constantly at my neck. Still, there didn't seem to be much of a choice in the matter.

Even if I could believe what I'd seen on the television, my face would still be getting far more attention than it deserved or I desired.

It wasn't the first time my face had been seen nationally. The last time it had happened, I'd become famous, albeit briefly. Five years later, almost, it was happening again, but the fame was now infamy. I wondered how long it would last this time.

Alena had bought more clothes, and I picked through the selections she'd made for me, getting dressed, telling her about what I'd seen on the news. It earned an arching of an eyebrow and a brief pursing of the lips.

"Very interesting."

"Someone's throwing up a roadblock for us."

"You were in the Army. Could it be someone you know from those days, someone now at the Pentagon?"

"No way. Even if I knew people in the E-Ring, which I don't. This is something else."

"Someone doing us a favor."

"Nothing's for free. They're doing us a favor, they'll want one in return." I pulled on the latest in what was becoming an endless stream of new blue jeans. She'd picked three shirts for me, as well, all of them plain, no logo, no slogans, one in white, one in blue, and one in green. I went with the green. My shoes, at least, hadn't needed to be replaced. "I don't want to think about what we spend on clothes."

"You think it's bad for you, it costs two to three times as much for me," Alena said.

I finished tucking myself in, then asked, "We have weapons?"

"The nearest cache from here is in Philadelphia. Clearing it would take too long."

"We might want to do something about that. Whether or not we're still number one with a bullet on the nation's Most Wanted list, I don't want to risk running into any more shooters working for Gorman-North."

Her expression tightened, and she shook her head slightly. "I tried reaching Dan this morning when I went out. I didn't get a response, Atticus."

"Vadim?"

"Nothing."

I thought about what the reporter and the pundit had been saying. "They've been picked up."

"I think that's likely. Where and when and by whom I do not know. Before I returned to you, I was inclined to believe it would be federal agents who had taken them in. Now, I am unsure. In either case, we must operate on the premise that one of them, if not both, are in custody."

"Would he talk?"

"Dan, you mean?"

I nodded.

"Not on his life, and not simply because of any fear or loyalty he might feel for either of us. It would be a point of pride to him."

"There's a lot of pressure they could bring to bear to convince him to change his mind. Especially if they have Vadim in custody."

"No, you misunderstand," Alena said. "He doesn't *want* to talk. Given the choice, he'll take their worst. He thinks of it as proving himself."

"To who?"

"God only knows," Alena said. "He's always been like that. Most of the *spesnaz* I dealt with seemed to feel they hadn't earned their place unless they'd been wounded or tortured first."

"If they've got Vadim . . ."

"He's younger, I don't know about him." She shook her head. "We will learn soon enough, I think."

The news sobered me, took the last of the joy I had been feeling at being reunited with her and turned it to air. Despite the sleep, I felt suddenly tired, and on that came another desire, almost childlike in its simplicity: I wanted to go home. I wanted to go back to Kobuleti, back to the house and Miata. The want didn't last for long, just long enough to make itself known to me, and then it was chased away with the knowledge that, much as I might want it, it wasn't going to happen, not as things stood now. It probably would never happen again.

Montana had changed the game, and if the cabin in the woods hadn't proven it, what had followed in Lynch sure as hell did, and the developments on the news made it even clearer. The further we went, it seemed, the less we knew, and instead of being manipulated by one force—presumably whoever it was who so badly wanted us dead—there was now a new player who maybe didn't. Or wanted something else from us entirely. There were strings being pulled that we not only couldn't see, we couldn't even begin to understand.

We weren't in over our heads. We were already under and about to lose our last breath. There was no getting off this ride until it ended.

"What are you thinking?" Alena asked me.

"Honestly?"

"Of course honestly."

"I'm thinking about the end to *Butch Cassidy and the Sundance Kid,* that's what I'm thinking."

She managed a smile. "I thought we were Bonnie and Clyde."

"Take your pick, they both end the same way."

The smile faded. "If we go, we go together."

There was nothing much more to say after that.

CHAPTER TWO

Louis Woodburn wore khaki slacks and a faded yellow shirt, and a tan that could only have come from a bottle or a bed. He didn't wear a tie.

Alena and I watched as he made his way over to us from behind his desk at Cape Fear Marine and Yachts, which was about as straightforward a name of a business as one could ask for. The receptionist who had beckoned Woodburn over, a busty blonde with lipstick the color of a stoplight, made the introductions.

"Louis, this is Miranda and Simon Cole," she said. "Apparently, they've been referred to you."

"Really?" Woodburn's face lit with unexpected pleasure. "Wonderful! What can I do for the two of you?"

"He wants to buy a yacht," Alena said. It came out flat, as if she was indulging her husband, but only barely.

"Well, that's what we sell here, yachts." Woodburn smiled

brightly at me, then at Alena. “You don’t sound convinced, Mrs. Cole.”

“I think they’re awfully expensive.”

“Some of them can be very reasonable, you’d be surprised. And you can’t forget it’s a great investment.” He leaned forward slightly, lowering his voice, his Carolinian drawl thickening slightly. “And, depending on your accountant and your business, a hell of a write-off.”

“See, that’s what I mean,” I said to Alena. “It’s an investment.”

“Exactly,” Woodburn said, taking a step back towards his desk, and motioning us to follow him. “Why don’t we take a seat, look at some of the brochures, figure out what you’re looking for. There are a lot of choices. Would either of you like something to drink? Iced tea, bottled water?”

“Bottled water.” Alena sniffed. “Still water, not bubbling.”

“Nothing for me,” I said.

Louis Woodburn ushered us to the leather-upholstered chairs opposite his desk, then went off, presumably to find Alena a bottle of still water. I took another glance around the showroom, at the shiny displays and brightly colored posters. There were two other salespeople working at nearby desks, and an older couple browsing one of the catalogues. I suspected this was the off-season for yacht sales.

Woodburn returned with a bottle of Evian, which he was wiping down with a paper towel as he approached. He handed it over to Alena with all the ceremony of a sommelier presenting the pride of his cellar, then took his seat behind the desk. I put him on the cusp of fifty, and despite his exuberance—or perhaps precisely because of it—he seemed to be taking to it well. If the ring on his finger and the photographs on his desk were to be believed, he was currently on his second, or perhaps even his third marriage.

“So, what kind of vessel are you thinking about? Something

like a Funship, or maybe something in the cruiser line? The Four Winns Vista series are excellent yachts, perfect for entertaining or for entertainment." He shuffled the papers on his desk, searching for brochures, beginning to lay them out before the two of us. "There's also the Cruisers Yachts line. I highly recommend looking at those. They're manufactured right here on the Cape Fear River. They're really the yacht of choice."

I extended my hand, and he filled it with one of the brochures.

"What size are you looking at?" Woodburn asked.

"Twenty-eight feet," Alena said.

"Closer to fifty," I said, examining the brochure.

Alena lowered her bottle of water and shot me a glare. "That's not what you said earlier."

"Let's see what he's offering," I told her, then turned to Woodburn. "The problem is, Miranda doesn't have an idea what we're talking about. She's got horrible spatial perception."

"Simon!"

"C'mon, it's true, honey, you know that. Admit it, you don't have the first idea between a fifty-footer and a yacht that's twenty-eight feet."

"Twenty-two feet," she said.

Woodburn laughed softly, and he was good, because he made it clear he was appreciating Alena's wit, and not the reproach that had come with it.

"It's a significant twenty-two feet," he said. "But, yes, it's certainly hard when you're dealing in the abstract like this."

"Twenty-eight feet, there's not a lot of room below," I told Alena. "Not like you're going to want."

"Tell you what," Woodburn said. "Let's go take a walk around the shop and the service department, you can see the different sizes. We can't really go aboard them, of course, but that way you can get a better picture of the kind of scale we're talking about."

"That's a great idea," I said, and got to my feet, Woodburn following suit. We both looked at Alena expectantly.

She sighed, and then, with convincing reluctance, got to her feet.

We let him do his song and dance for much of the next hour, following Louis Woodburn as he escorted us through the service shop, listening attentively as he pointed out the amenities on this model, the appointments on that one. He played more to Alena than to me, though he never forgot I was there, and Alena did a good job of allowing herself to be won over, little by little. By the time we'd finished with the tour, it was nearly four in the afternoon, and Alena was even laughing at Woodburn's jokes.

On our way back to the sales office, Alena said to me, "Jake was right. He's very good."

She indicated Woodburn, less for my benefit than to make certain he knew who we were talking about.

"Yeah, he was, wasn't he?" I agreed. "I'll have to thank him for the recommendation."

"Let's wait until we actually buy one of them," Alena said.

"Jake?" Woodburn asked.

"Our friend who recommended we come talk to you," I told him. "Jacob Collins."

He was smooth about it, and very quick, which I supposed was what made him so ideal as a contact person. "No kidding? Now, that's funny. That's . . . that's funny."

"Why do you say that?"

"I haven't talked to Jake in quite a while." Louis Woodburn checked his watch, then added, "Aw, Christ, I didn't realize how late it had gotten. I'm sorry, Mr. Cole, Mrs. Cole, I'm going to have to cut this short. My stepdaughter has a softball game I need to attend. Let me hand you off to one of my associates, how about that?"

"We were enjoying dealing with you," Alena said.

"I appreciate that, I really do, but I have to go." He smiled at us, and it was almost the same smile he'd been using before, but not quite. I wasn't reading fear in it, but instead something closer to confusion, perhaps mixed with a mild alarm. He reached out for my hand, gave it a firm and practiced shake, then nodded to Alena, and then he was heading for his car parked outside the sales office, a silver Cadillac, one of the new models.

We watched the Caddie pull onto Market Street and disappear into traffic.

"So, if he's still your guy, he does what now?" I asked Alena. "Calls the latest number Sargenti sent him and says that Miranda and Simon Cole came by?"

"Most likely."

"His reaction seem odd to you?"

"In what way?"

"I don't know. Like maybe we weren't the first people to actually mention Mr. Jacob Collins to him in person recently. Instead of, for instance, over the phone."

Alena nodded slowly. "We should head back to the hotel. I'll call Nicolas, tell him to check the box and report back to us."

We headed to where we'd parked our rental, and I took the wheel and started us back in the direction of the river and the hotel. I checked the mirrors a couple times, and twice I thought that maybe we were being followed by a blue BMW, but then I thought that maybe I was being overly paranoid. Market was pretty much a long, straight shot back into downtown, and while there were plenty of places to turn off of it, it was heavily traveled, and the BMW certainly wasn't the only car that seemed to be heading in our direction.

That's what I told myself, at least, until we'd parked back in the lot of the Wilmingtonian and I was out of the car and Alena was joining me.

"The car at four o'clock," she said, not indicating it in the slightest. "That car was behind us all the way here."

It had parked some sixty feet away, and there was a man getting out of the vehicle, and already I didn't like what I was seeing. It wasn't that he was big, certainly no taller than either Alena or myself, but there was something in his carriage that reminded me immediately of Dan. As he turned towards us I saw his right hand going into his jacket, and I liked that even less. If he was going for a gun, we weren't going to be able to do much but run or bleed. But the hand came out as smoothly and quickly as it had gone in, and there was no gun in it that I could see as he continued on his line towards us.

I put a hand on Alena's back, turning her and myself towards one of the five buildings that made up the Wilmingtonian Hotel, and, specifically, the suite we'd taken.

"Coming up from behind."

"So you give him our back?" Alena muttered.

"I want you inside," I said.

"You're being a fool."

She stopped and turned around and so I did, too.

The man had closed to about twenty feet. Both of his hands were visible, at his sides, but he was focused on us, and as we faced him he called out, saying, "Pardon me, I beg your pardon." He had a deep voice, not quite from the gravel at the bottom of the quarry, but not many feet above it, either.

"Can I help you?" I asked.

He slowed his approach, easing off and giving first Alena, then me, a quick eyeballing. His expression wasn't hostile, but it wasn't in neutral, either. Wary, perhaps. His skin had the rich warmth of a good tan or a Mediterranean heritage, and given the absolute black of his hair and the deep brown of his eyes, I was leaning to the latter. Maybe Italian extraction, more likely Sicilian. He was wearing khakis, with a black T-shirt under his open coat, and the coat itself was almost the same brown of his eyes, and thin, as if optimistic at the promise of spring. When I checked his feet, I saw he was wearing boots rather than sneakers or loafers, and that the boots had a squared toe. The clip to a folding knife hung over the lip of his left front pants pocket.

He was military, or he had been, and I wondered for a moment if this wasn't another of Sean's friends.

"You dropped this," he said to me, and then he closed the rest of the distance, extending his right hand.

"I don't think so."

"Yeah," he said. "You did."

Then he showed me what he was holding in his hand.

It was a picture of Natalie Trent.

CHAPTER THREE

His name was John Panno, at least according to his driver's license and the business card he showed us when we got into our suite. The license had been issued by the State of Maryland. The business card had come from a firm calling itself Phoenix Resource Consultancy. Apparently, Phoenix Resource Consultancy didn't have a street address, just an e-mail address and a phone number. I didn't recognize the area code on the phone number.

"Another fucking contractor," I said, handing the card back to him. In my other hand, I was holding the photograph of Natalie.

"PRC is not Gorman-North," he said, easily.

"No, it's the People's Republic of China. You might want to change your name."

"Eight fucking months I've been watching Cape Fear Marine and Yachts. Eight months waiting for one of you to make contact with Louis Woodburn. Eight. Fucking. Months. You couldn't have maybe connected the dots a little sooner?"

I turned the photograph of Natalie in my hand. It had a date written on the back in script, and it wasn't Natalie's handwriting. If my memory was right, the date would've been roughly around the time we'd gone into business together. I flipped it around once more, examining the picture. It was a candid, reduced to wallet-size, caught while she was grinning at someone who wasn't the photographer.

I set the photo on the antique coffee table in the center of the sitting room portion of our suite, then stared at Panno, seated on the couch beyond it. He returned the stare evenly, as if telling me that whatever I might have thought of myself, he wasn't impressed.

"The picture got you in the door," I said. "Doesn't get you farther than that."

"How far do I need to go?" he asked. "Considering that you've got most of the law enforcement in the country coming down on your ass at this very moment, I mean."

Alena, seated to the side in one of the high-backed easy chairs, leaned forward. "You've been waiting eight months, you say. Why here?"

"It's where he told me to look." Panno hadn't moved his gaze from me.

"Who?"

"Who do you think?" He flicked his eyes to the photograph, then back to me. "Her father."

From the corner of my eye, I saw Alena look to me for verification.

"It's possible," I told her. "Elliot Trent was Secret Service before he started Sentinel. He even worked the presidential detail at one point. He has connections in D.C.—intelligence, military—

and I'd be surprised if some of them weren't at a high enough level that they could have dug up the protocol for him."

Panno shook his head slightly. "You don't know anything about him, do you?"

"I know enough."

"Trent was Army Intelligence before he went to Treasury. He's got more connections than you have hairs on your ass."

I glanced at Alena. "See, it's the sophisticated level of conversation you get from soldiers that makes me miss the Army most."

"He wants to talk to you," Panno said.

"Me alone or the both of us?"

"You, specifically, though the conditional was that, if she was with you, she was to come along."

"He retired," I said. "Trent. He sold Sentinel, packed it in."

"Last year. He had another heart attack. He's had three since she died. He's not going to run much longer."

The news bothered me, more than I would have expected. There was no love lost between me and Elliot Trent; there never had been, and I knew that there never would be. But the knowledge that he was dying brought a deeper sadness than I'd have imagined. He'd lost his wife, he'd lost his daughter, he'd given up his business. What else was there for him to do now but die?

Except, apparently, hire a contractor from an organization I'd never even heard of before to watch Cape Fear Marine and Yachts in the hopes that we would, one day, show up. If Panno wasn't exaggerating, if he'd really been on the job for eight months, that was quite a feat; someone should have noticed him, and if no one had, he'd done it very well, indeed.

I decided he had to be exaggerating, and turned away from him and Alena, running a hand over my mostly bare scalp. New hair was already coming in, and it felt like needles against my palm.

"Mr. Trent wants to talk to you, Kodiak. I'm supposed to take you to him."

"What does he know?" I asked, turning back and pointing to the picture of Natalie, resting faceup on the coffee table. "About how she died?"

"Almost all of it," Panno said. "It's taken him the better part of three years, but he's got almost all of it, now, from Gorman-North on up."

"He knows who bought it? Who put it into motion?"

"He knows that you were involved." John Panno tilted his head slightly to include Alena. "Her, too."

None of us spoke for a second.

"He hates your guts," Panno added. Then he smiled a smile that said based on that endorsement alone, he was going to, as well. "I mean, he *really* hates your guts."

"Yet he still wants to talk to me."

"Like I said."

"About?"

"That's for him to say."

"Where is he now?"

"He's got a house near Peden Point, maybe ten, fifteen miles away. He came here about a month after sending me down to watch for the two of you. Wanted to be close by if you finally showed up."

Panno waited a moment, to see if either Alena or I had any further questions, though I suspect, if we'd had, he wouldn't have answered them. Then he leaned forward, scooping the photograph in his right hand, making it vanish beneath the breadth of his palm. There was damage to his knuckles, scarring from one or more punches that had hit teeth, perhaps, rather than jaw. He slid the photograph carefully back into the inside pocket of his jacket, then got to his feet.

"I'll take you to him," John Panno told us.

Alena was staring at a point on the carpet, her brow furrowed. She glanced up to him, then moved the look to me, and I could see she was more puzzled than curious. Her association with Trent was negligible, and her only dealings with the man had left her unimpressed. It was Natalie she had bonded with. It was Natalie who might have become her friend if she had lived.

"Come on," Panno said. There wasn't impatience in his voice, just the command. "He knows you're here. I've already called him. He's expecting you."

"All right," I said, giving Alena my hand and helping her out of the chair. "Let's go see just how much Elliot Trent hates me."

CHAPTER FOUR

Elliot Trent hated me quite a bit, it turned out. I knew this, because the first thing he said to me was, "You don't deserve to be alive."

He said it softly, and he said it with conviction, and he said it in my face, and when I didn't respond immediately, he repeated it.

"You don't deserve to be alive," Elliot Trent said.

The last four years or so since I'd seen him hadn't been kind, and Panno was right: It was the last three of them that had really done the trick. He still stood ramrod straight, still had the head of steel-gray hair, the same eyes, but they were sunken now, in a complexion that had gone sallow, and that beneath the porch light of his beach house home verged on jaundice. New lines had multiplied from the old on his face, and the sunken eyes, while still sharp, were shot through with broken veins. They burned with ferocity and hatred, and they dared me to answer him, and since what he had said to me twice now was probably very true, I didn't respond.

He grunted, contemptuous, then turned and led the way for Alena and me to follow into the house. Panno took up the rear, and like everything else he'd done, there was nothing threatening to it other than his position.

As if Alena and I would have agreed to come this far only to make a break for it at the last moment.

Trent led us down a hallway, turning off into an open sitting room that afforded a view of the beach through three large bay windows. The walls had that whitewash-plank feel to them, the trim along the windowsill painted in a moss green. Everything in the décor and coloration should have been cheerful, but instead it felt melancholic, the way beach houses always do. There was a desk against one wall with a PC, switched on, and shoved beneath it was a plastic milk crate stuffed full of papers. Two framed photographs flanked the computer on either side, and at first I thought both were of Natalie, then realized only one was; the other was a portrait of his late wife.

Trent moved into the room, then turned, staying on his feet. He motioned to the various seating options, the easy chairs and the love seat, then put his attention on Panno.

"There's chili on the stove, get some food in you."

"We feeding them?"

Trent snorted.

Panno left the room the same way we'd entered it, leaving Alena and me standing at its entrance. Trent waited another few seconds, then repeated the refrain for a third time.

"You don't deserve to be alive." This time, I was sure that, along with me, he was including Alena in the declaration.

The view from the windows was spectacular. The house was off a street called Loder Avenue, and I could look out the windows and see the darkening beach in the sunset, the barrier islands disappearing beyond in the diminishing light. Come hurricane season, Trent would have a front-row seat.

Alena surprised me by speaking up, saying, "I am sorry for the loss of your daughter, Mr. Trent."

Trent's mouth worked slightly, as if he was searching for his teeth with his tongue.

"Was it your bullet?" he demanded. "Is that what you're trying to say to me, it was your bullet that killed her?"

"We didn't kill Natalie," I said.

"Yes, you did." It was a growl. "You didn't shoot her, but you sure as hell did kill her."

"You're wrong," I said. "And if you think that I had the power to make Natalie do anything she didn't want to do, you're deluding yourself. She went her own way, and she always did. She walked away from you and Sentinel. If she had wanted to, she would have walked away from me, too."

"But she didn't." Trent glared at me. "She chose you over me, and you let her die."

I should have let it pass. He was her father, and it was his grief, and if anyone was entitled to rage at the injustice of it all, it was Elliot Trent.

"No," I said. "You don't get to accuse us of that, me of that. You've got your guilt because you think you drove her away, you lost her, you're welcome to it. You earned it. You don't like me, fine, you never have. You hate me—fine, maybe I've earned that, too. But I don't own Natalie's death, and neither does Alena, and if that's what you've been waiting eight months or three years or all your goddamn life to say, then we're done here."

I turned my back on him, started out into the hall. After a fraction, I heard Alena moving to follow me.

"Don't you leave," Trent said.

I didn't stop.

His voice was hoarse, and pained with the strain of the volume he put upon it. "Dammit, Atticus, don't leave!"

Panno had appeared in the hallway to my left, coming out of the kitchen. He'd removed his jacket, and I saw that his T-shirt was actually a muscle shirt, missing its sleeves. There was light from the archway, and it spilled out, and I could make out a tattoo on his upper arm, a Chinese dragon in faded color. He had a bowl of his dinner in one hand, was eating a spoonful of it with the other. He didn't look like he was going to try to stop us.

"You don't blame me for that," I said, without looking back at Trent. "You don't blame Alena, and you don't blame me."

Behind me, I heard the creak of a chair, the sound of him taking a seat.

"No," he said, and he sounded as tired as I'd felt this same morning. "No, all right. That's fair."

I turned, and Alena and I moved back into the sitting room. Trent tracked us as we came back, then indicated the love seat. Alena took it, and I followed.

"It's hard to remember that she was precious to people other than me," Elliot Trent said. "And it's difficult to accept that she was precious to people I dislike as much as the two of you."

"Just had to throw that in there, didn't you?" I said.

"I'm not going to pretend." He pointed at Alena with his right index finger, as if trying to stab her in the heart. "She's a murdering bitch, and you're her partner now, or so they say. Even if you weren't, I know what you did for her, I've learned that much, at least. She's a killer, no matter how she tries to change her stripes, and now you're one, too. Two of The Ten, sitting side by side in front of me. If you think I like that, it's you who's delusional, not me."

Beside me, Alena didn't move. She wasn't looking at him, instead focused on the view out the bay windows. The room felt like it was growing darker, despite the lamps that burned on the wall and in the corner.

"You've gone to a lot of time and a lot of trouble to speak with us, Mr. Trent," Alena said. "Perhaps you'd like to come to your point?"

"In a moment. Given the time and the trouble I've taken, I'm allowed an indulgence or two. I've been waiting for this for almost three years."

"Panno said it was eight months," I said.

"*This* has been eight months, since the only thing I had left to go on was Drama's 'Mr. Collins' bullshit."

"And before then, Elliot?"

"Why did you come back?" he demanded, and it was as hostile as anything he had said to us before. "You and Drama, you were gone. No one would have ever found you. You could have stayed hidden until your sins finally found your address, you could have died from old age before anybody knew you were still even alive. Why did you come back, Atticus?"

"I had something to do."

"And is it done, now? Have you done it? While you were killing Matthew Bowles in Montana and wrapping the Lynch PD's pants around their fucking ankles, have you managed to do what you set out to do?"

"Not yet."

"Because you don't know how. Do you? You're missing that one little piece you need, and you haven't the first idea where to find it."

I stared at him, trying not to hope that he had what Bowles had died without sharing.

"We want the same thing," Elliot Trent said. "We want the son of a bitch who murdered my daughter dead."

■ ■ ■

Panno returned, wiping his mouth with the back of one hand, carrying a bottle of Budweiser in the other. He took the chair at the desk, turning it so he could watch the three of us while we spoke. Outside, night had dropped the curtain, and when there was silence in the room, all of us could hear the sound of the waves on the beach.

"Explain him," I said to Trent after Panno had settled himself.

"John's the son of a friend," he said. "He's going to help you out."

"We don't want his help."

"You're getting it whether you want it or not. I don't care how good she is, how good you think you are, you're going to need his help. He's got connections, he's my man on this, and the trouble you're in at the moment, you need both those things."

"Just give me the name," I said. "I'll handle the rest."

He laughed at me. "Simple as that, huh?"

"Simple as that."

"No." Trent shook his head. "You think if it was that simple, I'd need you? I'd need *her*? You don't have the first idea who you're going after."

"He's in the White House."

Trent reacted to that, mildly surprised. Panno gave a slight shake of his head.

"And that doesn't scare you?" Trent asked. "That doesn't make you pause? What if I told you it was the President of the United States, Kodiak? What if that was the name I gave to you? Would you still be so full of yourself, so damn stupid, you'd take that on?"

"Is it?" I asked.

He laughed again, in spite of the pain it caused him. "No, we're not going to work like that. I don't want favors from you. The last thing I want is you doing me a favor. I'm hiring you and your girlfriend there for this. I'm paying you. What's the rate?"

Now it was my turn to shake my head. "Elliot—"

"Dammit, what's the rate?"

"It depends on the target," Alena interposed softly. "If we're talking about the President of the United States, you don't have that kind of money. Nobody does."

"It doesn't go that high."

"I'm somewhat relieved," I said.

"Don't worry," Trent said. "What I've got for you will still shrink your balls to acorns."

"So give me the name."

"How much?" Trent asked. He directed it at Alena.

"As I said, more information is required before that can even be discussed."

"I want to do this right. The way it's supposed to be done. What happens now? We've made contact, what happens next? You vet me, right?"

Alena hesitated, glancing to me as if to check for my permission to continue. I didn't move my eyes from Trent.

"Yes," she said. "The next step would be to verify that you are sincere. And that you are not setting us up."

"You do that how? General surveillance? Background check?"

"That and more. But in this case it is unnecessary. You have already demonstrated your sincerity."

"Have I?"

"You once protected the President of the United States, Mr. Trent. No man who has done that job would even dream of joking about trying to assassinate him. It would be inconceivable to even suggest such a thing. Simply joking about the solicitation of such an act is a federal offense. Yet here we are, and you are ex-Secret Service, and you are talking about this to us here, now, in front of a witness. You are more than sincere, Mr. Trent. You may be insane."

Trent's expression changed, like someone was tugging its corners like smoothing the sheet on a hospital bed, and he lost his focus on her for a moment, considering her words. I had no doubt in the truth of what Alena had just said, though I hadn't consciously realized just how enormous a sin Trent was committing. For a moment, it seemed that Trent hadn't, either.

He got out of his chair, and he did it awkwardly, and it made me wonder if he'd had bypass surgery, and if so how many times, and how recently. At first, I thought he was heading to Panno, but then I realized he was after the shrine to his lost family. He picked up the photograph of his wife, staring at it for several seconds before setting it carefully back precisely where it had rested.

"You don't have children, do you?" He turned to look at us, on the love seat. "The two of you, wherever it is that you've been hiding, you haven't started breeding?"

"No," I said, and Alena glanced over at me, probably wondering why I'd bothered to even answer the question.

"Then you can't understand. You cannot possibly begin to understand. We're talking about my daughter, my only child, and the man who murdered her. We're talking about the life that her mother and I created between us. Our child. When Maggie died, I had Natalie and that was all. Breast cancer's genetic, you know that? It's not the only risk factor, but it's probably the most major one. There were times I'd look at Natalie and I swear my heart would stop at the fear of it growing inside her, too.

"You know how you can tell a real parent, Kodiak? It's not biological. I don't give a damn if you've adopted or warded or fostered, that's not it. You know how you can tell? It's a simple test, really. Doesn't take much to prove it.

"A parent would give anything, do anything, to keep his child from harm, to spare his child pain. That's what it means to be a parent. It means that the life of your child is more important than your own."

He stopped speaking, focused now on me, making certain I understood.

"If there was any chance the law would take the man responsible for what happened to her, I would let the law do just that," Trent said. "But the law won't. The law will never touch him, because he's protected himself from it. He's wrapped himself in it and then elevated himself high above it. He's not alone in that. There are a lot of them like that in Washington, there always have been, but these days I swear to God it's worse.

"That's why I want the two of you. We're at war here, the fucking country's at war, and there are bastards like this man more concerned with protecting what goes into his pockets than the people he purports to serve."

"I'm not taking your money," I said.

"You will," Elliot Trent told me. "Because I won't give you his name unless you do. I'm buying a murder, and I don't want any of us to have any illusions about it. And I don't want either of you forgetting that you're working for me on this. That's what my money's buying."

Alena moved her hand, resting it on the back of mine. I looked down, saw her long, strong fingers on my own. When I moved my eyes up, she met them with hers, and there was a sorrow in them unlike any I'd seen before, and it was all for me. Even if she forgave herself every other crime she had ever committed, this was the one she knew was coming and the one she would never allow to be absolved. This was what she had done to me.

I looked away from her, to Trent.

"All right," I said. "But we need the name."

"He's the White House chief of staff," Elliot Trent said. "His name is Jason Earle."

CHAPTER FIVE

Jason Earle was born in Point Au Gres, Michigan, the eldest of four children, with three younger sisters. His parents were both deceased. His father had worked in insurance. His mother was a homemaker, and took home the blue ribbon at the county fair for her bread-and-butter pickles thirty-three years in a row, up until the year she died.

I was born in San Francisco, California, the eldest of two children, with a younger brother. My parents and brother, to the best of my knowledge, are still living. My parents are both academics, my father a professor of religion, my mother a professor of English, which goes a long way to explaining how I ended up with a first name like Atticus.

■ ■ ■

Jason Earle grew up in Point Au Gres, with his family. He played football, was on the debate team, and was elected senior class president. He attended the University of Michigan, and graduated third in his class, with a bachelor's degree in economics. It was at Michigan where he first got involved in politics, working on both local and state campaigns.

Upon graduation, he was called up for service, but received a deferment, claiming undue hardship on a dependent; his wife of four and a half months, Victoria, was pregnant. He went to law school instead. Then he ran for the Michigan House of Representatives, and lost.

At twenty-nine, he took a job with Gorman Service Industries, a general service provider for gas and petroleum exploration and extraction. He remained with GSI for eleven years. For four of them, he was their assistant chief legal counsel.

He left to work at the White House, and served as the Deputy Assistant to the Secretary of Energy until that administration was voted out of office. He returned to the private sector, offering his services as a consultant. His services were sought by Northrop Grumman, General Motors, and again by GSI, and more specifically, by Gorman-North, the construction and contracting division of the parent company. He continued to practice law, and began to show an interest in policy and military affairs. He served as an advisor to the Defense Policy Board at the Pentagon.

He returned to the White House in the following administration, and, due in no small part to the number of connections and relationships he had forged in the last two decades, was named Deputy Chief of Staff. He held the position for two and a half years, until the then-chief of staff resigned, at which point he became the National Security Advisor to the Vice President of the United States until the end of the Vice President's term in office.

Again in the private sector, Earle pursued consulting work once more, his services now in wide demand. After three years, during which time he served on advisory commissions to the CIA, the State Department, and the President's Council on Economic Reform, he accepted a job with GSI as their Executive Vice President for Overseas Development and Policy. In this capacity, he also oversaw interests at Gorman-North, including Gorman-North's private military contracts.

He was with GSI when the newly elected President asked him to head his transition team, as a precursor to becoming his chief of staff.

Earle, of course, accepted immediately.

I grew up in Santa Cruz, California, and I ran cross-country, and I did some track, and I tried my hand at soccer and basketball, and I wasn't bad at any of it, but I was never exceptional. The only thing I was voted in high school was "Most Likely to Say the Wrong Thing." I was, in all ways, unremarkable.

Because it had always been assumed I would, I went to college, at Northwestern University. I made it through freshman year, and part of sophomore, and like in high school, I was a good student, at least as far as my GPA was concerned. But, like in high school, I was aimless and bored, and I dropped out in the winter of my second year. I spent the next eight months wandering around Europe, working occasional jobs, before enlisting in the Army back home. My parents, who had barely managed to contain themselves at my departure from higher education, all but disowned me.

I completed basic and AIT, did a turn with the MPs, and then volunteered to go to Fort Bragg and do a new course in what the Special Forces Command was calling "Executive Protection." I completed it well, got my sergeant stripes, and was assigned an officer named Wyatt to protect and to serve. Things got complicated, and when my service was up, I passed on reenlistment, pissing off a wide variety of superiors who felt they had wasted a lot of taxpayer money on my training.

I moved to New York with an Army buddy, we got an apartment in the Village, and I tried to find work as a personal security agent, but everyone else called me a bodyguard. I went to the big firms—like Sentinel Guards, run by Elliot Trent—in search of work, and I got a couple of interviews, but they didn't go well. I was outspoken and probably too full of myself, and my résumé wasn't anything to be crowing about. I ended up working alone most of the time, but every so often I would cross paths with others in the field, and that's how I met Natalie Trent, and that's how we became friends.

I did pretty well as a bodyguard, and worked for a lot of people, some of them worth my time and more of them not. My Army buddy died and Natalie and I had some rough times as a result. I ran into the officer I'd protected in the Army again by running into his daughter first, and that changed my life, and I fell in love, or thought I did, on more than one occasion. I kept on trying to protect people, and a lot of the time I succeeded, and then Natalie and I and a couple of others found ourselves protecting a man from one of The Ten that everyone called John Doe, because no one had a better name for him.

John Doe turned into Drama, and, later, Drama turned into Alena Cizkova.

■ ■ ■

The number of people Jason Earle is responsible for killing, either with tacit approval or by direct order, either deliberately or inadvertently, is unknown. Only two were ever verified to my satisfaction. There are possibly hundreds more, if not thousands.

He is suspected of committing Gorman-North resources to the forcible relocation of six hundred and seventy-three Goajiro Indians in northern Venezuela, in pursuit of an exploration contract given to GSI by the Venezuelan state-owned oil company, Petróleos de Venezuela S.A. The land this particular Goajiro tribe lived on had been ceded to them in a very well publicized treaty with their government, and their refusal to move was understandable.

The story, unsubstantiated, goes that there was some sort of accident upriver, a chemical spill into the water supply for the tribe. Fish died first, and then members of the tribe began to fall ill. Emergency aid workers arrived with uncharacteristic speed, attempting to treat those Goajiro who had already become sick and to secure a new clean-water source for the rest of the tribe. They delivered medicine and bottled water, food and blankets.

Despite their swift arrival, however, almost all of the tribe perished.

From drinking the contaminated water.

Instead of the water in the bottles.

Or maybe what made them sick was the water in the river, and what killed them was the water in the bottles.

The emergency aid workers and their supplies were sourced from Gorman-North.

There's another story, goes like this:

In a country in the dry and hot and fairly sandy part of the world, where there is an awful lot of oil apparently to be found buried not all too deep beneath the ground, GSI had a very large contract to help build the machines that would bring this oil to the surface. They maintained certain fields of pumps and pipes, and they built a little piece of America in the middle of a very Islamic country so they could do their jobs in comfort, and without bringing offense to their hosts through any cultural insensitivity or inadvertent misunderstandings.

And this was well and good for a great number of years, and GSI found themselves making pretty good money as a result of this arrangement.

Then, one day, the Old Prince who was the country's Minister of Oil died, and a New Prince took his place. The New Prince looks around, and cannot help but notice that everywhere his country's oil is coming to the surface, it's coming there through no fault of his own nation. There are a lot of young people in his nation looking for work, and this is their most precious resource, the New Prince reasons, and he announces his intention to end his country's contracts with those foreign service providers who are doing what, he now believes, could be done just as well by his fellow countrymen.

This affects not only GSI, but other companies like it. Needless to say, GSI and the other companies like it are not happy at this news. They feel it's imperative that the New Prince understand the relationship is a mutually beneficial one, and that terminating it would be detrimental to all the parties involved. The New Prince reportedly responds by saying that, while he sees the detriment to their interests, he fails to see it to his own.

Men at GSI and the other companies like it begin to do everything they can to stop the New Prince. They entreat him, and his father, the King, and failing both, then turn to their own governments in the hopes of bringing appropriate political pressure to bear. Nothing works.

Then the New Prince's plane goes down in the desert, and there are no survivors. No one sees the plane go down. It just disappears from radar. There's a lot of desert, and not a scrap of wreckage is ever found.

The concessions remain in place.

Then there's the story about the reporter from *Der Spiegel,* a man named Kurt Hayner.

Herr Hayner, it seems, had asked himself one day just how it was that a certain nation in Central America had been able to suddenly crush a revolutionary movement that had plagued it for almost two decades, and that, in recent months, had begun to gain more and more popular support. How it was that, after years and years of combating these revolutionaries to no appreciable result, the country in question had so quickly solved its problem.

In the course of his investigations, Herr Hayner learned that an envoy from the country in question had paid a visit to certain representatives in Washington, D.C., asking for their assistance. The envoy argued that the revolutionaries in his country certainly would not have a good relationship with the United States as their political ideology was not one the United States approved of, and perhaps, for that reason, the United States might wish to offer some assistance in dealing with the problem.

The answer the envoy received was, at first, not at all what he had hoped for. No, he was told by these representatives, we cannot help you, much as we wish we could. Politically, it's impossible for us to get involved at the present time.

But, they told the envoy, you might wish to talk to someone at Gorman-North.

So the government of the country in Central America paid Gorman-North an immense amount of money to come and "advise" its military on methods to combat the revolutionaries.

This is not what made Herr Hayner a threat. What made him a threat was when he learned just *how* Gorman-North had been "advising." The words "intimidation" and "fear" and "preemptive action" and, most of all, "coercive interrogation techniques" were going to most likely feature very prominently in his piece for *Der Spiegel.*

That made him a threat.

So someone called a man in Wilmington, and asked if he could speak to Jacob Collins. No, the caller was told, I haven't heard from Jake in twenty years, not since high school, I figure. But, hey, what the hell, you can leave your name and a number, and if I bump into him, I'll make sure to give him the message.

Herr Hayner died in a house fire at his home outside of Berlin sixteen days later.

My crimes are yet to be numbered.

CHAPTER SIX

At Trent's insistence, we were staying with him at his home, and his arguments for us doing so were both persuasive and logical. Regardless of what CNN might be reporting, Alena and I were still ranking high in the Most Wanted category, and while we'd made it this far without anyone picking up the trail, there was no reason to push our luck. The last thing Trent wanted, now that he had us, was a sharp-eyed police officer or a concerned citizen with a memory for faces making us as we were moving from point A to point B. For the duration of the planning of the job, at least, we were going to remain his guests. It was, he insisted, one of the things he was paying for, the right to look over our shoulders.

It was his way of dealing with his guilt, I knew, though what, precisely, he felt guilt over was less clear. He knew he'd bought himself a murder, and that couldn't have sat well on his already weakened heart, no matter how much he wanted Natalie's death answered. Or perhaps it may have come from the fact that Alena and I were now his surrogates, commissioned to do the thing he wanted done, but could not himself do.

It didn't matter; we were staying, whether we liked it or not. While unspoken, the implicit threat of what would happen if we refused was perfectly clear.

It was Panno who drew the line from Hayner to Alena, from Alena to Gorman-North, and from Gorman-North to Jason Earle.

Panno had run back to the hotel the previous night to gather our things and check us out, and had gone out again early this morning to chase down the shopping list Alena had prepared. The list wasn't anything fancy, but it had been specific, with the groceries we wanted, the nutritional supplements and the like that she and I both now made a habit of taking. Panno had rolled his eyes when he'd looked over the list.

While he was out, we tried to get some exercise in without actually leaving the house. There was some workout equipment in a sunroom on the first floor, an elliptical trainer and rowing machine, both of them with only the barest signs of use. We did our yoga and then used the machines, and Panno returned from his errands as we were coming up on ninety minutes. Seven minutes after that, according to the timer on the elliptical, he joined us in the sunroom, a cup of coffee in his hand. He walked slowly around us, watching Alena rowing steadily away and me running at a good clip to nowhere. Then he sat on the windowsill in front of us, so we could both see him.

"You killed him," Panno told her. It was a simple statement, devoid of judgment.

"Who are we talking about?" Alena asked. She asked it the way you ask after the health of someone you barely know, as a courtesy, a little breathless from her exertion.

"Kurt Hayner, with *Der Spiegel.* You turned him into a crispy critter."

She continued rowing, staring at a point past his shoulder, then nodded slightly.

"You killed him for Gorman-North," Panno said.

"When was this?" I asked.

"Six years ago," Panno said. He was watching Alena for a reaction, and not finding one. "She toasted him in Berlin, made it look like an electrical fire. Took everything in the house, including his notes."

"Yes." Her expression hadn't changed, nor had the pace of her strokes, and for a moment there was only the clack of our respective machines and the resistances they posed. Panno was watching her exactly as before. Today he was wearing blue jeans and a black T-shirt, and in the daylight, I could make out the details of the dragon living on his upper left arm. The scale work on it was excellent, and it must have taken a lot of ink and a lot of time, and a fair threshold for pain.

On the face of it, the murder of Kurt Hayner gave Jason Earle his motive for wanting Alena, and by extension me, dead. GSI had wanted Hayner dead and Earle had been the head of GSI at the time of the murder. She was carrying knowledge that could certainly destroy Earle and, depending on how it came to light, even collapse the administration in which he served. Knowing that I had been with her for several months, suspecting that she had taken me into her confidence completely, he had added my name to Earle's hit list right beside hers.

It was a motive.

I just wasn't certain it was a very good one, and at this point I knew Alena well enough to see that she didn't, either. Yes, it was possible the truth of Kurt Hayner's death could threaten Earle, but the more I thought about it, the more I realized that was really all it could hurt. The administration would survive it, the way administrations seemed to more and more. Unless there was oral sex involved or photographs or video, the public would let it pass, and the rest of the White House could spin it any way they wanted to; they could disown Earle, fall on him like the proverbial ton of bricks, even ignore it.

That was without considering whether or not Earle could truly be damaged by such an allegation. His reputation would take a hit, certainly, but I couldn't see the man himself facing criminal proceedings. Where was the evidence? It wasn't as if Alena could be relied upon to testify in court about Earle's involvement, assuming he'd been directly involved in commissioning the murder at all.

I tried not to think too much or for too long about Kurt Hayner, whom Alena had taken money to kill for doing his job.

"Doesn't work," I said. The elliptical was on a random hill climb, and I took that moment to raise both the angle and the resistance I was working with. I tried to, literally, take it in stride.

Panno sniffed, squinting at me, as if surprised I had anything to offer. "You don't buy it?"

"This guy may be chief of staff, but he's been burning through favors and money for three-plus years now trying to get at us. That's a huge expense, not just in dollars but in influence. Jesus Christ, first the guy covers up murders in Cold Spring, then he dumps the media on us in Montana? That's not done through official channels, not most of it, at least. It doesn't track. You don't burn that much power just because you're afraid either she or I might go talking about something we probably couldn't prove to begin with."

"You're talking like you know the guy," Panno said. "You don't know the guy."

"I know the job," I said. "I know what the White House chief of staff does, at least in the abstract, and we're talking about a man who's been in that position for nearly seven years, now. Most chiefs of staff make it for, what, two or three? This guy's smart, he's discreet, he's not going to go to these lengths on the basis of something that never would happen."

"You both had heat coming down on you." Panno pointed a finger at Alena. "She had a goddamn book coming out about her. How long you think it was going to be before someone connected the dots?"

"Until the end of time. You hire one of The Ten, one of the things you're buying is their silence. That's assumed, it's part of the contract, or else the whole mechanism falls apart, nothing is ever done. Even if Alena had been taken into custody and interrogated, she never would have copped to the crime, nor named names. Not in a million years."

"I never met with Jason Earle," Alena added. "I would not have been able to indict him directly even had I desire to do so. The job you're speaking of was acquired through the channels. It was delivered by a woman named Audrey Daudin, a Swiss national and private banker. She had many clients, and I was unable to determine which of them I was serving."

From behind us, a voice said, "God, you're both such arrogant fucks, it disgusts me."

Panno grinned. Past him, in the reflection on the window, I could see Trent standing in the doorway behind us. He was dressed, a coffee mug in hand.

"Bowles called me the same thing," I said, without turning around.

"That's because Bowles knew more than the both of you put together about what's going on."

"Obviously," Alena remarked, still continuing her steady row.

Trent moved between the machines. Panno got to his feet as he approached.

"That's decaf?" he asked Trent.

"It's what was in the pot," Trent countered, and I took some pleasure in the fact that he sounded as bitchy to Panno in that moment as he sounded to me and Alena in every other.

"You want another heart attack?" Panno took the mug from Trent's hand and set it on the sill. "Lay off the caffeine."

"Greed," I said. "Money."

Both Panno and Trent looked at me. Alena didn't, but said, "It would have to be an incredible amount of money."

I switched off the elliptical, stepped down from the rails. I was sweating, and I didn't have anything to wipe my face with, so I used the front of my shirt.

"Money, sex, or power," I said. "Those are the reasons for murder."

"Protecting your own," Panno said.

"We call that self-defense. It's not sex, so it's either money or power. And Hayner, that's not enough to steal Earle's power, not all of it, at any rate. So it's money. And Alena's right: We have to be able to threaten an incredible amount of money for Earle to go to the lengths he's gone to."

Panno glanced at Trent, who was staring at me as if waiting to see how many more words the monkey could string together.

"Gorman-North, is that it?" I said. "We're not threatening Earle: We're threatening Gorman-North."

"All it took was spelling it out for you," Trent said.

"So why don't you spell out the rest?"

He made an almost contemptuous snort, then said, "John."

"The three of you aren't the only ones who want Earle taken care of," Panno told me. "There are other people who have an interest. People who have been trying to get him removed from his position of influence for a few years now, and who haven't been able to do it."

The sound of the oars slowed, Alena coming to a stop.

"Phoenix Resource Consultancy," I said. "Just who do you consult *for*, John?"

"Right now? Not working for anyone." He smiled at me. "This is a favor for Mr. Trent. But if you're asking for people I've worked with in the past, the only one who should interest you right now is a man at the Pentagon."

Alena got to her feet. "The conflicting reports."

I looked at Panno, at Trent, and then back to Panno. "Is there *anyone* who doesn't know we're planning to kill the White House chief of staff?"

"There are eight people who know," Trent answered. "Four of them are in this room."

"And the other four?"

"They're in the E-Ring."

"Jesus fucking Christ," I said. "You're using us for a coup."

"It's called profiteering," Panno said. "Whether you like it or not, whether you even believe it or not, we are at war, and will be for the foreseeable future. There's something FDR said during World War Two that's relevant. He said, 'I don't want to see a single war millionaire created in the United States as a result of this world disaster.' Harry Truman called the act of war-profiteering treason.

"It is. People die as a result. Soldiers, civilians, ours, theirs. Our people don't get what they need, or when they get what they need it doesn't do what it's supposed to, or there isn't enough of it, or it falls apart because the suppliers are cutting corners, massaging the bottom line.

"Gorman-North provides services to American military personnel all around the world. They build our bases, they staff our bases, they supply our bases and our soldiers with matériel and support services. They are everywhere in the system.

"And they're making billions on the deal. Billions and billions of dollars, and when we talk about that much money, even one percent of it not reaching the battlefield is a problem. When we talk about that much money, we're talking about hundreds of millions of dollars. And like I said, this thing isn't going to end anytime soon. There are going to be more and more contracts. And more and more of that money isn't going to make it where it's supposed to go."

Panno stopped speaking, his eyes locked on mine.

"It's not a coup," Trent told me. "Don't make it worse than it already is."

"It's already pretty fucking bad," I said. "If the Pentagon knows, if four fucking people there know, then that's the fucking military moving against the civilian government. What else do you want to call it?"

"No one is talking about bringing down the government," Panno said.

"Earle has been in the White House shepherding contracts for Gorman-North? You guys know this for a fact?"

"Yes."

"And we're just supposed to take your word for that?"

Trent gestured to the desk, the milk crate. "There's the paper, you want to go through it."

Alena seized on that. "So who exactly is it we're working for, Mr. Trent?"

"I'm a private citizen," Trent answered.

"Of course you are. Perfect deniability for your friends at the Pentagon. Where did this task originate? Somewhere oblique, I should think. The Office of the Assistant Secretary of Defense for

Special Operations and Low-Intensity Conflict, perhaps? Something similar?"

"Earle can't be budged," Panno said, studiously ignoring everything Alena had said. "And nothing gets past him if it's about Gorman-North. You're going to do the job anyway. This doesn't change that, because it doesn't change why you're doing it, or why Mr. Trent wants you to do it. It's just an added benefit."

"We'd be doing your friends in the E-Ring a favor," I said.

"That's probably a good way to look at it, Atticus," he said easily.

"What do we get in exchange?" I asked.

"Logistical support, intelligence. Money, if it's needed. All of it indirectly, of course."

"We're already being paid."

"You're going to incur added costs."

"I want something more. Something else."

Panno knew exactly what I was talking about. He didn't even blink.

"For both of us," I added. "For Alena and for me."

"You do this right," John Panno told me. "You'll get it."

"Then let's figure out how we're going to kill this son of a bitch," I said.

CHAPTER SEVEN

Several years ago, I was drinking at Paddy Reilly's, just sitting at the bar and killing the afternoon slowly. This was before Paddy's got discovered and got hip and you couldn't squeeze your way inside, and just after my car wreck of a girlfriend at the time had introduced me to the place. The bartender, who had come over from Belfast, and I got to talking, and the subject of my profession came up, as it does, when someone asks, "So, what do you do for a living?"

"I'm a personal protection specialist," I'd said.

"What's that when it's at home, then?"

"Bodyguard."

Which had, in turn, led to a conversation about protecting people, and my thoughts on it at the time. Being from Belfast, and having grown up with all that entailed, the bartender had a very intimate view on violence, very different from that of most of the people you meet. In the course of the conversation, the difference between assassination and murder came up.

"I've known the rough shooters, mate," the bartender told me. "They'd make you wet yourself you saw them coming."

"That's not what makes me wet myself," I said. "What makes me wet myself is the ones I *don't* see coming. The professional assassins, the ones you don't know were there until they've already left."

The bartender, who was a couple years younger than even I was at the time, shook his head. "That's James Bond bullshit. You want somebody dead, whyn't you just come at them with a bomb or a gun, eh? Why muck around with all that other garbage? Just seems to me like more ways it can go wrong."

"You're talking about killers, not assassins."

"Same difference, mate."

"No," I said. "A killer is who you use when you don't care if people know it was a murder. An assassin's who you use when you don't want *anyone* to know it was a murder."

The bartender had digested that, then bought me another Guinness on the house.

The trick wasn't simply killing Jason Earle, it was doing it in a way that wouldn't look like murder, either before, during, or after the act. It was going to have to be a snow-white hit, with not even a smudge left behind. Trent and Panno were both very clear on this, which, I suppose, meant that whoever it was back at the Pentagon who had given this particular execution of nastiness his blessing had been, as well. (I was sure it was a him; to my knowledge there had yet to be an Assistant Secretary of Defense for Special Operations and Low-Intensity Conflict, for example, who had been female.)

No blowback at all. Not even a hint of it.

Not that it would have been that much easier if we hadn't much cared how it looked from the outside. While the White House chief of staff did not enjoy the same Secret Service protection as did the President, Vice President, and their families, he was a hard target all the same. Striking at him in the White House wasn't only out of the question, it was patently impossible. Even if it had been, by some insane confluence of coincidences, chance, and luck, viable, I don't think any one of us would have gone for it, anyway, including Alena. It was the White House. It wasn't just off the table; it wasn't even in the same room where the rest of the game was being played.

Panno and Trent had prepared a bundle of intelligence for Alena and me to start with, and for the first six days, that's what we focused on. Trent had a wireless connection in the house, and between the documents in the milk crate and Alena's MacBook, we must have reviewed several thousand pages of data on Earle, his life, his relationships, his family, and his work with GSI and Gorman-North. "Target immersion" was what Alena called it; learning everything so you can forget most of it later; learning everything because you didn't know what might prove important.

"Video," Alena told Panno after we'd been at it a week. "There's little by way of photographs, and there's no video."

"Earle doesn't like the spotlight."

"We don't care," she told him. "We need both. Get it."

Three days later, Panno handed us a CD of compressed video footage and various photographs of Jason Earle. The photographs weren't so much to assist in a visual confirmation—we knew what Earle looked like, and unlike us, he wasn't going to any lengths to conceal his features. As far as that went, there was still heat on Danielle and Christopher Morse, meaning there was still a manhunt ongoing for both Alena and me, but in the media, at least, the story had begun to play out. The world, being the world, had moved on, and once the Pentagon had thrown a spanner into Earle's smear campaign, confusion had dampened the media enthusiasm for selling that flavor of fear.

That didn't mean we were taking anything for granted. Alena bleached her hair, killing the glorious copper in it, then replaced it with something from a bottle that said it was "Superstar Blonde" but which came out looking like melted yellow crayon. She did her eyebrows, as well, which must have hurt like hell, but she didn't complain.

"Cuffs and collar," she told me, and I laughed at that.

For my part, I was letting the beard grow in while refusing to let the hair on my head do the same. The itching was finally beginning to pass, which made it bearable. The last time I'd done a beard, it had been a tiny and almost fashionable thing on my chin. This one wasn't. This one was full, and combined with my cue-ball pate, remarkably unflattering.

I didn't even like looking at myself.

With his place of work off-limits, we turned our attention to his place of residence, and rapidly discovered we didn't much care for that, either. He maintained a home in Chevy Chase, Maryland, and while it was by no means a fortress, it was alarmed and patrolled, and had to have been checked on a regular basis by White House Security, at the least.

It was also occupied by his wife, and she didn't like to be alone. While both Jason and Victoria Earle, it seemed, were entirely faithful to one another, she was the social butterfly he was not. She had a wide number of friends who came to visit, she enjoyed entertaining, and she was active in several groups and societies. The house was heavily trafficked, and that meant while it might be easier to slip in or out with a crowd, the possibility of collateral damage was enormous. We didn't want to set the trap for Earle and end up killing his wife by mistake.

So hitting him at home was out, too.

"Schedule," I said to Trent. "Can you get us his schedule for the next few months?"

"How many months are we talking about?"

"I don't know. If you can get it out to three, great. Six, even better."

"It's going to take you six months to do this?"

"It's going to take as long as it's going to take, Elliot, and rushing it isn't the way to see this done right."

Trent told me he would see what he could do.

The White House chief of staff is one of those jobs that everyone has heard about, and most people have no idea what it entails. Considering that the person holding the position has often been called "The Second-Most Powerful Man in Washington," that's a little disconcerting.

The chief of staff is the highest-ranking member in the Executive Office of the President of the United States. He is responsible for controlling access to the President—a duty that has oftentimes earned him the nickname of "the Gatekeeper"—because there are always people who want the President's time. The chief of staff vets these requests, turning away those that, for one reason or another, do not meet either his own, or, more importantly, the President's requirements.

He oversees the work of the White House staff. This means everyone—the maids, the butlers, the gardeners, the staffers in the West Wing, and the caterers in the galley. He makes the White House run, each and every day, and he deals with preparations for all state visits and the like.

He often is one of the President's closest advisors, which goes a long way to explaining why he is considered to be such a powerful figure. Given that he oftentimes has a front-row seat for and even participates in major policy decisions, he needs to be reliable, smart, and frank. He must be willing to offer his own opinions, while ultimately abiding by the President's final decision.

These things being said, not every administration has had a chief of staff. In some instances it has been deemed unnecessary; in others, the position has been simply unfillable. Where there is a strong and actively involved President, the chief of staff can find himself with little to do, especially with regard to formulation of policy and issues of governance. By the same token, there have been Presidents who had demonstrated very little interest in the day-to-day minutiae of governing, and as a result the chief of staff becomes very powerful indeed, sometimes even referred to as a "quasi-prime minister."

Most of them don't last in the job very long, the average time of service being two and a half years. There's high burnout due to stress. Jason Earle had the distinction of being the longest-serving chief of staff, at seven years, beating out the previous record-holder, John Steelman, who served under Harry Truman for six.

Panno found that as ironic as I did.

Then there are the unofficial duties. A good chief of staff maintains strong relationships with both the first lady, the Vice President, and the wife of the Vice President. He is trusted by all, and endeavors to facilitate communication between each of their staffs. In many cases, he adopts some of their projects and preferences as his own. A bad relationship with any of them can undermine his key relationship with the President, and therefore, a good chief of staff—or, at least, a chief of staff who wants to remain in the position—makes it a point to work with, and to make himself available to, the other three.

"He was hospitalized for chest pains last spring," Alena told me. "He complained of shortness of breath and a sharp pain in the side while in the office last April, and was taken to Bethesda for examination and observation."

"And?"

"There was no complication, and it was attributed to stress on the job."

"You think they're covering up a heart attack?"

She shook her head. "There is no shame in it, so why bother concealing it?"

"Still."

She gnawed on her lower lip. "Worth considering."

Trent, via Panno, via whoever, got us a copy of his schedule. We were in the beginning of the third week, now, and Panno was spending more and more time away from the house, presumably running between us and whoever he was messengering for in Washington. I hoped whoever it was he was reporting to—if he was reporting at all—was discreet. The last thing we wanted was for our location to be blown.

The second to last thing we wanted was for Earle to find out he was in our sights. If he knew—or for that matter, even suspected—that Alena and I had grown tired of being hunted and had decided to turn the tables on him, he wouldn't be simply a hard target; he would become an impossible one. He would go to ground, wrap himself up inside his protective bubble. Then there would be no way we could pierce it to reach him.

When Trent finally got us Earle's schedule, it took less than a minute to realize that what we'd feared was exactly what had happened.

"There's nothing here," I said. "No public appearances, nothing. He's got one trip with the President to Camp David, that's it."

"It's his tentative schedule for the next three months." Trent fixed me with his sunken eyes. "Tentative. Don't read too much into it."

Alena shook her head in disgust, tossing the paper onto our ever-growing stack of research, which now dominated the dining room table.

"He knows," she said. "Someone tipped him, and he knows."

"No one tipped him," Trent said. It wasn't defensive; it was defiant. He looked from Alena to me as if suspecting us of lurking betrayal.

"Then he suspects," Alena said. "For whatever reason, he suspects, Mr. Trent. Look at this schedule. There are no public appearances. None. He is the chief of staff at the White House, and yet he has not taken a single public engagement, not a single appearance. According to this schedule, he is behaving in all ways like a man who knows he is being targeted."

"The schedule's considered tentative, at best," Trent said. "It may change."

I shook my head. "Not unless he thinks the threat's gone."

"Then you'll just have to convince him it is."

"Well, the easiest way to do that, Elliot, would be to use the phone there and turn us over to the cops."

"No," Alena disagreed. "It would be easier to kill us."

"Don't tempt me," Trent said.

"We can't fake our deaths," I said to Alena, ignoring him. "Earle would never buy that."

"He will not expose himself until he is certain that our threat is removed," Alena said, flatly. "Until he believes without doubt that we pose him—or mean him—no harm. He can afford to wait."

"I can't," said Trent.

"Stannous acetate," Alena said.

We were in bed, each of us on our backs, staring at the dark ceiling and listening to the not-so-distant waves. We weren't post-coital; we hadn't made love since moving into Trent's house, and it wasn't out of any deference to him or concern for what he might think. It was hard, I suppose, for either of us to feel romantic while planning what, in its most naked terms, was murder. It wasn't that we were no longer comfortable with each other, nor that we no longer felt as strongly as we once had. There was a time and a place for it, and that time and place just wasn't here and now.

"Tin?" I asked. It took me a moment. I'd been lost in my own thoughts, missing Kobuleti, and wondering how Miata was faring with the Raminisshvillis and their Internet café in Kobuleti.

When Alena spoke, her voice was soft, and her tone one of resolve. "You dissolve it in glacial acetic acid, you get a solid, stannous acetate." She rolled onto her side to look at me in the darkness. Her almost-blond hair seemed luminescent. "The CIA used it to induce heart attacks during the Cold War. It can be dissolved and then ingested as a liquid, or placed as a contact agent."

"How quickly does it work?"

"Ingested, it works very quickly. Within minutes. As a contact agent, absorption is slower unless aided by a solvent of some sort."

"How traceable?"

"Anything can be discovered if one is to look for it. The question is whether or not an autopsy will be performed."

"White House chief of staff dies of an AMI—"

"After complaining of chest pains and shortness of breath the previous year," Alena interrupted.

"—I'd think an autopsy is standard operating procedure."

She considered that, then rolled onto her back again.

"Bethesda," I said, after a moment. "They'll do the autopsy at the naval base in Bethesda."

She turned her head to look at me. "Performed by military personnel?"

"Oh, yes."

She almost smiled. "Problem solved."

We were left with three questions—how, where, and when. It was one thing to have resolved that we would kill Earle by poisoning him with stannous acetate. It was another thing entirely to figure out how, exactly, we'd get the poison into his bloodstream.

The answer came while we were watching the video Panno had acquired for us. We watched it on the laptop, a random sampling of media appearances and round tables and talk shows, and the most recent was already four months old, from December of the previous year. There was nothing after that, which only reconfirmed what Alena and I now knew as true; for some reason, Earle suspected he had been targeted, and was taking steps to deny exposure. As a result, most of what we watched was older, dating from early in the first term of the current administration.

The piece that caught us was almost five years old, and shortly after it started I realized what I'd been looking at all along and stopped the playback, then rewound it. We watched it a second time, and then a third.

"You're seeing that?" I asked her after the last time through.

"Yes," she said.

"I think we've got him."

"Yes." Alena sighed, not unhappy, not pleased, just the sound of someone who had completed a particularly arduous and not particularly enjoyable job. "Yes, Atticus, I think we do."

We had the how. We knew how we would kill Earle if we were ever given the chance.

But as things stood, there was no where and there was no when, and as best as any of us could tell, Jason Earle was doing everything in his power to make certain there never would be, either.

Three weeks and three days after we started, we sat down with Trent and Panno at the kitchen table. Panno had the latest version of Earle's schedule he'd been able to obtain, and once again, it appeared that the White House chief of staff was far too busy chief-of-staffing in the White House to come out and play, let alone be murdered.

I passed the schedule off to Alena, who glanced at it, snorted, and set it aside. Getting Earle out into the open was something we'd come to later.

"We're going to need some stannous acetate," I said. "It's easy enough to acquire from just about any chemical warehouse, any supplier to schools or labs. However you get it, you obviously don't want it to be traced back."

Panno took notes on a pad he had produced from a pocket. He took the notes in pencil. "Spell it."

I spelled it for him.

"How much will you need?"

"Not much," Alena said. "Five grams will do; it costs about one hundred dollars per gram. Ten grams would be ideal; it would provide a backup supply."

"Done," Panno said. "You want it brought here?"

"We'll come to that."

"What's it do?" Trent asked.

"You'll like this, Elliot," I told him. "For all intents and purposes, it induces a heart attack. It'll look like he had an acute myocardial infarction."

Trent actually smiled.

"What happens if someone gets paddles on him in time?" Panno asked.

"Won't make a damn bit of difference, not if it's still in his system. He'll just arrest again. It'll look like he had multiples, instead of just the one."

"Vector?"

"It can be ingested, but we're going to try for a topical application."

Trent stopped smiling. "I don't like that."

"We're talking about murdering a man, but *that's* the part you don't like?"

"It's imprecise. What happens if someone else touches the surface in question first?"

"Won't be a problem." I looked at Alena. "Show them."

Alena opened her laptop and switched on the video we'd cued up. It was the oldest of the clips we had, taped five years prior, and showed Earle speaking to an auditorium full of fresh young faces at the Harvard Business School.

"Watch his hands," Alena told them.

They watched.

Alena cued the next clip, this time with Earle at a podium in front of a cluster of reporters.

"Again."

They watched again.

She cued and played the next three, and at the last said, "It's compulsive behavior, and entirely subconscious. He approaches the podium in each instance, he adjusts the microphone, and then he plants his hands on either side, as if to support himself. In every video where a podium has been present, Jason Earle does the same thing. Adjust and plant."

"We get him at a speaking engagement," I said. "We find the right venue, something where he's speaking after dinner, say, then we apply the stannous acetate to the podium just prior to his taking the stage. We dose the ridges on either side, where he plants his hands."

"He'll be introduced." Panno shook his head. "C'mon, Kodiak. He's the featured speaker, someone will stand there to introduce him first. What happens if whoever is doing the introducing puts his or her hands on those sides?"

"The way we'll fix the dose, it'll require contact with both hands," I said. "Ideally, we get him at a smaller function, something more intimate, where the introduction will be brief by necessity. If whoever does the introducing touches only one side, we should be okay. It's the combination of doses that'll do it."

Trent stared at the monitor on the laptop for several seconds.

"How long will it take?" he asked.

"Fifteen minutes, maybe longer," Alena said. "He will be well into his lecture when he goes into arrest."

"Will it hurt him?"

"It is a heart attack, Mr. Trent. You have suffered several yourself. What do you think?"

"I think it'll hurt like hell."

"That is what I think, as well."

"Good," Elliot Trent said, pleased. "When do you do it?"

I closed the laptop.

"We don't," I said. "There's no opportunity. You saw the schedule. He's not speaking in public, and as far as we can tell, he won't speak in public ever again if he thinks there's even a remote chance that Alena or I will try to hit him. We've seen four versions of his schedule, and they're all the same. Either he knows he's being targeted, or he suspects he is, but whichever the case, he's going out of his way to deny us any opportunity to hit him."

Trent didn't like that, shaking his head. "No. Dammit, no, not good enough. He doesn't live in the damn White House. You can take him at his home."

"According to your friend John, there, his home is now protected by the boys from Gorman-North," I said. "If you want us to hit the house with RPGs and automatic weapons, then maybe—maybe—we can make it happen. But not without collateral damage. And not without making it look like exactly what it will be, which is a goddamn hit."

"It's not an option," Panno said. "Needs to be clean."

"Then why did you show this to us?" Trent demanded, gesturing at the laptop. "You tell us what you need to do it, you tell us how you'll do it, and then you say you can't do it? What the hell is the point of that, Kodiak?"

"To show you it's possible—"

"You just said—"

"—just not possible at the present time."

Trent started to retort, then stopped himself.

"Do you understand what I'm telling you, Elliot?" I asked. "I'm telling you that we can get you what you want. We can kill the man responsible for Natalie's murder. I'm telling you that we can do it, and we can even get away with it. But not unless the situation changes. Not unless Jason Earle believes—absolutely, positively, and without question believes—that it's safe to emerge from his bunker. He has to believe that the threat Alena and I pose to him is gone. One way or another."

Trent's mouth worked, as if he were tasting each of the things he wanted to say before swallowing them instead of sharing them. Then he found something that didn't taste quite so bad.

"It's you and Drama he's afraid of," he said. "Natalie died because he was coming after you. He's afraid of you because he thinks you're threatening him."

"Yes," I said.

"And all of this bullshit he's pulled, it's for the same reason. Because he's afraid of the two of you."

"Yes."

"The son of a bitch is wrong. He should be afraid of me."

"That's what we were thinking," Alena said.

Trent closed his eyes, dropping into dark thoughts, and I was right there with him. Beside him, Panno was frowning, suspicious, as if sensing that suddenly Trent, Alena, and I were having an entirely different conversation from the one he'd been privy to.

"Then I'll kill him myself," Trent said, opening his eyes. "You two just tell me how."

"The same way your daughter would have done it, Mr. Trent," Alena told him. "With a rifle."

CHAPTER EIGHT

I woke early the next morning and found Trent already gone, and that Panno had presumably gone with him. There was no note, there was no message, but the two pictures that had formed the shrine to his family were missing. In the room Panno had been living out of on the ground floor I discovered a weapons bag tucked beneath the bed. Inside the bag were two pistols, both semiautos, a Colt and a Smith & Wesson. The Smith had been fitted to take a suppressor, and I wasn't surprised to find one waiting for me in the side pocket of the bag. I left them where they were and went out onto the front porch to do my yoga in the morning mist.

Alena joined me about fifteen minutes later, and since we were suddenly without baby-sitting, we decided to go for a run on the beach. We were back at the house ninety minutes later, and I made breakfast while Alena showered. We ate at the table, surrounded by our research and our notes.

"You want me to do it?" Alena asked me while we were doing the washing-up.

"No," I told her, and went to take my shower.

The next morning Panno came back, driving a green Acura I'd never seen before. Alena and I were waiting for him at the door. He came onto the porch like he was preparing to slug me.

"Baltimore Marriott Waterfront Hotel," Panno said. "Inner Harbor. Room fourteen-oh-four."

I held out my hand, and he dropped the car keys into my palm.

"You are a cold-blooded son of a bitch," he said.

"We both know someone colder," I told him.

Then I got in the green Acura and drove to Baltimore.

I parked a couple blocks away from the hotel, then walked the rest of the distance. It didn't quite feel like spring yet in Maryland, and the wind off the water was cruel, and it made me wish I'd brought a watch cap or some other sort of cover for my naked scalp. I had the Smith tucked into my pants and the suppressor in my left pocket, and the metal of each conducted the cold. It was early evening, already dark, and there were plenty of people about, and I had to wait for a group of conventioneers to exit the lobby before I could make my way into the hotel.

It took a couple of seconds to find the elevator, and two minutes of waiting before a car came to carry me to the fourteenth floor. I rode up with three others, a very carefully prepared blonde in her mid-thirties and her two J. Crew-appointed children, the eldest of them perhaps ten years old. He accidentally stepped on his mother's foot as they followed me into the car.

"Dammit," she snarled at him. "It wouldn't kill you to apologize."

The boy looked at her with the same contempt she was directing his way, then backed against the wall of the car for a slouch. Without any sincerity whatsoever, he said, "Sorry."

Mom sniffed, and then the car came to a halt on the fourteenth floor, and as I was exiting I said to the mother, "You treat him like a monster, he'll become a monster."

I lost her response behind the closing doors.

Trent let me into the room without a word, turning away as soon as I stepped inside, and I took the opportunity to pull the Do Not Disturb sign from where it was hanging on the knob and place it on the outside handle. Then I closed the door and followed after him, found him standing at the desk, pouring from a bottle of Maker's Mark. He added ice to the drink, using his fingers instead of the provided tongs, then offered the glass to me.

"No, thanks," I said.

His response was to tilt the glass and deliver half of what he'd poured down his throat.

The room was a queen, and Trent had kept it orderly. On the nightstand closest to the window he'd placed the photographs of his wife and daughter. The golf bag he'd used to transport the rifle was visible leaning against the wall beside the closet, and the weapon itself was lying on a bath towel on the bed, as if he had just completed a fieldstrip of it. Perhaps he had. The rifle was a Robinson Armament M96, the same model that Natalie had favored, the same model that Alena had used to kill Oxford three and a half years earlier.

Trent finished his drink, and set the glass down on the papers resting on the desk. From where I was standing I could see the rows and columns of numbers Alena had helped him to prepare.

"She liked you," Trent said, and he was looking at the pictures on his nightstand. "That counts for something, I guess."

"She loved you," I told him. "That never changed."

"No, it wouldn't have." He kept his eyes on the photographs, speaking to them as much as to me. "I wanted to protect her. I hated that she followed me into Sentinel because I worried she would get hurt, and I loved that she wanted to follow her father."

I rolled the suppressor out of my pocket and into my left hand, then took the Smith & Wesson from my waist. The suppressor fit it perfectly, tightening smoothly into place.

"She was the most precious thing in the world to me."

Trent coughed, clearing his throat, then faced me again.

"I don't care why you do it, Atticus," he said. "Do it for your country. Do it for the money. Do it for her. But make that bastard pay."

"We all do," I said.

Then I shot him twice in the head.

CHAPTER NINE

According to Panno, the fallout went like this:

Fifteen hours after I'd killed him, Elliot Trent was found dead in his room by housekeeping. The hotel called the police, and shortly after their initial analysis of the crime scene, a homicide lieutenant with the Baltimore Police Department in turn called the FBI. Said lieutenant then informed the Special Agent in Charge that he had reason to believe the murder victim discovered in the Baltimore Marriott Waterfront Hotel had been planning to assassinate White House Chief of Staff Jason Earle.

The FBI took over the investigation, and as a matter of course, took all of the evidence that the Baltimore PD had collected, including the victim's personal belongings and those items deemed to be in his possession at the time of his death. They found a high-powered rifle, suitable for sniping. They found two maps of Chevy Chase, Maryland, and each had been marked with notations by a hand determined to be Trent's, and each highlighted Earle's home, as well as the most likely routes he was liable to take to and from work. They found three sheets of what at first glance were determined to be math computations, but were quickly identified as firing solutions of the kind that would be prepared by a sniper. They found two photographs, one of Trent's late daughter, another of his late wife.

They found nothing by way of evidence that might explain who had murdered Trent, or why.

Three days after the discovery of Trent's body, a special agent from the Bureau's headquarters in D.C. met with the White House chief of staff to brief him on what had been found. While the identity of Trent's killer remained a mystery, the circumstantial evidence surrounding the discovery of Trent's body led to an alarming conclusion. At the time of his death, Elliot Trent had quite clearly been planning to assassinate Jason Earle.

Whether or not the attempt would have been successful, the agent could not say. But without a doubt, Trent's intention, ability, and willingness to attempt the act were clear. As to his motive, all the agent could offer was that, given the presence of the two photographs, it was possible that Trent felt that Earle was in some way responsible for the deaths of his wife and daughter. Why Trent would think that was anyone's guess.

Upon being asked, the agent assured the White House chief of staff that every effort was being made to locate and apprehend Trent's killer. The agent confessed that, without either witnesses to the crime or any evidence at the scene, he didn't hold out much hope.

Even before Trent's body was discovered, I was back in Alena and Panno's company, this time in Charlotte, instead of Wilmington.

With Trent's death, the location on Peden Point had to be abandoned, and upon my departure the two of them had gone to work on the house. They'd removed all signs that anyone other than Trent had ever lived there, and left behind just enough of the research we'd done on Earle to hopefully support the FBI's theory of the crime should a search of the premises take place.

Then Panno and Alena drove the almost four hours to Charlotte. By the time I met up with them shortly after one the next morning, they were already settled into the house Panno had rented off Commonwealth Avenue, opposite a power substation. It was a small place, two bedrooms and one bath, and with the three of us in it and the strange energy now flowing between us, it was going to be both awkward and intimate. Alena greeted me with a wan smile and a cup of herbal tea. Panno took my arrival as his cue to start drinking.

Panno left for D.C. the following afternoon, and for the next eight days, Alena and I occupied ourselves as best we could. Mostly, we stayed indoors. The Danielle and Christopher Morse story had all but vanished from the news cycle at this point, but we were still wary.

Elliot Trent had gambled his life on a chance at drawing Jason Earle out into the open. Neither Alena nor I wanted to do anything to diminish that sacrifice, nor to squander the opportunity we hoped it would create.

Panno returned nine days after Trent died, arriving in the early evening and driving yet another car, this one a big blue Ford pickup. He'd brought groceries and other household necessities to restock our stores, and as we unpacked everything in the kitchen, he told us the good news.

"Earle's scheduling appearances again."

Alena, who had been sorting the fresh fruit and veg into the refrigerator, actually blew out a sigh of relief.

"What do you have?" I asked him.

In answer, Panno handed over four folded sheets of paper, and I settled with them and him at the kitchen table. Alena finished with the groceries and then went to fetch the MacBook, and when she joined us I gave her the pages and booted up the Web browser, jumping online via a neighbor's unsecured wireless connection.

"It's a pretty full schedule," I remarked to Panno.

"Figure he's been saying no so often he was eager for a chance to start saying yes." Panno scratched at the rough stubble along his cheek. "You guys took a hell of a risk. Hell of a fucking risk."

Alena, looking over the schedule, said, "Earle had to believe the danger Atticus and I pose to him is ended. By making Trent the threat, and by allowing Earle to conclude that we were the ones who dealt with it, he can now believe the matter is finished."

"And that's not assumptive as all hell? You don't think that Earle just looked at the situation and concluded that instead of just one threat—the two of you—there were actually two of them?"

"Assumptive or not, his schedule tells us he bought it," I said.

"Or maybe his schedule is telling you that you're being set up."

Alena was on the third of the four sheets, and she didn't look up. "That is, of course, possible."

"But you don't think it's likely."

"Maybe," I said. "Earle's spent four years trying to solve the problem of Alena and me, John. He's burnt capital, connections, favors, and something like twelve of Gorman-North's best guns. He has to want this over and done with as much as we do. He *wants* to believe we're walking away."

"I see it, Atticus, I get it, I really do." Panno got up from the table, heading to the refrigerator. "But all of this is built on the assumption that Earle saw the report of Trent's death, saw the assassination plot, and then concluded that it was you and Killer, there, who took care of Trent."

"It's a reasonable assumption on his part," I said. "Earle knows about the Jacob Collins contact. The FBI will have told him that Trent had a home in Wilmington. If they did any search at all—and we all know they did—then they also learned there were at least three people living there, even if they don't know exactly who those three were. It's enough for Earle to make the connection, to put Alena, myself, and Trent in the same place at the same time. So he's got to ask why we were together, and what's he going to conclude, John?"

"That Trent brought you two in to help him plan or execute the hit."

"And then Trent ends up dead," I said. "Our peace offering to Earle, our way of saying that we're quits."

"It's a hell of a long path for Earle to follow to get where you want him to go."

"Has to be that way. Any shorter and it would've made him suspicious. The only way this could work was to let Earle reach his own conclusions."

There was a snap of a church key freeing a bottle cap, and Panno came back to the table with a long-neck bottle of Budweiser in his hand. "Maybe."

Alena finished with the fourth sheet, set it down, then motioned for me to slide the laptop over to her. "We have the schedule. Either it worked, or it did not. Either we will kill him, or he will kill us. But Trent's death has given us what we hoped it would. It has given us our opportunity."

"Or it's given Earle his," Panno said.

Then, having taken the last word, he left Alena and me to figure out when and where we would murder Jason Earle.

CHAPTER TEN

We worked the schedule for two days, checking and double-checking the listed appointments, meetings, and appearances. There was a day near the end of April coming up, almost four weeks out, now, that we liked the looks of. Earle had two events scheduled, one out at Georgetown, the other at the Watergate, and when we had Panno double-check them it looked like nothing had changed, that neither had been canceled.

At the Watergate, Earle was going to be the featured after-dinner speaker at the national meeting of Women for the Preservation of the American Heritage. This was, apparently, something he was doing as a favor for, or at the request of, the first lady, as WPAH was one of her pet projects, a foundation that she had been active in even before meeting her husband. Earle, according to the schedule, was to speak for forty-five minutes following dessert, but the schedule had blocked time from five until seven-thirty that evening, apparently to provide wiggle room.

Georgetown, on the other hand, was far more tightly scheduled, at fifty-five minutes. It was another speaking engagement, from one in the afternoon until just before two, and there was nothing in the schedule specifying where he was speaking on the campus or what he was speaking about, only that he was going to. Using Alena's MacBook and the Georgetown Web site wasn't much help; the April calendar indeed had an entry for "Lecture by White House Chief of Staff Jason Earle," and said the lecture would be given in McCarthy Hall, in the McShain Lounge, but that was all.

"McShain Lounge," I said. "Sounds intimate."

"For alumni and alumnae," Alena remarked.

"Easy enough to fake that."

"You think?" She considered. "There are many other ways to gain access to the campus and the hall prior to the engagement."

"Sure."

"Many of them."

I could see the wheels spinning.

I let them spin.

We had a fight about it the following morning, as we were finishing up our yoga in what passed for the living room. We'd shoved all of the furniture to the sides to give us room, and even with that accommodation there still wasn't nearly the room either of us would've liked. In the kitchen, I could hear morning radio and the sounds of Panno apparently making himself a very large breakfast.

"So I'm thinking the best way to do this is to go up to D.C. in the next week and get into position," I told Alena. "Get a job on the campus, maybe, doing maintenance or something similar, get the layout."

"Agreed."

"Verify that everything is as we think it is."

"Yes."

"Then the other one follows maybe a day or two prior to the hit, prepares the exfil and stands by."

"Again, agreed. We stay only long enough to verify the kill."

Each of us stretched, turning into new poses. From my angle, she was now upside down.

"That's about a month without contact," I said. "That's a long time."

"We will survive it."

"I'll be careful," I told her.

Alena bent backwards, the move smooth as a line of molten glass. "You are not going to do it."

"Like hell, Alena."

"No, you are not thinking. I am better for this, and you know that." She left the position, exhaling long, then getting to her feet. "I have the experience, and I am marginally harder to recognize than you are, at least at the moment."

I tumbled down and got my own feet beneath me. "I need to do this."

"Why? Because Natalie was your friend? Is it not enough that Jason Earle will die for what he did to her? Is it not enough that you will be as guilty as I or Trent or Panno in this?"

"No, it's not. I need to do it. I need to see him die."

"That is unprofessional."

"Fuck professional. This entire thing is unprofessional. Elliot Trent let me shoot him in the goddamn head to give us this, you think he was giving a rat's ass about professional? Nothing about this is professional, Alena! Nothing."

Alena stared at me, unblinking, a sheen of sweat on her skin.

"Don't talk to me about professional," I said. "Not about this."

"Yes, Atticus, about this. If no one is being professional, then one of us must be. That person is me."

"This isn't Oxford; this isn't you trying to save me from what I might become. I've become it, Alena. For better or for worse, I've become it."

"I know. And you know that I am better for this. If a job cannot be obtained, I can pass as a student. I can get onto the campus, I can place the poison, and I can get out again. And it is not that you cannot do these things, Atticus, it is that I can do them better, with less risk to myself."

The thing was, she was right. She was absolutely right. She could pass for ten years younger if she tried, with the right clothes, the right hair. She could play the Russian émigré and get a job on the maintenance staff, or she could play the postgrad student, or she could play the alum. And maybe I could do all of those things, too, but I wouldn't be able to do half of them as well.

And it was unprofessional, and she was right about that, too. Whatever the reasons behind the crime, when it came to the task, the task was the only thing that should have mattered. Anything else, any agenda or emotion, would only get in the way of that, and make it harder to do the job right.

"You're right," I said, and I left it at that.

Alena left two days later, with Panno. She left with a new cell phone and a new identity to match her blond hair, and eight days after she arrived in D.C., she had a job in custodial services on the Georgetown campus. That information came from Panno, not from her, because she was running silent now, and would until I arrived in advance of the hit.

Panno's job was to serve as the link, and on the day of the hit, to provide the overwatch, to confirm that Earle was en route, that we were good to go. For the next three weeks he gave me updates at regular intervals, and he came down to Charlotte twice, to meet face-to-face and keep me posted. He had dead-dropped the stannous acetate to Alena before the first week was out, and confirmed that she had retrieved it and brought it back to the apartment she was subletting in Annandale. To the best of his knowledge, she was running safe, and had not been made.

What little remained of the media pursuit of Danielle and Christopher Morse became more and more infrequent, and then, almost as abruptly as it had come, ended.

I waited.

For almost a month, alone in a house in Charlotte, I waited, and it nearly killed me. I was worried for Alena, but it wasn't like it had been upon leaving Lynch. That had been fear, honest and true, and what I felt now was nervousness, nothing more. But I was stagnant, and once I took care of those few things that remained for me to do in Charlotte there was nothing else, and there was nothing to be done for it. I was stir-crazy before the end of the fourth day, and on the fifth I risked venturing out and bought myself a membership at a Gold's Gym located two and a half miles from the house. Then I went in search of the local library and, finding it, began dividing my time between the gym and the stacks. I packed, unpacked, and repacked my go-bag multiple times. I cleaned the house. Thoroughly.

And everywhere I went, in everything I did, I walked with ghosts.

Pulling a book from a library shelf and seeing Natalie Trent with the blood trailing from her mouth, where it had formed a puddle on brittle, dry leaves. Doing the dishes and hearing the sound of her father's suddenly dead weight collapsing all at once to the hotel carpet. The shudder and wheeze of the dying hidden behind the threads of spring that had come to Charlotte.

I walked with ghosts, and they gave me no peace.

The day before Earle was scheduled to lecture at Georgetown, I packed up my go-bag for the last time and drove north to D.C., in a used Honda that had been purchased for precisely the purpose two weeks earlier. I had a new ID provided by Panno, and the old ones that Sargenti had given us back in Boise, and I had eighteen thousand dollars in cash. I had two changes of new clothes, spring weight, because it was April and though the weather was forecast to be mild, it could just as easily turn hot.

I spent the night in a Red Roof Inn just off the Capital Beltway, and Panno met me in the bar there just past nine. He had another Budweiser and I had mineral water, and there were a couple of businessmen and women in there with us, and there was enough noise that we could talk.

"You're good to go," he told me. "She'll expect to hear from you tomorrow morning at oh-nine-hundred to confirm coms. I've got both your numbers, I'll keep you posted."

"You're not worried about putting this over a cell phone in the heart of D.C.?"

"Not the cell phones I've supplied you guys with, no." Panno slugged back some of his beer and cracked a grin at me. "You're covered."

I nodded, and we fell into silence for several minutes.

"Did you know Natalie?" I asked him.

"From the time we were kids," he said, running his eyes around the bar. "Right up until college, yeah."

"Didn't stay in touch?"

"Got difficult to. I was in the service, here and there. We fell out. My mistake, I could have reached out if I had wanted to, and I didn't."

"Why not?"

"I was in love with her." Panno quit his survey of the bar, brought his eyes to me. "We had a thing for a while, high school, like that. Ended when we went to college. She ended it. I didn't take it well."

"I thought you were in this because of Trent."

"It's as much about her as it is about him. Let me ask you something. You were in the Army. Why'd you leave?"

"I wasn't very good at it. You?"

"Special Forces."

"That wasn't what I meant. Why'd you leave?"

"I have a problem following the orders of idiots," he said. "There weren't a lot of them, but I seemed to have a knack for finding the ones that were hiding in the woodwork. My problem is I look like I'm dumber than I actually am, and I was dealing with people who were dumber than they looked, you know?"

"Too well."

"You got a future at this."

"I'm not sure I want it."

"You're good at it. That move the two of you pulled in Wyoming was fucking brilliant."

"That was her, not me."

"Not according to your wife. I asked her."

"What'd you call her?"

"C'mon, man, if you don't have a common-law marriage I don't know what one looks like."

I shook my head slightly. "She's being generous about Wyoming."

"She says that putting yourself out there in Montana, that was your idea, too. That took balls. That took more than just guts—that took passion."

I looked at him. It wasn't a word I was hearing much, and I wasn't feeling terribly passionate at the moment. I was feeling cold, to the world and to myself.

"Some people need killing," Panno told me.

"I've heard that before," I said. "I'm not sure I disagree with it. I'm just not sure I'm the guy to be making that call."

He nodded, then raised his beer.

"For Natalie and her dad," he said.

I met his glass with my own.

"For Natalie and her dad," I agreed.

I didn't sleep well that night, and was up again before the dawn. I tried yoga and couldn't get myself to breathe properly. I took a shower and shaved off the beard, but kept the mustache, turning it into something that drooped deep around the sides of my mouth. I liked the look better than the full beard, but that wasn't saying much. After I had dressed again, I turned on the television and watched the news, and nowhere did my face or Alena's appear.

I checked out early, got into the car, and headed across the Potomac. I drove out to Arlington, parked, and waited for nine o'clock to roll around. When it did, I took the cell phone Panno had given me the previous night and switched it on, then dialed the number for Alena.

She answered on the first ring. "Hello."

"I love you," I said.

There was a pause. "Coms are working," Alena said, softly, and I wasn't sure if it was uncertainty or surprise in her voice. "Call me at noon to confirm."

"Noon," I said, and cut the connection.

■ ■ ■

Panno called five minutes later, also to confirm that coms were working, and that everything was still on schedule. That left me most of three hours to kill, so I drove over to the Mall. It was the heart of spring in D.C., and it was already muggy, but that wasn't stopping the tourists. It took me a while to find a place to park, by which time it was a little past ten. I started at the Lincoln Memorial and walked from there for the next hour and a half. I stopped for twenty minutes or so at the Vietnam Memorial, found it as affecting as I always did, and spent much of it just staring at the three soldiers, at their fatigue and their honor and their sorrow.

I took my time heading back to the car, and if I was being surveilled, it was beyond my ability to spot it. It was twenty-three minutes to noon as I was climbing back behind the wheel, and that was when the phone Panno had given me began to ring.

"Go," I said.

"He's canceled," Panno told me. He was doing a very good job of keeping the frustration from his voice.

My heart jump-started again.

"Is he spooked?" I asked. "Did he get tipped?"

"Fuck if I know. My information says he's just canceled the Georgetown gig, that's all. Could be a thousand reasons why he would do that, it doesn't mean he knows anything."

"Can you find out if he's still planning on being at the Watergate?"

"He only canceled—"

"No, I know that, I'm asking can you confirm that he will be at the Watergate tonight?"

"I'll get on it. You'll tell her?"

"I'm heading out there now," I said, hung up, and then hit my redial. Alena answered as she had the first time, before the first ring was through. "He's canceled."

"Why?"

"We don't know. I'm trying to confirm that he'll still be going to the Watergate."

"What are you thinking?"

"I don't know yet. Where are you?"

"At work, on campus. It's confirmed, he's not coming?"

"He's not coming," I said. "I'll be there as soon as I can."

"There's a lot on the north side, just off Reservoir Road. I'll meet you there."

I hung up and started driving. After a second, I switched on the radio, punched my way through the AM presets, finally landing on an all-talk station. Nobody was saying anything about any new crisis in the world, and that was a good sign, I thought, because it meant that whatever the reason Earle had canceled his trip out to Georgetown, maybe it wasn't a reason that would cause him to cancel his evening plans as well. And I needed him to keep his evening plans. I needed him to go to the Watergate.

If we didn't hit him today, I didn't know when, or if, we would get another chance. It had taken almost three months and Elliot Trent's death to put this together. Another three months would be all the more complicated, and all the more dangerous for us. It didn't matter that we weren't in the news anymore. The public's memory is for shit, but it's not *that* much for shit.

Alena was exactly where she said she would be, wearing her custodial coveralls and carrying a ratty-looking backpack that went with the ensemble. She had cut her hair very short, and maintained the blond look, and I guessed that was why she'd had to cut her hair; it had been bleached one too many times.

I pulled in and stopped, leaving the engine running, and she opened the passenger door and slid in, dropping the backpack at her feet. I started to turn back to the wheel, but she surprised the hell out of me by reaching out and grabbing me with both hands. She put her mouth to mine, kissed me fiercely and for not long enough, then released me.

"I love you, too," she said. "Drive."

I pulled back onto Reservoir, turning right, heading once again in the direction I had come.

"Has he called you back?"

"Not yet. I'm trying to get confirmation about the Watergate."

"You want to try to hit him there?"

"You see another alternative?" I asked. "There's no way we can take him at his house, and I'm thinking the window on this is rapidly slamming shut."

"We can't dose the podium there," she said. "The first lady will be speaking, we can't take that risk."

"We won't dose the podium. We'll find another way. How do we get to your place?"

"You're heading the wrong direction. Turn left up ahead."

I took the left, followed her directions, turning towards Annandale. "You've already packed up?"

"There wasn't much to pack." She nudged the backpack at her feet with her sneaker. "Why are we going there?"

"We need to stage," I said. "And you're going to have to change clothes."

"Then we'll need to stop somewhere to buy some. How nice?"

"Watergate nice."

"You do have a plan."

"I'm working on one."

"If we don't do this today, we're going to have more than just Earle as a problem," Alena said. "I don't think Panno's friends will be very happy with us."

"I'm trying not to think about that."

"Probably wise."

My phone rang, and I handed it to Alena to answer, heard her side of the conversation. It lasted all of eleven seconds before she was hanging up.

"According to his information, Earle will be honoring his commitment to the first lady this evening."

"Call him back, tell him that we're going to need to know the second he's on the move, and then tell him that he's going to need a suit, and he needs to meet us at the Watergate."

She did so, relaying exactly what I'd said. There was a pause, and then she handed the phone back to me. "He wants you."

"What?" I asked him.

"I'm not playing on the field," Panno said.

"Like hell you aren't," I said. "You want to use a sports metaphor, here's one: You're off the bench. We may need you there."

"You're seriously going to try this?" Panno asked. I couldn't tell if he was impressed or worried. "You're seriously going to try to do this, there?"

"Hell yeah."

"If he's twitched—"

"Then I'll die trying," I said.

CHAPTER ELEVEN

There are certain constants to be found in hotels around the world. They differ, of course, in levels of service, in the amenities they provide. Some offer twenty-four-hour room service, or same-day laundry, or an on-call masseuse, or a video library for your viewing pleasure. Some have concierge services that will literally bend over backwards to get you anything you could need or desire. Some have more, some have less.

But all of them—all of the good ones, at least—have two other things, and you can rely on them being there every single time.

They have a housekeeping staff, and they have a maintenance staff.

They have to. Otherwise, they can't call themselves a hotel.

■ ■ ■

It took us until three minutes to three to reach the Watergate, and because Alena had bought new clothes at Abercrombie & Fitch on Wisconsin, and because I didn't look that ratty to begin with, no one paid us any attention at all when we walked into the lobby. It wasn't crowded, but it was busy, and it was easy to pass without drawing notice, just a couple looking at the famous hotel, the woman carrying a natty, new backpack over her shoulder, the man with a small duffel in one hand.

We spent nine minutes walking through, admiring the décor and using the opportunity to scope out the hotel security. Once we'd made the guards and the cameras we headed for the elevators. Nobody stopped us because nobody had a reason to.

We went down, not up, and when the elevator stopped we got out like we knew where we were heading, moving down a slate-gray cinder-block corridor lined with laundry carts and pieces of broken furniture stacked atop one another. There were signs posted saying that this area was for employees only, and there was a bulletin board near where we'd exited with various notices posted, some of them official, some of them not. I stopped long enough to scan the board, and not finding what I wanted, moved on.

At the end of the corridor was a T intersection, and another bulletin board. We could hear the sounds of the hotel's engines working away, the physical plant nearby. The Watergate has two hundred and fifty rooms, and when it's hot, every one of them that's occupied is running its air conditioner. That's a lot of stress on the compressors, and it makes a lot of noise. Add to that the demands for power to all of those rooms, and to the kitchens, and the laundries, and the common areas, and the front desk, and it's amazing that more things don't go wrong in such places.

There was another corkboard, outside a locker room, and while Alena glanced through the door to confirm it was for the housekeeping staff, I found what I was looking for, thumbtacked beneath an admonishment to always wash my hands. It was the master room list, prepared each morning for the housekeeping staff, and it indicated which rooms were in use and which ones weren't, and in some hotels, it would even list the last name of the occupying party. The Watergate's list wasn't that generous, confining itself to providing room numbers and a notation as to whether they were occupied or not.

I heard a jangling of keys, glanced to my left to see a Latino man maybe in his late forties coming our way down the corridor. He was wearing a gray maintenance uniform, baggy on him, a radio on his belt beside his ring of keys, and I saw a lanyard hooked to his belt loop, disappearing inside his left rear pocket. He glanced our way with curiosity, but he didn't say anything. Class is a factor in hotels, and more often than not housekeeping and custodial services are handled by recent immigrants. The last thing a new arrival wants as he works his new job, trying to build a new life, is trouble.

The hallway was narrow, and he had to squeeze to get by, and as he did I reached out with my right hand and caught the clip on his lanyard between my thumb and index finger, squeezing to free it from his belt loop. It came loose, and I snapped my wrist up, and the key card the lanyard was holding came free from his pocket. I made the move as quick and sure as possible, and once I had it, I stuffed the card into my own pocket, the lanyard after it.

If he knew he'd just been pickpocketed, he didn't show it, and he didn't stop.

Alena moved back to my side, and I indicated the list, and she pulled it from the board. I glanced after the man who'd passed us by once more. He was heading for one of the service elevators, and he wasn't looking back, so I checked the direction he'd come, and saw a second locker room. While Alena scanned the papers she'd freed from the corkboard, I peered into the room, and confirmed it was the men's locker room, and that it was empty. No one was within. If the shift hadn't changed at three, then it likely wouldn't be changing until four, at the earliest. I stepped inside, pulled Alena in after me, and closed the door.

Here's something else you can count on in hotels. They have security in the lobby, and maybe they have a security office on the ground floor, or in the basement, or in the subbasement. But that's it. Where the worker bees congregate, they don't have cameras; certainly not in the locker rooms.

"Anything?" I asked her.

She was scanning the list quickly. "There are over one hundred suites."

"It'll be marked, it'll have a notation of some sort. 'VIP' or a star or something."

She grunted her agreement, kept scanning the pages. While she did so, I moved along the lockers. Most of them were padlocked closed, but a couple weren't, and in one of the unlocked I found a maintenance jumpsuit that I thought I could squeeze into. I pulled it free and bundled it up, stuffing it into my go-bag.

"They're marked with a star, you were right," Alena said. "There are four of them."

"Unoccupied?"

"Two."

"It'll be one of those," I said.

She glanced from the sheets to me, worry in her eyes. "You're so certain."

"He blocked two and a half hours for this on his schedule. He's the featured speaker; he's the main attraction. They're catering to him, they'll have a suite for him to rest or get some work done, whatever, but he sure as hell isn't going to stand around outside the banquet hall waiting to be called and they're not going to ask him to, just in case the dinner goes long. They'll call him when they're ready. He'll go down then."

A slight smile played at the corner of her mouth. "All right."

I pulled the key from my pocket, handed it to her.

"Hurry back," I told her.

She was gone for thirty-seven minutes, during which time three things happened.

The first was that I got out of my pants and into the maintenance uniform. It fit, but only barely, and I had to leave the front unzipped. I swapped shirts with one from my go-bag, a plain white T, then took a moment to drop it to the cement floor and rub up some dirt. Then I put it on.

The second thing was that Panno called. The reception was bad, the phone giving me almost no signal.

"He's on his way to the hotel." His voice was choppy with static.

I checked my watch. "Can you beat him here?"

"Not easily."

"Try," I told him, and hung up.

The third thing was that the day shift began to file in, making for their lockers. I caught a couple of eyeballs, including one from the same man whose pocket I'd picked.

"How you doing?" I asked him.

"I'm all right." His accent was thick, more Central American than Mexican.

I offered him my hand, smiling. "Jerry," I said. "Nice to meet you."

"Ramón. You're new?"

"Just starting tonight. Don't know where half of anything is."

One of the other crew, in the midst of changing, laughed. "Yeah, that sounds about right."

"They didn't even give me orientation," I said, keeping it cheerful. "Figure I get that after my first check?"

"If you're lucky," another one said. "Let me get changed, I'll show you where everything is. My name's Monte."

"Man, Monte, that would kick ass," I said. "Seriously, I'd appreciate that more than you know."

During the course of my orientation I picked up a radio, a toolbox, and a can of WD-40. Then I went to use the bathroom, and parked myself on the toilet until I heard the last of them leave the locker room. I made a lot of noise with the toilet paper, flushed, and came out to find I was alone in the room. I moved my new toolbox to the nearest bench, popped it open, and checked the supplies. Most of them didn't interest me, but there was a rag, stained but dry, and I stuffed that in the breast pocket of the coveralls.

The radio was a Motorola, and I switched it on, then put it back on my belt. There was a little traffic, and I listened to it carefully, trying to get a handle on how the calls were taken, how they were dispatched. The dispatcher was a woman named Janet, and she sounded pleasant enough. No one was using codes of any sort, and the communications I heard were straightforward and verged on terse.

Alena peered into the locker room then, her expression curious and a little frightened, but as soon as she saw me she dropped the act and came the rest of the way inside.

"Done," she told me as she handed me back the master key on its lanyard.

"He's on his way, might be here already. Panno's supposed to call from the lobby. You want to head up there, you probably should."

"You're going to wait down here?"

"Safer," I said. "Here I'm one of the workers and we're united. Upstairs, management might notice me, and maintenance just standing around in the lobby is going to draw attention. Let me have it."

She slid the backpack from her shoulder, catching it and quickly unzipping one of the pockets on its side. "What if he recognizes you?"

"I'm hoping he won't."

"But if he does?"

"What do you want me to say? If he makes me, it's over; you know that."

From the pocket on the side of the backpack, Alena handed me a small metal container, the kind used for fancy breath mints and expensive chewing gum. I put it in my pocket with the key card.

"You need to get up there," I said.

She nodded, kissed my cheek, then my lips, and said, "Be a professional."

"There's a first time for everything," I said.

CHAPTER TWELVE

At nine minutes to six, my radio squawked, and I heard the call I'd been waiting for.

"One-four-four-one, air-conditioning not working," the dispatcher said. *"Can maintenance get up there and check the thermostat, please? VIP room."*

"Janet? Les. I can handle that," came the response. *"Be about fifteen minutes."*

"Thanks, Les."

I used my cell phone to call Panno. "Here's what I need you to do—"

"Wait," he said.

"There's no time to wait. I need this done, and I need it done now," I said. "You have to get to a house phone, you have to call the switchboard, the operator, and you have to tell them that you're in fourteen-forty-one, and that you just called down about the thermostat in the room. You need to tell them that it's working again, that you don't need anyone to come up, that they can cancel the call. Do you understand?"

"He's got guards with him."

I stopped halfway to the door of the locker room. "How many?"

"Three. I think they're all Gorman-North. Killer has a plan for getting one of them down here, but I don't know about the other two."

"Use the house phone, then call me back," I said, and hung up, and waited for my Motorola to speak once more. It seemed like it took a very long time before it did.

"Les, honey, you there?"

"I'm on my way up there now, Janet, tell them to hold their horses."

"No, they just called down to say it's working again, you don't have to bother."

"No kidding? Okay, then, I'm taking my break."

"You enjoy your dinner, hon."

My phone rang.

"Done," Panno said. "We've got one of them off the room now; your wife made a point of asking some questions about a certain guest at the front desk, and she was insistent enough to make them nervous. This guy's down here, talking to the manager."

"Where is she?"

"She's outside, but you've got two either in or on the room. I don't know how you're going to manage that."

"Don't worry about it," I told him. "I'll call you when it's done."

"Good lu—"

I hung up before he could finish, took my toolbox, and headed for the service elevator.

■ ■ ■

It was as I stepped out onto the fourteenth floor that two of the things I'd missed struck me at once. The first was that fourteen-forty-one could, conceivably, not be the room Jason Earle was in; Alena had disconnected the thermostats in two of the rooms, and he could only be in one of them. I was quite possibly headed to the wrong place.

The second thing was more irrational, and struck me just as I was able to confirm that I, at least, was headed to the right room. Panno said the guards were Gorman-North. That Earle had brought guards at all worried me, and that there were only three of them confused me. If there had been more, I'd have believed he'd been tipped to our attempt at Georgetown, and was building protection around himself. But only three, I didn't know what to make of that, if it was only for show or for ego or for something else entirely. If it was a trap then it wasn't enough muscle. If it was for his protection it wasn't enough coverage.

So what the hell was it?

I came out of the service corridor and into the carpeted hallway to see two men standing post perhaps fifty feet away. They saw me as I emerged, and both turned to watch my approach, and I raised my free hand in greeting, trudging towards them. They didn't wave back, but one of the two knocked on the door they were guarding, then stuck his head in, most likely to announce my arrival.

"Sorry," I said as I drew closer. "Sorry, it's been crazy this evening, I got up here as soon as I could."

"Can I look in your toolbox, please, sir?" the larger and older of the two asked me.

"Yeah, sure." I handed it over to him. He set it down on the floor and opened it, began rifling through the contents.

The other guard, perhaps six or seven years younger than his partner, was looking at me closely. I met his eyes and he looked away, checking down the hallway. He hadn't liked the eye contact, which had been the point of doing it.

His partner closed the box and handed it back to me, saying, "There you go."

Then he opened the door, and held it until I had stepped fully into Jason Earle's suite, before letting it fall closed behind me.

CHAPTER THIRTEEN

"Maintenance," I called.

"Go ahead."

I looked to the source, saw a man seated at the desk by the window off to my right. He was bent to his work, a large pen visible in his hand, and I watched as he put pen to paper, scribbling quickly. He didn't raise his head at all. The two words were the extent of his acknowledgment that I was even there.

I stared at his back for a moment, then moved to where the thermostat was on the wall. I set the toolbox down at my feet, snapped it open, then used a flathead screwdriver to pop the faceplate free. It dangled on its wires, and, now exposed, I could see where Alena had disconnected the mercury switch to render the thermostat useless. I ignored it, fiddled for several seconds, then dropped the screwdriver back into the box. It went in with a clatter, and at his desk, the man stiffened for a moment in annoyance, then resumed what he had been doing.

From my breast pocket, I pulled the rag I'd grabbed and sprayed it with a hit from the can of WD-40. I stood up again, using my body to block any view he might have if he turned around, pretending to work the thermostat some more while running the rag over the two buttons on the faceplate. The smell of the solvent was rich in the air.

I went back to the toolbox again, clattering through it, then pulled the small metal box Alena had given me and popped open the top. I took a second to glance to the desk, and the man still hadn't even turned to see me, now moving a new set of paperwork in front of him. With the top of the toolbox as a shield from his view, I tapped the contents of my little tin onto the corner of my rag. The granules were fat and almost chalky, light gray. I closed the tin with one hand, stuffed it back into my pocket, then turned to the faceplate one more time. I smeared each button with the rag.

The room seemed very quiet, just the sound of two men working to two very different ends.

I folded the edge of the rag over into itself, then folded it again, and then used it to protect my fingers as I fitted the plate back into position over the thermostat. Then I folded it a final time and tucked it carefully back into my pocket. The buttons glistened slightly from the WD-40, but against their own almost-white, the powder was nearly impossible to see.

I cleared my throat, and when he didn't respond, said, "Pardon me, sir?"

He straightened in his seat, half turning. "Yes?"

"I've done everything I can, but I don't have the parts I need with me. I'm going to have to go back downstairs to get them."

"I see."

"If I can bother you for a moment to come over here, I'd like to show you the reset, though. That way, if it starts working, you'll be able to get it set how you like without me needing to come back up here."

Even from across the room, I heard his sigh. Then he capped his pen and pushed back his chair, got to his feet, and started over towards me. I turned away, to face the thermostat.

"All right, go ahead," he said.

I indicated the two buttons on the faceplate. "Once it's in reset, you need to reinitialize it. The way you do that is by holding these two buttons down together for about five seconds. You do that, you should hear a click. You want to try it, you should be able to hear it now. Won't do anything, but you'll know what I'm talking about."

"Both of the buttons at once, like this?" He pushed his index and middle finger of his left hand against the buttons, depressing them firmly.

"Just like that, now you hold it."

He held them down for several seconds, then released, saying, "I didn't hear anything."

"I'm sorry, sir, are you sure?"

"Yes, I'm sure."

"Sometimes it doesn't work first time."

He shook his head slightly, finding me tiresome, and again depressed the buttons with his index and middle fingers. He held them longer this time, and I could see the circulation in his fingertips diminishing from the pressure he was applying. After almost ten seconds, he released.

"Nothing." He looked at his fingers, searched for a place to wipe them, then gave up. "Don't you clean your work surface after you're done with it? It's covered with oil."

I pulled the rag again, still folded, and used it to wipe the faceplate down, saying, "Sorry about that. I forget sometimes."

“I didn’t hear anything that time, either.”

“Must be something in the power source, then, like I was afraid of.” I replaced the rag in the same pocket as before. “I’ll see if I can’t find a replacement, bring a whole new unit up here.”

“If you could. It’s getting stuffy in here.”

“Shouldn’t take me too long, sir.”

I turned to face him, and Jason Earle was looking at me, and our eyes met.

I thought about everything I wanted to say to him. How I wanted to tell him that he was a dead man and he didn’t know it yet and that I had killed him. I wanted to tell him why I had done what I had done to him. I wanted to tell him that Elliot Trent had taken my bullets with a smile all in the hope of this moment. I wanted to tell him that he had taken my best friend from the world, and that I didn’t care who the hell he was or thought he was, she hadn’t been his to take. That he shouldn’t have done it, he should have let it all go, because I would have been happy to do the same. I wanted to tell him that I almost had, but that, like Elliot Trent, I had someone who was precious to me, even more than Natalie had been, and he had threatened her, too, and that I wouldn’t—I couldn’t—let that stand.

I wanted to tell him that there were some things that had to be answered, and that I knew one day I would have to answer for this.

All the things I wanted to say to him.

I didn’t say any of them.

Because Jason Earle looked me in the eyes, and he didn’t know who I was.

He had no idea who I was.

“Sorry to have disturbed your work, sir,” I said, and I closed my toolbox, and I walked out of the suite.

I didn’t look back.

CHAPTER FOURTEEN

An ambulance crew was rushing through the lobby when I came out of the elevator, and I had to sidestep them as they rolled their gurney into my car before I was even all of the way out. I'd changed back into my earlier clothes, replaced the toolbox and radio where I'd found them, stuffed the coveralls into the duffel I had in my hand. I rubbernecked until the elevator doors slid closed, then turned to find Panno waiting for me. We headed out together, into the warmth of the evening.

"She called three minutes ago," Panno told me. "She says she'll meet you at the Jefferson Memorial."

"No trouble?"

"None. You?"

"He didn't know who I was. I think, even if I looked exactly as I did four years ago, he still wouldn't have known."

"You're probably right," Panno said. "C'mon, I'll give you a lift."

■ ■ ■

She was exactly where she said she would be, and Panno walked with me to where Alena stood waiting, watching the last of the daylight reflecting off the river. There were cherry blossoms still in the trees, and the air was heavy with the scent, and she turned when she heard us approaching, watching as we came closer.

"You did it?"

"It was on the radio on the way over," I told her. "It's done."

"So are we," Panno said. "The IDs you're carrying will work another two days, should be long enough to get you both wherever it is you're going. After that, they'll be useless. Danielle and Christopher Morse will be discovered, dead, before the end of the week, and when that happens, Interpol will update their entries on Drama and Patriot to reflect the same thing."

"Thank you," I said, still looking at Alena.

"It's what you wanted? That's what you wanted in return?" Panno asked.

"I want one more thing," I said.

"What's that?"

"I want to go home," I said, and I took Alena's hand in mine, and together, we walked to the car, to begin the long trip back to Kobuleti.

ACKNOWLEDGMENTS

The dark days of this novel were illuminated by several people. A handful of them are named here.

Keith Giffen, Geoff Johns, Grant Morrison, Mark Waid, and Stephen "Sarge" Wacker, all of whom helped far more than they realized, in manners they could never have foreseen. MG3 or the Fab Four (plus Pete Best), call it what you will; you all create the remarkable, and are all remarkable in your own right. It has been an honor to serve with you, and to my dying day, I will remember and cherish what it is we have created.

Morgan and Matthew. A simple thanks. Now give me a Will save, DC 20.

Eric Trautmann, weapons-grade wiseass and steely-eyed missile man supreme. Your assistance, guidance, and friendship are unparalleled. Both you and Gabi enrich our lives.

Matt Brady. Yes, Matt, you can be my sidekick. Now get to work.

Irwyn Applebaum and Nita Taublib. Thanks for giving me the time. I hope like hell you're soon rewarded for your faith, patience, and passion.

Kate Miciak, for enduring Kateness, and for really, *really* pissing me off this time. But then again, if it was easy, everyone would do it. Right? Right?

Angela Cheng-Caplan. It's done, now. I'll get to work on the other stuff.

Maggie Griffin. You are a light in dark days, and a joy at all times. I could thank you for a thousand things, but for now, I will thank you for this—Bristol, where your sorrow and your strength first broke my heart, and then mended it. And if anyone asks just what it was we were doing in my hotel room, just smile knowingly.

David Hale Smith. I owe you more than just Scotch, my friend; I owe you Kevlar and a long vacation. Thank you for everything that you do, and the passion, style, and intelligence with which you do it. You're still the second-best decision I ever made in my life.

And finally, once again, to Jennifer, Elliot, and Dashiell. You are my heart.

ABOUT THE AUTHOR

GREG RUCKA is the author of *Private Wars, A Gentleman's Game,* and six previous thrillers, as well as numerous graphic novels, including the Eisner Award-winning *Whiteout: Melt. Whiteout* is currently in production as a major motion picture starring Kate Beckinsale. He lives in Portland, Oregon, with his family.